T0247948

SMOKE
AND
MIRRORS

SMOKE AND MIRRORS

A Greer Hogan Mystery

M. E. HILLIARD

NEW YORK

Copyright © 2024 by Macaire Hill

Published in the United States by Crooked Lane Books, an imprint of The Quick Brown Fox & Company LLC.

Crooked Lane Books and its logo are trademarks of The Quick Brown Fox & Company LLC.

Library of Congress Catalog-in-Publication data available upon request.

ISBN (hardcover): 978-1-63910-619-6
ISBN (ebook): 978-1-63910-620-2

Cover design by Alan Ayers

Printed in the United States.

www.crookedlanebooks.com

Crooked Lane Books
34 West 27th St., 10th Floor
New York, NY 10001

First Edition: June 2024

10 9 8 7 6 5 4 3 2 1

For my family near and far,
always my biggest fans and supporters

Chapter One

~

A walk among the tombstones gives a girl perspective, especially when the tombstones in question tell the tale of the neighborhood you grew up in, the grammar school you attended, and the parish church where you were married. Here lies the first little girl who spoke to me on the playground when I was the new kid in school. She was dropped to the pavement by an aneurysm the day before her twenty-ninth birthday. To my left, the class clown, a bright-eyed boy dead at thirty-seven from a cancer both stunning and horrifying in its lethal efficiency. Just ahead was the ornate headstone of a girl whose fancy house and designer clothes I'd envied all through high school. She'd spent the fifteen years after we graduated drinking herself to death, finally finishing the job a week after our class reunion. Safe to say, none of us had ended up where we'd thought we would.

I moved on. There'd been a funeral that afternoon—no one I knew: I'd checked the online parish bulletin—and I made my way around the freshly dug earth and blanket of flowers. There were a couple of nice arrangements of early spring blooms mixed in with the usual funeral floral offerings. I wrinkled my nose. I hated the smell of lilies. I left the cloying odor behind as I moved into the older part of the cemetery. In use before the parish got larger and wealthier, it was close to the church and the rectory. When the school was added, the trustees had had the foresight to buy up as much of the nearby land as they could, adding a schoolyard on one side and expanding the cemetery on the other. I liked this original graveyard, with its trees and flowering shrubs. Here the air smelled of late winter, cool and damp, with an earthy note from the mud left by the melting snow. It was twilight, and the quickly changing temperatures that accompanied the change in seasons created a light fog. It blurred outlines, making the monuments seem to shift and the paths between them come and go. No matter, I had the place to myself, and I knew where I was going.

And there it was. The grave I'd come to visit, its dark granite marker as solid and unassuming as the man himself. Daniel Fitzpatrick Sullivan. My late husband. Danny had been as straightforward as they come, never one to keep secrets. But something had been bothering him right before he died, something he'd wanted to tell me about one morning. I hadn't made time to listen, and by that night he was dead. Whatever it was he had known, it was a secret someone wanted to keep, and they'd made sure he took it to his grave. Danny had been murdered in our apartment, and I'd found him there, dead, nearly four years ago. The guilt and shock had worn off. The rage remained.

I sat on a small stone bench a few feet from the grave. Behind and above me was a statue of the angel Gabriel, sans trumpet. He gazed down, lips parted, expression earnest, with one hand outstretched. A hedge had grown up over the decades, creating an alcove that sheltered both bench and statue. It was a private, peaceful place, and the reason I'd chosen the small plot. I could sit, unobserved, yet still hear anyone approaching on the gravel path. I studied the stone in front of me. The fog swirled and drifted, never quite obscuring the inscription, never quite disappearing. I leaned forward, elbows on my knees, and sighed.

"We need to talk, Dan," I said. "I know you were trying to tell me something. I think you still are. But you're going to have to spell it out. The dreams aren't enough."

Silence. I tried to clear my mind and let my thoughts drift. I didn't expect a direct download from Danny, though that would have been nice. I'd have been satisfied if my subconscious burped up some fact I'd missed previously. Instead, I got one of the same scenes that played out while I slept—my husband at the end of a long, dark hallway, holding out an envelope. I shook my head.

"I already know about that," I said. "The spreadsheets you sent to Ian." Ian Cameron, my long-ago first love, and longtime friend and mentor to the man I'd eventually married, had received several pages of information from Danny via snail mail. They'd been sent right before he died. Dan had tried to call Ian too, in the days before he was murdered, but the two hadn't been able to connect. Ian had hung on to the spreadsheets, although, as he'd told me recently, "Without context, I can't make any sense of them."

"What am I missing?" I pounded my fists on my thighs. "What—" I stopped. I'd heard a faint sound. I leaned forward again, so I could see past the hedge. An indistinct shape, muffled in fog, was moving toward me. A few seconds later, a tall figure, clothed entirely in black, stepped into view and stopped beside me.

"Greer. I thought I'd find you here."

"Father Liam," I said. "I thought I had the whole place to myself."

"Saw you from the rectory window. Figured you'd come to have a chat with our man Daniel."

Father Liam Sullivan was my late husband's cousin, and of all his relatives, my favorite. Though he was ten years older than Dan, the two had always been close, more like brothers than cousins. Handsome, charming, and bright, Liam had been a successful stockbroker. At the age of thirty, he had come to Sunday dinner at his parents' and announced that, after much reflection, he had joined the Society of Jesus and was going to become a priest. The entire family, with two exceptions, was stunned. Liam's grandmother, in spite of having always considered Jesuits a bit too free-thinking for her taste, was thrilled to have a member of the clergy in the family and said she always knew Liam would find his way someday. Danny hadn't been surprised either. "It always felt like Liam was looking for something, and then once he went to seminary, it didn't feel like that anymore," he'd told me. Father Liam had officiated our wedding and Dan's funeral. I liked him, and I trusted him.

"I have, though the conversation's been a bit one-sided," I said. I slid sideways on the small bench. He perched on the end of it. We both sat and studied the headstone. After a moment, Father Liam sighed, pulled out a packet of cigarettes, and lit up.

I raised an eyebrow. "Thought you'd quit," I said.

"I have, when I'm where anyone can see me," he said, blowing out a stream of smoke. "Parishioners, at least. You're family."

"Hmm," I said, but before I could make a point about splitting hairs, he started to speak.

"I've spoken to the prison chaplain, out there where they've put the man the cops said killed Dan."

"Pete Perry," I said. "And?"

"This Perry isn't religious, and Father Andrew isn't there all the time, but he did make a point of speaking to him."

I waited. Liam took a long drag on his cigarette.

"Well," he said, "Andrew said Perry seemed happy to have someone to talk to about the whole thing, someone who would hear him out. He admits he broke in—says he was paid to, and to look for certain things—and that Dan came home unexpectedly, and so he hit him. He swears he left Dan alive but unconscious."

"That's what he told me," I said. "And he was an amateur boxer, so I think he would know if he hit Dan hard enough to kill him."

"He still boxes," Liam said. "And according to Andrew, he's still pretty good. I don't know, Greer. I admit, I thought you were reaching with this, just not able to let go, but Andrew's been doing this a long time, ministering to the incarcerated. He thinks the man's telling the truth."

"Thank you for telling me—and for asking around, even though you thought I was off my rocker."

"I never thought that, Greer, but grief is a strange and difficult thing. It hits people differently. I just didn't want you to get stuck."

"I'm not stuck. Not anymore. I was stuck for three years. Now I'm looking for answers. You understand if Pete Perry didn't kill Dan, someone else did? And that somcone is still out there?"

"It did occur to me, yes. But what will you do? This isn't enough to take to the police."

"I'm not sure what I'll do next," I said. "It's possible I can find something the police would be interested in, enough to take another look."

"And if they won't?"

I shrugged.

"The thing is, why would anyone want to kill Dan?" Liam sounded frustrated and angry. *Join the club,* I thought.

"That's the million-dollar question, isn't it?" I said. "If we knew why, we'd know who. At least I think so."

He gave me a long look. "What will you do, Greer?" he asked again.

"Find out. Why and who."

"And then?"

I took a deep breath. "I don't know," I said, staring at the headstone.

"Hmm. Well. Stay on the side of the angels, Greer."

"Only if I can be the one with the flaming sword, Father."

Liam shook his head. I stood. I was getting cold, and it was getting dark. Liam ground out his cigarette and stood as well.

"Would you like to come for a drink? Or stay for supper? The Rangers are playing tonight. We could watch and catch up on the family news," he said.

"No, thanks. I've got some things to take care of. But I'll take a raincheck."

"Well, you know you're always welcome. At Mass, as well. You can come without your mother dragging you, you know."

"Nice try, Father. I'll take you up on the drink and the hockey game sometime." I gave him a quick kiss on the cheek. "Thanks again for listening and helping me out."

"Anytime, Greer. You know where to find me." He turned toward the rectory, and I followed the path to the front gate, moving faster this time. I'd made the trip out to Riverdale to have lunch with my parents. They were leaving the next day for an extended trip to visit my sister and her family in Florida.

I suspected my mother was trying to give my father a taste of retirement. I also suspected this would not be effective.

As far as my parents knew, I had gone straight back to Manhattan after lunch. There were a few things I'd needed to do that I didn't want to discuss with them, though, this visit to the cemetery being one. I'd have to tell them something about my investigation of Dan's death eventually, but not yet. I didn't know how it would end, and I didn't want them involved.

Some things a girl has to do on her own.

Chapter Two

My subway ride was uneventful. Rush hour hadn't started, and I was headed into Manhattan rather than leaving it. I'd been back in the city long enough to get my game face on and have my commuter muscle memory kick in, but I still held my tote bag a little tighter than usual. I wanted to keep it close without looking like a nervous out-of-towner waiting to be mugged. I'd made a couple of purchases I couldn't exactly put on a police report, and was carrying more cash than usual. The trip was quick and not too crowded, but I still breathed a sigh of relief when I locked the door of my apartment behind me.

My temporary gig came with temporary digs. I'd been hired by the Archive of Illusionists and Conjurers as an all-purpose cataloger, abstracter, and indexer. They'd received a bequest that included a large collection of books pertaining to the history and practice of what my new supervisor referred to as "the conjuring arts." In other words, magic and magicians. While I had no experience with either, the colleague who had recommended me had stated that I had the appropriate "curiosity, initiative, and discretion" for the job. I was also willing to work for a modest salary supplemented by free lodging in an unrenovated, fifth-floor walk-up apartment across the street from my worksite on the Upper West Side. Said worksite was a classic brownstone with a large library and collection of magical ephemera. It was situated near the corner on a quiet cross street. The apartment was in a mid-rise fronting the avenue, but my windows had a direct view of the brownstone.

"I'm afraid the apartment hasn't been updated in decades," Ava, the Archive librarian, had told me before I arrived. "And, of course, there's no elevator. But it's a co-op and they do provide Wi-Fi. I had enough money in the project budget for a new bed and some kitchen items—microwave, decent coffeemaker, things like that. The brownstone where the collection is housed also has new kitchen appliances and good internet connectivity, but other than regular cleaning and maintenance, nothing has been touched in seven or eight years, maybe more. The former owner was a bit eccentric. The hours are flexible though—you can work anytime between six AM and midnight."

For thirty flexible hours a week and free lodging, I was in. I needed a paycheck while the Raven Hill Library was being rebuilt, and I needed to be in the city to look into Dan's murder, whenever and wherever the trail led. The apartment wasn't bad. It was a small one-bedroom with a living room and separate, if tiny, kitchen. There was an alcove off the bedroom. It was long and narrow, but it had a window and enough room for a reading chair, lamp, and bookcase. There were two oddly shaped closets, and if the bedroom door was closed, the living room got no natural light, but I found it quite acceptable, and it was more than I'd have been able to afford on my own. The furniture had a definite mid-century modern feel and had been scrupulously cleaned. The new coffeepot was so high tech it was clear Ava and I placed a similar value on the importance of a well-brewed cup.

I stashed my purchases in various hidey-holes I'd found—another unexpected bonus—and then took a quick shower. While I dried my hair, I contemplated my wardrobe options for the evening. I was meeting someone for drinks. April Benson was the almost ex-wife of the late Frank Benson, who had served as corporate counsel for New Leaf, the company Dan was working for when he died. The divorce was contentious and not yet final when Frank met his untimely end. I'd met her at the wedding of a mutual friend the previous fall. The weekend had involved lots of booze, some great parties, and a murder. Maybe more than one.

Frank Benson had attended the wedding with his fiancée, Shelby. I'd been chatting with them not long before Frank had a heart attack. He'd been whisked away from the festivities to the local hospital. He'd seemed to be on the mend but had suddenly died while briefly alone in his room. Unexpected but not unreasonable given the state of his health. The fact that he had had a visitor no one could identify shortly before he died had my girl detective senses tingling. That's what I wanted to talk to April about.

I considered my approach to the subject as I pulled things out of my closet. Opening with *"So I'm pretty sure the person who killed my husband is still running loose, and I think this same person may have offed your husband too"* was a little blunt, even if it did put the whole situation in a nutshell. It would convince most people I was crazy, but I'd floated some suspicions to April at the time, and she'd been willing to consider them. Still, a more indirect approach might be best.

"Tell me, April, are you entirely satisfied with what the hospital and the police told you about Frank's cause of death?" I said aloud to the empty apartment. Something like that would work, with the right balance of concern and curiosity. No lie—I was both: concerned because I believed Dan's killer was still out there, and I didn't know what might happen once I started stirring things up; and curious because I knew the police had done at least a cursory check into Frank's death, since it had occurred in close proximity to another crime, but I hadn't heard anything about it. April would have, if there was anything to know, because she was still next of kin at the time he'd died.

Satisfied with my plan, I applied some lipstick, checked the outside temp, and added a scarf and gloves to my ensemble. I'd gone for the all-black, low-key professional look. I'd spent most of my workdays in jeans lately, so it was nice to feel a little more pulled together. Besides, April was an attorney, and she'd be coming from work. We'd look like two women of business having a few glasses of wine, not a couple of amateur detectives nosing into a possible murder.

Not that anyone would notice, I told myself as I fastened all three locks on my apartment door, then double-checked them. It was just that a couple of times since the wedding, and several more since I'd been back in the city, I'd had the feeling of being watched. Nothing concrete I could point to, only a creepy back-of-the-neck feeling. It usually happened when I was out and about, running errands. Once or twice, I'd also thought something was not where I'd left it at work, but I hadn't been at the job long enough to have a standard place for everything. Logical explanations for all, I was sure. But still.

April was already seated when I arrived at the restaurant, a bistro with an eclectic menu and nice wine list. The clientele were mostly neighborhood residents looking for a good meal at the end of the day. That was one thing I'd really missed about the city—never having to cook for myself. I slid into the chair across from April. She'd snagged a table far enough from the bar to be quiet, but with a good view. We exchanged greetings—thankfully, she was neither a hugger nor an air kisser.

"Nice little place," she said, once we'd each ordered a glass of wine and an appetizer. "Do they do lunch? I've got a new client up this way."

"Yes, and a really good brunch on the weekends."

"I'll have to keep it in mind," April said. "You're looking great. I guess being back in the city is agreeing with you."

"It's nice to be doing so much walking again, and I move around a lot for my job. And I broke down and joined a gym, just to make sure I got out and talked to people. It offers some fun classes."

Truth be told, I was in the best shape of my life. Between the walk-up apartment, all the stairs in the brownstone, and moving and shelving the collection I was working on, I got plenty of exercise. The gym did provide a chance to meet people and chat, to the extent you could chat during a mixed martial arts class geared toward self-defense. In the past year, I'd nearly been drowned, I'd been stuck in a burning building, and I'd run into an attempted stabbing, all in the service of justice. At this point, I wasn't taking any chances. Plus, I now had discernible triceps, which had me pretty impressed with myself.

"Hmm, I'll have to try one of those classes sometime," April said. "And the new job?"

I gave her the basics and finished up with, "But it's only temporary. I'll be here a few more months, and then it's back to Raven Hill."

"Well, that should give you enough time," April said.

I raised my eyebrows. She leaned forward.

"To figure out what actually happened," she said. "To your husband. And maybe to mine."

No beating around the bush with April.

"I'd love to," I said. "But tell me—what makes you think Frank didn't die of natural causes? Have you learned something?"

At that point the waiter appeared with our order. We sat in silence while he served, then thanked him. With a quick look around, April leaned forward again. I did the same.

"I got Frank's phone back. Useless, since it went into the lake with him. But I also got the records and all the medical examiner's findings. After our chat in Lake Placid, I asked for an autopsy. Took a while. Apparently, it always does."

"And?"

"And I wasn't entirely satisfied. I saw him right after he died— I had to take care of all the formalities. I took a good, long look. I know we were in the middle of an ugly divorce, but I'd been married to him for decades. We grew up together. He was the father of my children. It was a moment to say goodbye, I guess."

April paused and sighed. I stayed silent. She took a deep breath and continued. "Anyway, I noticed an unusual redness around his eyes. Even with the high blood pressure, Frank always had enviable skin. He'd flush a bit, but these were more like little pinpricks."

"Petechiae, I think it's called. Something like that."

"Yes, that's what I was told. I'd heard of it, probably some crime show or medical drama. I thought it only happened if someone tried to strangle you."

"Or smother you," I said.

"Looks like we watch the same shows," she said. "But the medical staff said it can happen during cardiac arrest. That's what killed him."

She went on a little more about the medical details and ended with, "So what they said all makes sense, I guess. But something still didn't seem right. I don't know—maybe they were worried I was looking for a reason to sue. Job-related hazard when you're an attorney."

"Did you ever find out who the visitor was? The one who said she was a friend of Shelby's?"

April shook her head. "That still bothers me too. Shelby checked with any friends, hers or Frank's, that were in the area—nothing. But I'm not sure how a total stranger could sneak into Frank's room. It's a busy hospital. There always seemed to be someone around."

"But all of them in scrubs and often masks" I said. "Would one more be noticed? Or someone who had one of those visitor badges?" I shook my head. "It does seem to be a reach."

"Yes, it does. But then there's this: he was using his personal phone when he went into the water. Based on the records, he'd been using it all weekend. Frank was a big believer in disconnecting from the office when he was on vacation." April rolled her eyes. "Even when the kids were small, I at least checked my messages. He'd be on the beach with them, looking for seashells and building sandcastles. Anyway, the night of the cocktail party, Frank made a call to the New Leaf office, then one to a cell phone registered to the company. Both of those were short. Then, right after that, he got a callback and was on the phone for a few minutes. Then nothing else."

"Shelby said he stepped away for a call. That's what he was doing on the dock," I said. "Was it at the right time?"

April and I had both been at the cocktail party, but she and Frank had kept their distance from each other.

"It was. It's the last call made or received on that phone," she said.

"And he was on the phone when he went into the water," I said. "So who was it?"

"This is where it gets interesting. There's no record of the number anywhere that I can find. I tried calling it back—no response, no message, nothing. My son the spy thriller reader tells me it was probably a burner phone, or a pay-as-you-go."

"You can use an app to do the same thing, but if it were me, I'd get a prepaid, and then ditch the phone." I'd read a few spy thrillers myself.

"Me too."

"It's possible the police could find something out about those calls to New Leaf, but they've got no reason to try," I said.

"No. But get this: the day Shelby got back from Lake Placid, she got a call from New Leaf, asking if they could send someone to pick up Frank's computer and phone, and anything else he had at home related to the business. She thought it was a little insensitive—Frank's body hadn't even been released yet. But it was William Warren, Frank's boss, and he was insistent. He told her they contained proprietary information relating to a time-sensitive deal. So she said yes. They were there within twenty-four hours. Cleaned out his home office."

"Plausible, but still awfully quick. So they took everything?"

"Not quite. Shelby was a little put out. She went in that night and took out everything that didn't have the company logo on it, as well as some pictures and personal items. She had a couple of file boxes stashed in her trunk while the company crew were in the office. She turned over anything he still had on paper, his personal laptop, and some drives to me, since I'm his executor."

"Awkward," I said.

"Very. She was hurt, I think, that Frank hadn't made changes to his will when they got engaged, but he had changed his life insurance. Amazing, given that no one ever really believes they're going to die. Shelby's smarter than she looks. She knows she lucked out there."

"Find anything interesting in the files?" I asked.

"No. I haven't gotten through everything, but I don't think there's anything to find. As I said, Frank was big on keeping work and home life separate."

April signaled to the waiter for more wine, then sat drumming her fingers on the table.

"I'm going to keep digging through what I've got," she said. "I smell a rat."

"Big time. I still think there's some connection to Dan's death. I had been asking Frank questions about what was going on at the office around that time, and that's when he clammed up and started making calls."

"I agree. I've never trusted those people. The whole business plan seemed sketchy, but Frank liked the idea of being in on the ground floor. He thought of it as the new, sexy business opportunity."

"It didn't start out that way. When Dan was brought on, it was strictly a natural products company. Very hippy-dippy, you know? Dan used to laugh and say the new investors wanted to be the Ben and Jerry's of personal care. They had CBD oil products, but not in a big way. Then next thing you know, it's a grand vision of holistic wellness centers and cannabis dispensaries."

"The laws around that are tricky, and changing all the time," April said. "If you want to talk to an expert, I can put you in touch with someone. His name is Noah Leonard. He's an attorney. I've referred a few potential clients to him. It's a fascinating business, and there's money to be made, but it requires a specialist."

"Thank you, that would be great," I said. "My practical experience with all this is limited to helping a couple of people navigate the application for medical marijuana use, but that area seems like the tip of the iceberg."

April nodded. "It's indicative of the complexity of the regulatory environment—Big Pharma would be all over that if it were simple."

"Dan mentioned something like that once," I said. "I've been trying to remember everything he said about the business, but so much of it was offhand comments, you know?"

"If it's not too painful, could you tell me what happened? To Dan, I mean. I've heard parts of the story, but maybe if I hear it from you, I can help."

"It's okay," I said. I gave her the whole story, from Dan's distraction and worry in the weeks leading up to his death, to his request for help that morning and the texts from the office when he was supposed to be downtown with me. Then coming home to an unlocked apartment door and finding Dan on the living room floor. April was a good listener, asking the occasional question, but otherwise quiet. I wound up with, "So unless it really was a random break-in, which I don't believe, I'm sure it's tied to Dan's work."

"And Frank was somehow involved and then became expendable," April said, her tone grim.

"It looks that way to me. Too many coincidences. But I can't prove anything."

"You're going to have to rattle some cages," April said.

"Yes." I had an idea how to do that, but I was hesitant. I was in information-gathering mode, but I couldn't do that forever. My friends and neighbors, Beau and Ben, had been doing some nosing around and had come up with a few leads. There were a couple of people in the building we had all lived in that I needed to talk to, who'd been unavailable in the few weeks I'd been back in the city. I'd see them soon. I'd add April's expert to my list and set up an appointment once I had a better idea of what I needed to know. That was the problem—I was casting about with no clear idea of what I was trying to catch. And time was passing. I might just have to wing it.

"It's been nearly four years. That's an issue," I said. "People forget things."

"When, exactly, did it happen?"

"April the fourth."

"A night that will live in infamy," April said. "That's when I first suspected Frank was cheating. Our daughter's senior year— she was the lead in her school play. I barely made it by curtain time—work and traffic. Frank arrived late, smelling like a perfume I wouldn't be caught dead in. Caitlyn had a fit. I thought things were bad at the time. Who knew it would end in all this? I'm sorry, Greer."

"Thanks," I said. "I appreciate your time, and your offer to help. It may turn out that what happened to Frank didn't have anything to do with Danny's death, and even if it did, we may never be able to prove it."

"But if it did, I want someone to pay. Our marriage was all over except for the shouting, but I'm the one who had to tell our children that their father was dead."

Chapter Three

I overslept the next morning. Though my hours were flexible, I had a meeting with my boss at nine for a status update. I made myself presentable and zipped down the stairs and across the street. I was unlocking the front door at a quarter to nine, which gave me time to disarm the security system. According to Ava, the previous owner had installed a customized system that monitored the house for everything from attempted break-ins to sudden temperature drops. "I don't even know what some of this equipment does," she had told me when teaching me how to code in. Based on the terms of the will, only the very exclusive company that installed it could modify or update it. "They provide an excellent monitoring service," she added, "so I'm fine with it." I'd become quite familiar with the whims of wealthy eccentrics while working in Raven Hill—my job might not exist without a family trust set up in a previous century—so none of this fazed me. Once all the control panels were blinking green, I raised the temperature a smidge and put on a pot of coffee. Ava had promised to bring breakfast from the bakery near her apartment, and my stomach growled in anticipation.

I set up my laptop on the kitchen table. The door and windows to the back garden let in some natural light. That and its proximity to the furnace made this the most comfortable spot in the house at this time of day. I did most of my work in the library on the first floor, but this was a better spot for a meeting. I was getting out mugs when I heard the front door slam, followed a minute later by the sound of footsteps above me.

"I'm in the kitchen," I yelled.

Ava appeared, bakery box in hand. She was a bit younger than I, with curly brown hair, big brown eyes, and a porcelain complexion. She credited the latter to being a career archivist, saying "I started working at sixteen, and I've spent most of my professional life in basements. You know what sunlight does to print." Her passion was old manuscripts and preservation. I liked her—she was smart, knowledgeable, and had a good sense of humor.

"Ah, coffee! It's a bit chilly out there, and I had to stop off at the Archive and pick up those keys you asked for. We'll try to find the ones that go to those storage rooms—I thought we'd opened everything up. But first let's take a look at the inventory and see what kind of progress you're making."

We went through the inventory spreadsheet I'd created, where I was trying to create some order out of the multiple partial inventories I'd been given. The best of these had been created by the man who had owned the brownstone and amassed the collection, Lars Christopher. He'd once been a magician, "The Amazing Christophe," but his career had been cut short by an injury. He'd turned to collecting books, manuscripts, and ephemera, and become an expert on the history of the conjuring arts. The rest of the information had been compiled by a combination of interns and archive personnel, and some of it was handwritten. The brownstone was about twenty minutes from the actual archive, and Ava had admitted that they had been sending people up whenever they could spare someone, which wasn't often. Hence the decision to hire me.

"You're making good progress," Ava said. "I like the way you've attached bib numbers to titles wherever you can. We can link to the catalog records."

"I'm doing pretty well with the newer stuff—there are records out there. It's the older stuff that's harder, especially if it's not in English. I'm all right with the French and Latin—I've studied those—but there are a number of items in German, Italian, and Spanish."

"I can help you with the German, and we have a Spanish speaker on staff. I'll see what I can do about the Italian. There are quite a few rare items in this collection. We're going to have to do some original cataloging."

Ava made some notes as we went over a few more details, then stretched and said, "I say we take a break for strudel and then start trying some of those keys."

She had me at strudel.

We cleared the table, poured some more coffee, and pulled out the pastries. We chatted for a bit about general trends in libraries and publishing. Once we'd demolished the strudel, Ava reached into her bag and pulled out a small box labeled "LC house spare keys."

"Now let's see what we've got," she said. "Several of these are duplicates to the outside doors—those are labeled." She put those aside, and we spread out the rest.

"That's quite a collection," I said. "The storage rooms have newer locks. Pretty standard, so we'll want the full-size keys for those."

"I was so sure we'd unlocked everything before you came," Ava said as she sorted. "I'm going to leave all these with you just in case. I'll take the spares to the house in case someone from the office needs to get in."

"That'll work. If I discover what any of the rest of them go to, I'll label them."

We went down the hall that led from the kitchen to a small apartment at the front of the house, what the Brits referred to as a bedsit. It was half a floor below street level, so it didn't get much light, but it did have its own entrance from the front. This was locked up tight. Though it had a galley kitchen, the bathroom was in the hallway, along with two small closets. Both were locked. After trying a few keys, we were able to open them, and found nothing more exciting than linens of all types—bedding, tablecloths and napkins, and a variety of towels. A faint scent of cedar wafted out.

"They don't make them like they used to," Ava said. "Imagine having a cedar closet for your linen napkins!"

"And some efficient soul even left sandpaper to freshen it up once in a while," I said, pointing to something tucked onto a lower shelf.

"It would've been Fritz. He was a detail guy, kept everything running. He worked for Lars for a long time. Now let me take a few quick pictures. I'm sure all of this is on the inventory of household contents we gave to the trustees, but I'll have to check."

"Why didn't Fritz live here? There's a lot of room."

"From what I understand, he did for a while. Once Lars stopped performing, he bought the place across the street, where you're staying, and Fritz moved in there. Even though they'd worked together for a long time, I think what it came down to was privacy. Lars trusted Fritz more than anyone else, but one thing I've learned since starting this job is that magicians are a secretive and even paranoid bunch. Now, what's next?"

We left the two linen closets unlocked and headed to the main floor.

"What happened to Fritz? Did he move away when Lars died?" I asked as we climbed the stairs.

"No, actually, he died first. Lars was away, and the smoke alarms started going off in the house. Fritz got the call and raced over. He was hit by a car. Hit and run, about three AM, so no one saw anything. The fire turned out to be some smoldering trash near the door to the ground-floor apartment. Some idiot tossed a lit cigarette. Tragic. Lars never really recovered. Wow, I never even realized there was a closet here!"

We were on the first floor in a little alcove tucked beneath the stairs. There was an empty shelf that had probably once held a phone, and enough room for a small chair. In the ornate carving decorating the wall under the stairs, there was a discreet knob and a keyhole.

"I found it when I was looking for someplace to hang my coat," I said. "It's not easy to spot. And I think the hall tree might have been in front of the alcove for a while. See the difference in how the wood is faded?"

"I see what you mean," Ava said, examining the floor. "I think you're right—the hall tree must have been moved. But I never would've noticed the door. You're very observant."

"You should see the building I work in upstate," I said. "You wouldn't believe what's in some of the nooks and crannies there." I pulled out my phone and shone a light at the keyhole. "I think we're looking for an old-style key, but not a very big one."

We pulled the likely candidates out of the box and began to try them.

"Third time's the charm," Ava said as the current key turned smoothly in the lock. The mechanism was clearly old but had been well-maintained. So had the hinges—the door swung open with nary a creak.

"Here, you hang on to this," Ava said, handing me the key. "Now, let's see if there's a switch." She felt around inside the door. "Ah, here we are." With a faint click, a low-wattage bulb just inside the door went on, illuminating shelves to one side and a rod with some empty hangers directly in front of us. Beyond that were a couple of boxes, then darkness.

"This goes farther back," I said, shining my phone flashlight into the depths of the closet. I stepped in and moved the light around, revealing more shelves and boxes. Some were closed and labeled, others were open, and there were items hanging on hooks on the wall. I started reading what was written on the boxes.

"Cards. Coins. Cups and balls." Those seemed straightforward enough. "And here we have locks, lockpicks, chains, and—sponges?"

I turned to Ava. "I know I'm supposed to inventory the ephemera, but I'm not sure I can even identify all of this correctly."

"No," she said. "I had no idea there was so much of this stuff here. I believe this is what the trustees' list of contents called "miscellaneous magic supplies." She sighed, and pushed a couple of boxes around, then turned to me and said, "You're going to need a magician."

Ava left about an hour later, after we'd investigated the one remaining locked area—a wardrobe filled entirely with hats. As promised, she left me the box of unidentified keys.

"I'm sure we've gotten everything unlocked, but then I was sure of that before you arrived. Some of those are small—you may find a trunk or cabinet somewhere that they fit. Just label them if you do. I'll order the archival storage materials you need—those shouldn't take long to arrive. And as soon as I get back to the office, I'll work on getting you some help with the foreign language titles."

"And the miscellaneous magical supplies?"

"I have an idea," Ava said. "It won't be the first time I've pulled a rabbit out of a hat!"

With a laugh and a cheery wave, she was off. I spent the next few hours sorting and cataloging, then had a quick lunch. I tidied up and then put some scraps in a napkin and went into the backyard. There was a stone bench outside the door. Weather permitting, I sat in the sun for a few minutes every afternoon to get some fresh air and clear my head. I'd noticed a couple crows perched on the fence my first week on the job, and had decided to try to befriend them. Every afternoon, I bribed them with scraps from my lunch. They'd learned pretty quickly that the food only stayed on the pavers in front of me while I was out-side—I picked it up and put it in the trash when I went in. So they'd decided to take their chances with me, and now hopped down to eat whenever they saw me come out. The original two had recently been joined by a third, smaller crow. Now that we had a regular lunch date, I'd named them Oliver, Charles, and Mabel. It wasn't the same as my regular chats with the manor ravens upstate, but it was nice.

The trio was arranged on their usual perch. I opened the napkin, recited the day's lunch menu, and took my seat. The three flew down immediately, cawing occasionally and keeping an eye on me. At one point, Mabel hopped over, tilted her head, and studied me. I'd heard corvids could recognize faces, so I let her have a good look. Who knew? Maybe they'd start showing up with crow treasures for me. Probably only bottlecaps or bits of foil, but it's still nice to be appreciated.

Once my new friends were done with their meal, I picked up the napkin and then walked to the back of the yard. It was a long, narrow space. The small patio by the kitchen gave way to patchy dead grass. I could see the outline of what looked like a garden, but nothing grew in it now. The yard was surrounded by fences on three sides, with the house at the other end. There was no access to the street, but there was a gate at the back. It was bolted shut on both sides. All the houses on this block had a small patch of outdoor space to the rear, fenced for privacy initially, and now security as well. No alleyways nearby.

I studied the brownstone. The Amazing Christophe, and later the executors of his estate, had kept the house in good repair. It was part of my job to give the place a good once-over, inside and out, on a weekly basis. It saved the Archive staff from having to make the trip. I spotted no broken windows, falling gutters, loose roof tiles, or any other cause for alarm on the exterior. The curtains on the second and third floor were closed, as I always left them unless I was working in a room. The attic windows were bare, the space within empty. So was the wine cellar. Both were badly lit but clean. I'd thought the brownstone would have a certain air of neglect after having been uninhabited for so many years, but it didn't. Though it felt more watchful than welcoming, the house didn't feel abandoned. It had a sense of expectation about it, as if it were waiting for something.

"Waiting for me to get back to work, probably," I said. I shook my head. Perhaps I was missing the atmospheric Raven Hill Manor more than I thought.

Once back inside, I settled into the front room with my laptop and a small rolling book cart. A wall of bookshelves surrounded a small fireplace, with comfortable chairs and a love seat placed in front of it. A bar cart was at one end, near two pocket doors leading to the library. These I always left open, giving me a view of the length of the house on this side of the hall. At the front of the room, near windows facing onto the street, was a desk with a comfortable chair. I liked to work there in the afternoon. The collection in this room ran more to modern titles and pleasure reading, so it was easier to inventory and catalog. I could also see what was going on in the neighborhood, which was nice since I spent so much time working alone.

I tuned in some classical music on the old but high-quality sound system and got to work. I spent a pleasant and productive afternoon working steadily through a few short shelves, only occasionally distracted by an interesting volume. It was a job-related hazard, and I'd learned to put those aside to look at later. Once I reached a good stopping point, I saved my work, backed it up, and stretched. The sun would be setting soon, and I wanted to get the rest of my house inspection done while I still had some daylight. The electricity worked just fine, and I always carried a flashlight, but some of the rooms had only older overhead light fixtures. I'd open the curtains and let in some natural light, and use the flashlight for any dark corners and cabinets.

Flashlight in hand, I climbed to the attic. I started at one end, turning on lights and checking windows. The space could easily be converted into usable rooms—the ceilings were high enough, and it was insulated. That would add value to a building already worth a small fortune, given current real estate prices. The brownstone needed some updating, but it had been well maintained. I'd no idea what the Archive planned or if the will had any stipulations regarding the disposition of the building. This one wasn't my problem.

I turned off the attic lights and worked my way through the third floor, which housed a few smallish guest rooms and a full bath. Each room had a freestanding wardrobe and a small bookcase in addition to the usual bed and armchair. The largest room even had an antique escritoire with all sorts of drawers and cubbies. I opened every wardrobe and cabinet, using my flashlight to check for problems, from termites to leaks.

"You never know," I said as I finished up in the third-floor bathroom and headed down the stairs. It was unlikely I'd find anything amiss, but I didn't mind what some would consider a tedious job. Truth be told, there was little I enjoyed more than being alone in some building or home that wasn't mine, and poking into anything that caught my interest. Some people were satisfied with snooping through other people's medicine cabinets. I preferred the run of the house, unsupervised. If I wasn't actually supposed to be there doing what I was doing, it added to the illicit thrill. I'd always been partial to the more genteel housebreakers of literature—Raffles; the Saint; Bernie Rhodenbarr; and that girl in *Midsomer Murders* who stole from the rich, as well as the police superintendent, and ended up returning everything to Barnaby's living room when he caught on to her—and felt I understood their motivation. Fortunately, I'd always had a paying job, and thus far at least, no reason to break and enter. Being nosy wasn't illegal.

The second-floor inspection went as uneventfully as the third, though here there were only two bedrooms and one very large bath. At some point closets had been built, creating some odd angles in all of the rooms. The bedroom at the back of the house was where we'd unlocked the wardrobe full of hats. I thought it must have been Christophe's—there was a distinctly masculine feel to the decor.

"Almost done," I said to myself as I returned to the first floor. The light was beginning to fade. I made sure all was in place in the library and that the cases holding the rare books were all locked. Then I crossed the hall to the other side of the house, which held a butler's pantry, a half bath, and the dining room. There was nothing remarkable about any of the rooms, with one exception. In the corner of the dining room, where one would expect to find a hutch full of china or the family silver, was a fortune teller, and an old one at that.

Once I had all the lights on, I walked over and studied what I had come to think of as the "permanent resident." It was an automaton, with the traditional turban and beard, in a colorfully painted glass case. When activated, his head and arm would move, and the machine would spit out a card with your fortune on it. The paint had faded, but it was possible to read the phrase "Ask Alexei" in ornate script across the top of the case. I had never asked Alexei anything—I wasn't even sure if he worked—but I greeted him politely when coming and going.

"I'm leaving for the night," I said as I turned off the lights. "Good evening."

I collected my bag and coat and finished locking up. Darkness was falling on the brownstone, and I checked the time as I set the alarm and began locking up. Perfect. With a brisk pace, I should be right on time.

I had a dinner date with a doorman, and I didn't want to be late.

Chapter Four

～

Suleiman Aydin had been the night doorman for the building my husband and I had lived in. He'd taken the part-time gig while working on his degree at Hunter College. Since I'd moved away, he'd gotten his bachelor's and recently started a job at Columbia. I remembered him as a studious and soft-spoken young man, both thoughtful and observant. If he'd seen something he thought was important on the night of the murder, I wanted to know about it.

We arrived at the diner we'd chosen at the same time. Once we were settled in our booth and had ordered, I congratulated him on his new job.

"I know you must be busy," I said, "so I appreciate you taking time to meet me."

He waved off my thanks. "It's no problem," he said. "I have a work event tonight, and I have to eat, right? And I was glad when your friends started asking questions about that night. Your husband was a good man, and the police weren't interested in what I saw."

"Well, they thought they had their man. They still do for that matter. And maybe they're right."

"But you don't think so, and I'm not sure either. I'm sorry I didn't go to them sooner, but I had just finished a big project for school that day, and I'd been up all night the night before. I was off for the next two days, and I went home and slept for most of the time. When I heard what happened, they had already talked to Oscar and arrested that man, and they didn't take me seriously."

Oscar was the full-time doorman. He worked days and had been there for as long as I could remember.

"What did you see? What made you think it was strange?" I asked.

Suleiman frowned. "It was what I didn't see that was strange," he said. "Look, I was running late from school. I'd called Oscar and he said he'd wait, but he sounded annoyed. So I was hurrying. I had gotten off the bus, and I was at the end of the block, sort of weaving in and out of the other people, you know? Then I saw a man in a suit just stop right in front of the building. He looked around, and then he fell down. Right down, right on the sidewalk. I thought he'd fainted or had a heart attack or something. So I started to run. I saw Oscar come out—we got to the man at about the same time."

Suleiman paused. He was staring into space, as though watching the scene play out on a screen. He took a sip of his water and continued.

"The guy started to sit up. He looked at both of us, then looked around like he was confused. Then he said, 'I'm all right, I'm okay—I just tripped.' But he didn't trip, he just fell down. I saw him. And he kept sitting there, turning his head and sort of looking at the door or something in that direction. It was hard to tell—he had on these big sunglasses, like a snowboarder wears. I thought that was strange, you know, with his suit, and this old leather briefcase. Anyway, he started to stand up. Oscar was trying to help him, but the man kind of waved him off. That's when the delivery man showed up."

"Pete Perry? The man they arrested?"

"I think it must have been him. He was wearing a hoodie and carrying one of those insulated boxes, and he turned and walked into the lobby. I started to go after him, when the guy in the suit sort of swayed. Oscar grabbed his arm and said something like 'Help me here, that's just dinner for 6B.' Then once the guy was steady on his feet, Oscar told me to go ahead in and get ready for my shift, that he'd be happy to help the gentleman. The last bit, though—I think he was just looking for a tip."

"Probably," I said. Oscar was always looking for a tip. "Did you see the delivery guy again?"

"No, I didn't. At first I thought I'd just missed him while I was putting my stuff away and getting my jacket on. But then about fifteen minutes later another delivery showed up, and *that* guy said it was for 6B. I rang up there and they said sure, send him up, it's about time. I didn't really think about it. I was so tired. I'm sorry."

"You didn't do anything wrong," I said. "There's always a lot of stuff going on in the lobby at that time of night."

"I know. Everybody seemed to be getting food delivered. After the order for 6B, someone else got a pizza, and there was sushi for the penthouse. Then FedEx made a late delivery. A while after that your neighbors, the Ginsburgs, got something from the kosher deli. A big container of chicken soup. Mr. Ginsburg had a cold. But there was something else strange."

"Go on."

"All the while this was going on, I could tell the door at the back, the one from the fire stairs, was opening and closing. The lobby door was open—it was a nice night—and when the lobby door is open, and someone goes out the back door, there's a little draft, and kind of a sucking noise, you know? But not loud. And the fire door bangs when it shuts."

"And it wasn't the usual? Smokers, people taking a shortcut?" I asked. Everyone used the stairs when the elevator broke, but we technically weren't supposed to be going out the fire door at the bottom. It opened onto an alley connecting to another alley that led to the cross street on the side of the building, rather than to the avenue in front. It could be used as a shortcut, depending on where you were going. I'd done it myself. And the few resident smokers who didn't want to light up in their apartments would go into the alley and prop the door open. It locked automatically when it shut and couldn't be opened from the outside. Propping it was even more illegal than using it as a shortcut, but the people who did it were careful—they lived in the building, after all.

Suleiman was shaking his head.

"I don't think so. In fact, I'm sure not, because there were times when the air changed but the door didn't bang. The second time it happened, I went and looked, but it was closed. No daylight around the frame."

"Did you go push it?"

"No, I only looked from the lobby, through the mailroom. I didn't want to leave the desk. But I looked at the security monitor for the camera by the back door. I went back to the beginning of my shift. I saw the man with the hoodie leave. He closed the door very carefully, slowly. Then Mr. Norton went out to have a cigarette. But then someone came in, like the door wasn't all the way shut. They even stopped and felt around, like they were checking the lock. Then they shut it from inside."

"Could you tell who it was?" I asked.

"No. The camera isn't very good, you know? I recognized the man in the hoodie because of what he was wearing and the insulated bag. Mr. Norton I know well, and he always wears his Mets cap. This other person could have been a resident, a newer one, but I don't think so. It was someone in a raincoat, with a hat—a beret, I think, or some kind of flat cap. I am sorry," he said again. "I'm not even sure if it was a man or a tall woman. The picture quality is so poor, and it's black and white."

"It's not your fault. You tried to tell someone. The police looked at the security footage, I know they did. It's how they spotted Pete Perry. The hoodie guy," I said.

But had they looked further? And even if they had, would they have tried to identify a random person walking in through the back door? Even though it was supposed to be locked, someone could have left it open. John Norton was careful, but he was also getting older.

I thought for a minute. What Suleiman had said was not a lot to go on, but he knew the building and its residents. If he thought there was something strange happening around the time of Dan's murder, then I believed him. Was it evidence? No, but it could lead to evidence. I slid my dishes aside and tore my paper placemat in half.

"Listen, I think this is important. I'm not sure how, but I want to keep it straight. Could you write down what happened, everything you just told me, in order? Maybe with the time, if you know it?"

"Yes, I know the times, pretty close, because I was running late and kept checking. So a timeline?"

"Yes, and I'm going to make some notes, to make sure I remember."

We each pulled out pens and went to work. When he was done, Suleiman looked over what he'd written, and said, "This is as close as I can get, but I think it's accurate." I read my notes to him, and he added a couple of details. Then he excused himself to go to his work event.

"But please call if you have any other questions," he said, adding all his contact info at the bottom of the timeline. "I would like to know what you find."

I thanked him again and he left. I ordered a cup of coffee. I now had a fuller, though not complete, picture of what had been going on in my building the night Dan was murdered, before I got home. Suleiman had been in the lobby, and he'd filled in some blanks and thrown some new information into the mix. Later in the week, I'd be talking to my former neighbors, the Ginsburgs, who had been out of town visiting their daughter for a few weeks. They still lived down the hall from my old apartment and had seen some things that hadn't made it into the police report. I owed all this new information to the careful detective work of my good friend Beau and his partner Ben, who were also building residents. Beau and I had worked together for years, and it was he who had let us know about an upcoming listing a few floors below him back when Dan and I were looking for a place to buy.

On the night of the murder, it was Beau I asked for when the burly uniformed officer who had responded to my 911 call offered to call someone for me. Beau had arrived, taken in the scene and my obvious shock, and gone into action. He'd talked to the cops and whisked me upstairs, where we were shortly joined by one of his friends who was a lawyer. Beau was a big believer in covering every base. The lawyer sat with me as I answered a few questions for the detectives that had been summoned by uniform, and then informed them that the shocked and exhausted widow would be happy to make a statement at a later date.

Once New York's finest had been banished and the lawyer had left me his contact information, I was tucked into the guest room. Shortly after, Beau appeared with a cup of strong, heavily sugared tea and little triangles of cinnamon toast, explaining that this was how his repressed, genteel Southern family dealt with trauma. After I'd had a little of each, he went down to my apartment to see what he could find out about the status of the investigation.

Once Beau was out the door, Ben appeared with a couple of sleeping pills and a mug of instant hot chocolate laced with brandy, explaining that this was how his loud, dysfunctional North Jersey family dealt with trauma. It did the trick, and by the time I woke up the next day Pete Perry was in custody, and my statement was a formality.

The two of them had also helped with packing up my apartment. Like me, there were a few things about the murder, the robbery, and the investigation that had them wondering. But I didn't say anything, so neither did they. But they discussed it with each other, and when I was ready to talk, so were they. When I was ready to start nosing around, they volunteered to help. Now that I was back in the city, we'd met a few times to put our heads together and see what we had. We would get together again once I'd talked to Suleiman and the Ginsburgs.

I studied the information in front of me. Suleiman was right. Like Sherlock Holmes's dog that didn't bark in the night, what didn't happen was stranger than what did.

The man that did not trip, but fell.

The door that opened, but did not bang shut.

The person that didn't live in the building, but knew a way in that only residents used.

Curiouser and curiouser.

I tucked away the notes, paid my bill, and left.

Chapter Five

I decided to walk home. I had a lot to mull over and hoped the brisk air would clear my head. I kept a steady pace, half my attention on the problem of solving Dan's murder, the other half on what was going on around me. The sounds of cars and buses, horns, people walking and talking on their cell phones, music drifting out of stores and restaurants as doors opened—it all combined into a steady, busy hum. I'd tune into different elements of it as I moved along, whatever was necessary to keep from bumping into something or someone, and to avoid being run over myself.

When I'd first moved to Raven Hill, I'd missed this noise. The quiet unnerved me. The absence of people all around me felt more dangerous than being surrounded by strangers. I drove more and walked less. But as the weather warmed and the place became more familiar, I made an effort to travel on foot when I could. Out walking my landlord's dog, going to and from work or out for coffee, I began to recognize the sounds of the village and the woods around it: less traffic noise, and voices were either off in the distance or close enough to greet me by name; the water of the Ravenskill either a mutter or a roar, depending on the season; the wind in the trees, and the sounds of animals going about their business, just out of sight; the sudden silence when those animals sensed a predator approaching, and the noises resuming when I moved along past them, my sights on different prey.

I turned off the avenue. The volume of the city decreased as I moved down the block. It was mostly residential, and any businesses were closed for the night. The occasional car passed, and I encountered one or two dog walkers, but other than that it was quiet. Here, I actually could hear the wind in the bare branches of the trees planted at intervals along the sidewalk. And something else—footsteps.

I slowed down, just a little. Whoever was behind me would start catching up if they maintained their own pace. I heard the footsteps get closer and then falter. After a brief pause they resumed, at a pace closer to my own. A car cruised by slowly. I could see the light of a cell phone through the passenger window. Someone looking for an address? Probably—the car stopped near the end of the block and someone hopped out. I kept walking. The space between avenues added up to a couple of blocks, but I was getting closer to the intersection. There was a convenience store on the corner, on the opposite side of the street. It wasn't one I usually shopped at, but any port in a storm. And depending on how the lights went, I might have a chance to sneak a peek at who was behind me.

I got to the corner. The traffic lights were in my favor. I'd have to wait to cross to the store. Whoever was behind me would either pass me and continue on across the avenue, or wait with me until the light changed. I turned to face the crosswalk and glanced back the way I'd come. I caught a glimpse of a figure moving into the shadows just beyond the streetlight. I looked to my right. There were a few people crossing the avenue toward me. When I looked to my left again, no one was in sight.

The light changed. I stepped off the curb and walked quickly, looking back over my shoulder when I entered the store. There was one person walking across the avenue, moving fast to make the light. I couldn't tell if it was the same one I'd seen behind me.

I roamed the aisles and picked up a container of half-and-half I needed and a package of cookies that I didn't. By the time I paid for my purchases, I'd thrown in a candy bar. You never know when you'll need emergency rations.

I took a good look around when I left the store. Everyone in sight seemed to be going about their business and paying no attention to me. Still, I took an indirect route home, staying on busier streets and zigzagging. The entrance to my building was on the avenue around the corner from the brownstone, so I was able to avoid the quiet cross street. Once inside, I made sure the door locked behind me, then began the trek upstairs to my apartment. By the time I'd walked in, relocked all three locks, turned on all the lights, and opened the cookies, I was beginning to wonder if I'd imagined the whole thing.

I went to the window and looked down onto the street. The only traffic, vehicular or pedestrian, was an older man walking his dog. I'd seen those two often around this time of night, so nothing unusual there. There were a few lights on in the brownstone. Those were on timers, and they went on and off to mimic the evening routine of a resident. Everything was on schedule from what I could see. I watched for another couple of minutes, then closed the curtains and went into the kitchen.

I put away the cookies and got out some ice cubes and a lemon. Once the glass was chilled and I had a nice twist, out came the gin and vermouth. Martini in hand, I retrieved the notes from my dinner with Suleiman and went into the alcove off the bedroom. This was where I'd come across some of the more interesting features of my new abode. The largest of these and my personal favorite was at the far end of the narrow room.

I set my drink down on top of the bookshelf, turned on the lamp, and closed the curtains. Then I went to what looked like an ornate, four-panel wooden screen hung on the wall like the work of art it was. It was carved with all manner of mythical beings in every imaginable landscape. The day I'd moved in, I'd been admiring the craftsmanship, and was running my fingers over a detailed depiction of the North Wind when it gave a little beneath my hand, and I realized it was a latch. The screen opened between the two center panels and folded back into itself. Behind it was a magnetic whiteboard. Beneath that was a shelf about a foot and a half deep and a scroll-shaped bracket, both attached to the wall with hooks. When unhooked, they swung out to form a desk.

I'd been delighted with it. Fritz, or someone who lived here before him, must have converted a shallow closet into this workspace. The board had been wiped clean, but there were plenty of magnets and I'd picked up a package of dry erase markers. Now, it was my evidence board.

I had to admit it wasn't quite as grand as the one used by my favorite detectives on television. Detective Chief Inspector Vera Stanhope had the entire wall of a squad room to work with. Senior Detective Mike Shepherd and his staff at the Brokenwood Police Department had a smallish, freestanding whiteboard. According to my friend Officer Jennie Webber, she used something similar in her office at the local police department. Since I'd always considered Brokenwood to be the New Zealand equivalent of Raven Hill, this made sense to me. My board was smaller still, more along the lines of the one the amateur sleuths had in *Only Murders in the Building*. But I figured I could do as well or better than a bunch of fictional true-crime podcasters, so here I was.

I retrieved my martini and placed it on the desk, along with the notes. I shifted the reading chair, swung it around to face the board, and settled in. As I sipped my martini, I studied what I had so far.

Centered at the top was a picture of Danny. It was a color printout of the photo he'd used on his company bio. I didn't want to use anything more personal—I was trying to maintain some distance, behave like a dispassionate observer. I needed to channel my inner girl detective and not give in to emotion.

I studied the rest of the players. I'd broken them down into two groups—likely suspects and witnesses. I used the term loosely—all of them had a close connection to either Dan or my suspects and might have information that could prove useful. I'd printed photos of all of them that I'd found online. Most worked for New Leaf, Dan's company. Like Dan, they had good headshots along with their professional bios. The one exception was Pete Perry, the man who'd gone to jail for the crime. I'd found a full-length promotional picture of him kitted out for a boxing match, but it gave a decent look at his face. I'd chosen that one, instead of the mugshot I'd also found, because I thought the fact that he was a trained fighter was important—he swore he'd only hit Dan hard enough to knock him out, and I figured he'd know.

Underneath each picture I'd written a few keywords. I'd put together a pretty extensive file on each of my suspects, but distilling the information down to the most salient points and adding it to the board helped me stay focused. I'd done the same for key witnesses. Then I'd drawn dotted lines between people who had connections to one another. I thought about what Suleiman had said, and added two cards to my suspect pool. Both had question marks in lieu of photos. The first said "the man who fell down" and the second read "Nonresident at back door." I wrote some details under each and reviewed my list:

Clarice Philips: CEO, charismatic, smart, young for the job
William Warren: COO, law degree, arrogant, losing his hair
Frank Benson: company counsel, mid-life crisis, average abilities
Pete Perry: boxer, petty thief, admits to B&E, hired to rob us
Man who fell down: didn't trip, oddly dressed, watching door
Nonresident at back door: ???

The obvious culprit was Perry, which was why he was in jail. The man Suleiman saw fall might just be a bit of an odd-ball—being clumsy and badly accessorized wasn't a crime—but he might also be an accomplice. Whoever slipped in the back door was a wild card—murderer, accomplice, or big fat nothing? I didn't have enough information to judge, but my instinct was they had something to do with the murder. I left both in the suspect group.

The remaining three people on the list were better-known quantities. They were also at the top of the food chain at New Leaf, so if there was something hinky going on, they had the most to lose. If they knew about it, they were crooks. If they didn't, they were idiots.

I didn't think any of them were idiots.

Frank Benson, though, was not of the same caliber as the other two. Dan had commented on it when he was hired. The Benson Group was a boutique law firm that had done some work for New Leaf as the company was expanding operations, but before they'd started wading into the cannabis dispensary business. According to Dan, Frank was an affable guy and decent lawyer who spent a lot of time golfing with clients. April was the brains of the operation. Yet it was Frank who was offered a big job and big salary. Even his wife had been surprised. It was strange. So was his behavior right before he died last September, but I hadn't considered him a serious suspect until April mentioned he had been in the neighborhood that night. I'd check to see what time his daughter's play had started. He was late, so the timing might work.

April Benson had been in the neighborhood as well. I'd given that some thought, but I couldn't come up with any kind of motive on her part. She was successful in her own right and had no use for the New Leaf crowd. I kept her in the "witness" pool, though, because she had insight into the business and access to some of Frank's records. She also had a personal interest in seeing this solved. That led me back to Frank's entry on the board to add one more pertinent detail.

Frank Benson: company counsel, mid-life crisis, average abilities, murdered?

Possibly. Probably, as far as I was concerned. But it would be hard to prove. Still, it had to be factored in.

William Warren. Successful, in an unremarkable sort of way. Went to the same good schools his parents had. Got a clerkship after law school working for someone his father knew. Made some useful connections and moved on to a big firm and bigger paycheck. Worked in a couple of different offices for them in the

United States, then spent some time in Europe. Came back to the states with a different firm, then took the job at New Leaf. Not a typical career path, but every position moved him up the ladder. Perhaps it was petty of me to add the bits about him being arrogant and losing his hair, but I'd met him a few times and found him insufferable. He thought he was smarter than everyone else in the room, no matter where he was. And he always seemed to be watching, waiting for someone to slip up. He never relaxed.

"Probably can't let his hair down for fear of ruining his comb-over," I'd whispered to Dan after a few drinks at the last company Christmas party we'd attended. My husband, one of the kindest people I'd ever met, had burst out laughing. So Dan hadn't liked him either. Warren definitely hadn't been hired for his charm.

Clarice Philips, on the other hand, had charm to spare. She could work a room like no one else I knew. It helped that she was attractive in an Eastern European model kind of way. Striking rather than pretty, as well as tall and lean, she dressed beautifully, and she never forgot a name or a face. She was also smart, a product of the Ivy League and then a top business school. She'd become CEO of New Leaf in her late twenties by leveraging her contacts and her charisma. I hadn't been able to find much about her more formative years, but I wasn't sure I needed to. The mystery of Dan's death started and ended with that company, I was sure of it. This mystery wasn't so much a whodunnit as a howcatchem, more Columbo than Poirot.

I decided to email pictures of my chief suspects to Suleiman. It was possible that either the man on the sidewalk or the unidentified person who'd come in the back door were already on my list, rather than additions to it. I had the headshots and some other, more informal pictures saved on my laptop. I'd send them in the morning.

Next up was the timeline Suleiman had made. This interested me because he was on the spot and could place certain people, identity known or not, in the building at specific times. I pulled out a big envelope I kept tucked into the desk and withdrew some folded pages. These were screenshots of the text messages Dan and I had exchanged the night he died. They covered nearly four hours. I laid them next to what I'd gotten from Suleiman. Then I rifled through the envelope again and pulled out the police report on Dan's death. Jennie Webber had gotten a copy and passed it on to me.

I read through it and then laid it on the desk as well. I studied my evidence board. What I needed was a complete timeline, one that covered the whereabouts of all my key players on the night of the murder. These documents were a good start. I got a notepad and made a rough draft. There were plenty of gaps, but I had some ideas about filling them in. The next step would be to get this on the whiteboard. Maybe color-coded by suspect? It would be a job, but useful. I yawned and checked the time. The timeline would have to wait.

I put everything away and closed the wooden panel. Empty glass in hand, I turned off the light and took another look out the window. The lights in the brownstone were mostly off. For a second I thought I saw movement in an upstairs window, but then decided it was a reflection of tree branches swaying in the wind. All was quiet on the block below. It looked like I'd be adding surveilling the street to my nightly routine. I was already doing multiple checks of the door locks, so why not? I should probably start varying my route home whenever I was out and about, I thought as I got ready for bed. Just because you're paranoid doesn't mean no one's following you.

I patted on some eye cream, checked the locks one last time, and crawled under the covers, expecting to be fast asleep in minutes. Not so much. I lay there, staring up at the ceiling, replaying my conversations with Suleiman and April and Father Liam. I was spinning and getting nowhere. I tried listing all the classifications of the Dewey Decimal system in order, including frequently used subclasses. It didn't help. I got up and walked through the dark apartment to get a glass of water.

When I returned to the bedroom, there were lights flickering through the gap in the curtains. Something was going on. I peeked out. A tow truck was moving slowly down the street, a whirling light on its roof flashing yellow, trailing a small, crumpled car with red lights on its bumper behind it. It had reached the far end of the block when a movement caught my eye on the sidewalk. Something small scampered away from a trash can and then paused, sniffing the air. A rat, most likely, at this time of night. Ick.

I watched to make sure it wasn't headed toward the brownstone. I was very careful with the trash for just this reason. It bounced a few steps closer to Christophe's, then turned and darted back the way it had come. Something had startled it. I watched, scanning the entrances to the three houses across from me, Christophe's in the center. I waited a couple of minutes and was about to go back to bed when a shadow detached itself from the wall of the house to the left of Christophe's. Avoiding the bright circle cast by the streetlight, it turned and walked swiftly away, seeming to disappear halfway down the block. Again I waited, but nothing else moved on the street.

I went to bed and fell into a sleep punctuated by dreams of walking down an endless corridor. Dan was at the end, but every time I got close, shadowy hands plucked at me, and a mist rose between us.

Chapter Six

The next day was both uneventful and rainy. I emailed Suleiman pictures of my suspects. He replied quickly—he didn't recognize Clarice. William Warren could have been the man who pretended to trip, but he wasn't certain—that man had been heavier. He didn't think he'd ever seen Frank Benson, and any one of them might have been the person who had come in the back.

I made steady progress on the collection and mulled over everything I'd learned. It didn't add up to much. I did get an email from April with the contact information for her cannabis expert and a brief note telling me she was still wading through stuff from Frank's home office but finding nothing of interest. I also heard from Ava, letting me know she'd found someone to help with both the Italian and the "magical supplies."

"He's been out of town but will be back this afternoon," she said. "He'd like to meet, but it would have to be kind of late. Is that okay?"

"Sure," I said. "Here?"

"No, but somewhere in the neighborhood. He said he'd text when he got in and let you know. You can always propose something else if it doesn't work for you. What can I say? Performers. They like to set the stage."

"Right, no worries. I'll let you know when I hear from him. Thanks."

I went back to what I was doing, which involved sorting through a couple of boxes from the closet we'd opened, as well as a few volumes from the collection. I'd been intrigued by the box labeled "lockpicks," and when I came across several books on the subject, one published by the CIA, I considered it a sign. After I'd read Ashley Weaver's Electra McDonnell series, I'd concluded that lockpicking was a useful skill to have. I didn't aspire to Electra's safecracking talent, which was just as well because, from the look of things, mastering lockpicking would take a lot of practice. No matter—I'd like to have something to do with my hands when watching television, and I hadn't taken to knitting.

I was in the process of laying out all the tools I'd found in the first box, comparing them to sketches in the books I'd found, and listing them on a spreadsheet, when my phone pinged. I didn't recognize the number. I opened the text.

Ava gave me your number. I'd like to
help. Can you meet me tonight at 9?
The Hungarian. Do you know it?

The magician. At least he used proper punctuation. I responded.

Yes. 9 is fine.

Great. See you then. I'll get a table.

He must be a magician if he could guarantee a table at nine. The Hungarian was always busy. This should be interesting. At least I'd have time to go to my self-defense class and then shower. With any luck, he'd be both knowledgeable and interesting. It would be nice to have someone other than Alexei to talk to.

I went back to my work. Time to inventory the box of locks and find one to practice on.

* * *

The Hungarian was an Upper West Side institution. It had been in business since the 1960s, across the street from the fantastical Peace Fountain adjacent to the Cathedral of St. John the Divine. I hadn't been there in a while, but nothing seemed to have changed. I stopped a waiter who was serving customers outside.

"Excuse me, I'm meeting some—"

"Inside. Back corner," he said, motioning with his head.

I walked in, inhaling the heady aroma of strong, fresh coffee. There was indeed an empty table in the back corner. With a lingering glance at the pastry case, I made my way through the crowded shop. The minute I sat down, a different waiter appeared.

"Your friend will be back in a minute. He said to go ahead and order."

You don't have to ask me twice where dessert is concerned. "I'll have a cappuccino and the chocolate torte," I said.

The waiter nodded and left. I took off my coat and looked around, enjoying the atmosphere. It was nice to be back, though, as I listened to the happy gurgle of the espresso machine, I felt a pang of homesickness for the Java Joint back in Raven Hill.

At that moment a lithe figure in black jeans and a dark

turtleneck slid into the seat across from me. His face was a collection of angles and shadows, with olive skin and grass-green eyes, and he had dark hair and the hint of a beard.

"I understand you need a magician, Ms. Hogan," he said, his voice low and melodious. He reached out. I felt a faint movement of air near my ear, and then I was being presented with a red rose. "Joseph Grimaldi, at your service."

I took the flower. I couldn't help but smile. "Call me Greer," I said.

"And you can call me Grim. All my friends do."

Of course. He certainly wasn't a Joe.

"Nice entrance, Grim," I said.

"I do my best," he said with a grin. "It helps that they know me here."

"I'll bet it does."

The waiter arrived with my order and what looked like a triple espresso for Grim. It was so dark it seemed to absorb light.

"Time change," he said, noticing my glance.

"When—"

"So tell me about the job," he said.

I gave him a summary of what I'd found, both in the library and in various closets, as well as some information on how we were inventorying and cataloging. He listened attentively, nodding once in a while. When I was done, I asked if he had any questions. What he said surprised me.

"So nothing in the attic or the wine cellar? Just stuff in the closets?"

I paused as I reached for my coffee.

"I didn't know you were familiar with the house," I said.

He looked surprised. "Doesn't every brownstone in the area have an attic and a cellar?"

"Undoubtedly, but you said 'wine cellar.' I'm pretty sure not all of them have floor-to-ceiling racks."

I got the mischievous grin again. "Good catch," Grim said. "Ava said you were sharp. As a matter of fact, I have been in the brownstone. It's been nine or ten years. I knew Lars professionally, though it was after he retired from performing."

"So you used to—what?—drop by to sample the occasional rare vintage and talk shop? Ava told me magicians were a secretive lot."

"True," he said. "But Lars was as much a teacher as a performer. Even when he was touring, he'd go to schools or summer camps and teach kids some basic tricks. He still did some of that when he retired, though he got much more into the history of magic and illusion. If he got a reasonable request from someone who wanted to use his collection to do some research, he'd invite them."

"And you had a reasonable request?"

"A few of them. I liked what he was doing, gathering all these books and manuscripts. The history of the art could easily be lost. It got to where I would look for things for him wherever I was in the world, and bring them to him. And I confess—I'm fond of a good French red, and he had a nice collection of those too."

"I'm with you there," I said. "Unfortunately, there's nothing left in the wine cellar. Not even dust. The cleaning crew is very efficient."

"Hmm. Attic the same?"

"Yep. Did he ever store anything up there?"

Grim shrugged. "Empty suitcases and trunks. Old props—top hats, zombie balls, the odd sword. You know—the usual."

Indeed.

"Well, I think the stuff in the attic was cleaned out and stashed on the lower floors. You can take a look around. Everything's unlocked now, and if it mysteriously relocks, I've got the keys."

Grim raised his eyebrows. "'Mysteriously relocks?'"

"Kidding. It's just that Ava thought everything was unlocked before I got there, but it wasn't the case. I think it's a function of several different interns being involved in previous inventories and in checking the house. According to Ava, they all want to see it."

"Hmm," Grim said again. "Well, you're probably right. The place does have a certain mystique."

"Apparently," I said. "Compared to where I work upstate, it's pretty low-key."

"Where's that?"

I told him about Raven Hill Manor and the library, and how I ended up with this temporary gig. I left out some of the details—like the fact that I had regular chats with the stuffed raven in Horatio Ravenscroft's old office, or the inexplicable smell of cherry pipe tobacco that sometimes wafted by. I also glossed over how I came to be the executor of a will relating to the premises, saying only that some of the provisions of the family trust were a bit convoluted, as was the family tree.

"What sounded good on paper is more difficult in the execution," I said. "The devil's in the details."

"No one ever really believes they're going to die, do they?" Grim said. "Or disappear," he added with a frown.

"A fitting end for a magician, though, isn't it?"

"We generally prefer to plan it and then reappear for maximum effect," he said. "Not just sail off into the sunset, never to be seen again. It's strange, though. He did the same trip every year."

"Ava said the weather was unusual, but he went out anyway. They found the boat, but no Lars. But you probably know more about this than I do."

Grim shrugged. "I was out of the country. Anyway, back to the brownstone. When would you like to get started? Tomorrow?"

"How about the day after? I have something to do tomorrow. Around ten?"

He winced. "You mean in the morning?"

"I do."

"Noon?" he asked. "Let me sleep in, get over the rest of this jetlag, and after that my entire bag of tricks is at your disposal."

"How promising," I said. "I'll expect to be thrilled and amazed. Noon it is."

He smiled and waved me off when I reached for my wallet.

"On me," he said. "I'll see you soon, Greer Hogan."

"Looking forward to it," I said.

Chapter Seven

April had suggested I rattle some cages, and I'd taken her advice to heart. I'd made an appointment to meet with Clarice Philips and William Warren at the New Leaf offices. After speaking briefly with a receptionist and making vague remarks about having to resolve some issues relating to my husband's death and some missing paperwork, I'd been put on a brief hold and then transferred to Clarice's assistant. He introduced himself as Austin, and in sympathetic tones informed me that New Leaf wanted to help in any way they could and had given me an appointment with Clarice for the very next afternoon.

I didn't know if that was a good sign or a bad one, but either way, I was going in with my game face on. Hair, makeup, outfit—it all had to help me make my case. A grieving but recovering widow, with the same expensive taste but less stable finances, deciding how to move on, and with many, many questions about her husband's last days in the office. It was a fishing expedition, and I intended to imply more than I stated, and see what bait they took. If any.

The next morning I got my hair trimmed and blown out. My former stylist, still working in the same salon, was happy to see me back and squeezed me in. What's more, she approved of my current cut and color.

"These layers are great—they really give you a lift. And the color is nice and rich, like your natural color, but better. You can probably go longer between touch-ups. Still, we'll need to do something about those roots in a few weeks."

Moira and I chatted about how the city had changed, and how it hadn't, since I'd left. She asked about my new job, and I told her my plans were up in the air at the moment. Once I'd finished the temporary job and settled some outstanding things related to Dan's death, I wasn't sure.

Moira snapped her fingers.

"I knew there was something! I wanted to thank you for sending me a new client. The woman who runs that company, the one your husband worked for. Clarice."

I was surprised. I'd recommended Moira to several people, but I couldn't recall saying anything to Clarice. I might have, though, while making small talk during some company function. It would have been before Dan died.

"I'm glad. So she's been with you for a few years now?" I said.

Moira paused, scissors in hand.

"Not exactly. She first came in around three or maybe four years ago. When did you move away? Four years ago, after Dan died but before you left. I remember because she would ask me if I'd seen you and how you were doing. She was concerned, you know? Anyway, after about a year, maybe a little less, she said she was moving way uptown. She'd inherited a condo or something. Then I didn't see her again until a couple of weeks ago. She came in and said she just couldn't find anyone she was happy with, and since I was close enough to her office, she wanted to come back. Don't know what she's been doing to her hair," Moira added. "It's a mess. Looks like she tried to cut it herself." She sniffed and shook her head.

I smiled. Moira had firm opinions about what her clients were allowed to do to their own hair. Beyond shampooing and brushing, very little.

"Well, I'm glad it worked out. For both of you, apparently. So, any good new restaurants I should try?"

We talked food for the rest of the appointment. I didn't tell Moira I would be seeing Clarice. I wasn't sure I'd mention Moira to Clarice either. It was a connection and a possible source of information. I'd play it by ear.

I left the salon and grabbed an early lunch on my way home. Back in my apartment, I redid my makeup and dressed in an ensemble I thought of as "power casual": tailored pants, fitted knit top, longer jacket. All classic and excellent quality, if not all up-to-the-minute fashion. And because I was back in my Manhattan wardrobe, all black, with one exception.

The deep red designer tote bag was made of a lightweight, recycled material. It had been a gently used hand-me-down from my colleague Millicent Ames. Millicent had been the archivist at the Raven Hill Library for most of her life. In her later years, she'd developed arthritis and adjusted her wardrobe accordingly.

"It was a well-intentioned thank-you gift from a genealogical society, Greer. It's light as a feather, but too big. I can't carry much without aggravating my shoulder. It would please me to see you use it. You'll appreciate the design, and I know you like a bright accessory," Millicent had said. "I've reached the age when I'd rather see things used than gathering dust in my closet."

I'd accepted the bag happily, and pulled it out now, comforted by the feeling that I was carrying some of Millicent's sharp intelligence with me. Once I'd packed it with everything I needed, I posed in front of the mirror. The pop of color elevated the outfit. Perfect. Off I went.

I made good time getting across town. Since I was a little early, I walked around the block before going in. It felt strange being there—I'd only visited the building once since Dan died. It had been shortly before I left town, and I'd had to take care of some things that couldn't be handled by email. The HR rep had been very apologetic and more than a little flustered when she was talking to me. I'd found being the widow of a murder victim had that effect on people. She'd even forgotten to give me something, a small box of personal items from Dan's desk, and had to race down to the lobby to catch me before I left. I hadn't had the heart to look inside it at the time, and now it was packed away with a lot of other stuff from my old home. Those boxes had been living in my parents' basement in Riverdale for years, and my mother never tired of reminding me that I needed to go through them and make some decisions about the contents.

Nerves steady, I went through the revolving doors into the building. Not much had changed. It was prewar construction, updated as needed but still sporting the woodwork and marble of an earlier age. The lobby had a combination reception and security desk in the middle, a half circle of gleaming polished oak. I stated my business and was given an adhesive pass to put on my lapel. I walked past the gleaming brass mailbox, topped by an eagle, the glass chute that fed it disappearing into the ceiling. The modern elevators whooshed beneath the original metal floor indicators, now only decorative. Call me an old-fashioned girl—I'd take this over a sleek, modern skyscraper any day.

I arrived at New Leaf to find Austin, Clarice's assistant, waiting for me at reception. He introduced himself and walked me

back to the executive offices. Nothing much had changed here
either. It was still an ugly cubicle farm, but at least they hadn't
gone to one of those ghastly open floor plans with sterile white
furniture and a clean-desk policy. I said as much to Austin.

"We're all about keeping costs down," he replied. "And I
think this suits the space better."

To the degree that portable carpeted walls stuck together
in squares suited any space, I guessed he was right. It was fairly
quiet, but I was still subject to curious stares as I walked through
the office. Every company runs on gossip. I didn't see anyone I
knew, though a couple of faces seemed vaguely familiar. One
twenty-something man came around the corner, saw me, then
stopped dead and stared. I couldn't place him, so I smiled and
nodded and kept going. Awkward.

Austin ushered me into Clarice's office. She was seated
behind her desk but rose and glided over to me immediately.
William Warren was also present, but on the phone. He turned
his back to finish his call. He'd ditched his comb-over in favor of
shaving off what was left of his hair. It was an improvement—I
could tell by the five o'clock shadow on his head that if he hadn't
buzzed it off he'd be looking like Gollum by now. He'd also lost
some weight.

I held out my hand to Clarice and smiled.

"So nice to see you again. And I absolutely love your pant-
suit!" I said.

"Oh, thank you. You don't think it's too nineties, do you?
I hesitated, but I fell in love with the color. And it's perfect for
days I have meetings—I can just lose the jacket while I'm working at my desk."

"Doesn't look at all dated, and the color is fabulous. That
silvery gray brings out your eyes. Good choice."

This was the type of conversation I'd always had with her, but at least I could be honest. The suit was the color of fog, and complemented the icy blue of her eyes and her dark hair, now cut in a chic bob. She wore a simple T-shirt under the suit jacket. It was understated elegance. That was Clarice.

Warren ended his call and walked toward us, hand outstretched.

"William, you're looking well," I said.

"Thanks. I've taken up running."

Which could be the difference between the heavier man that Suleiman recalled and the leaner William in front of me, I thought as we shook hands. When he attempted to crush my fingers, I recalled he'd always been the type to exert a lot of force during a handshake. I managed to smile instead of rolling my eyes, and returned his grip with a full-strength one of my own. I was pleased to see his look of surprise and decided all the time at the gym was paying off.

Clarice gestured to a small conference table in the corner, and we all took a seat. Austin popped his head in to see if anyone wanted anything to drink. Sparkling water all around. While we waited for him to come back, we made small talk about the weather and some new off-Broadway shows Clarice had seen. I hadn't realized she was such a theater maven. Warren followed the conversation closely but contributed little. He sat drumming his fingers against his thigh. When Austin reappeared and started handing round the Perrier, I saw Clarice shoot Warren a look. He stopped the drumming and reached for his glass. Once the door had closed behind her assistant, Clarice turned her attention to me.

"Austin mentioned that you had some questions, something about incomplete paperwork? Some confusion around the time Dan died? Tell me, what can we do to help?"

"There are a few things actually. I'm not even sure where to begin. It took a while to process everything, you know?"

"Of course. Take your time. Grief is such a strange thing, isn't it? Different for everyone."

There was genuine feeling in her voice. Clarice was good with people, but I'd put money on this being real empathy.

"Yes, it is strange. You don't just walk through dictated stages on a timetable. Some take more than others. It's surprising what comes up," I said.

Clarice was nodding in agreement.

"Hasn't it been about four years?" Warren said.

Clarice's mouth tightened. She took a sip of her water. I looked at Warren and said, "Four years in April, actually. You have a good memory."

"I checked when you called," he said. "I thought everything on our end should have been taken care of by now. You haven't had any issues have you? Life insurance, that sort of thing?"

"No. Your human resources person, Lucy, was very good. Walked me through everything, checked in with me later. She even met with me in person. I think she could tell I was in shock for a while."

"Who can blame you? It *was* shocking. A simple robbery gone awry. Infuriating. I mean, such a waste. And over what? Some jewelry?" Clarice shook her head.

"I think it's fair to say we were all shaken up," Warren said. "That's why I wanted to make sure there were no loose ends here. It wouldn't have been acceptable, but I can see how it might happen."

"It was nothing like that, though I'm glad you checked. I packed up our apartment right away, and I could have missed something. I'm only now starting to go through the remaining boxes. No, what I wanted to talk about was more—personal,

I guess you could say. I've always wondered about it but kept pushing it aside."

I paused. They waited silently. I took a deep breath. *Here goes nothing*, I thought.

"Dan mentioned that he was worried about something, a mistake, a discrepancy he'd found. He wanted to talk to me about it, but we didn't have time that morning, and then, well, you know . . ."

There was a brief silence. Nobody moved.

"Did he say what kind of—mistake?" Warren asked.

I shook my head. "No. He didn't. He said he'd need to explain it, it seemed crazy, and he couldn't believe he hadn't seen it before."

I stopped. The last phrase had just floated up out of my subconscious. *"I can't believe I didn't see this before."* I was once again standing in my apartment, getting ready to leave for work, and Dan was leaning against the kitchen door, coffee cup in hand.

"See what?"

That's what I'd said, but Dan had repeated that it was crazy, a lot to go into, and I'd told him we'd talk later, because I was late for work. It was only when I tuned back into my surroundings that I realized the question had come from Clarice, and that she and Warren were waiting for a response.

"Oh, I'm sorry. I just—I don't know what. That's what concerns me. I mean, he didn't make a big mistake on something, did he? I presumed it was some accounting thing, someone's expense report didn't add up or whatever. But he'd been so distracted, I began to worry. I'd hate to think he made an error and didn't own up to it right away, and I brushed him off. You know, your mind goes in all sorts of directions after something like that, but I've been feeling bad. About that whole day."

The bit about Dan making some kind of big financial error was a stretch—he was both intelligent and meticulous. But my mind *had* gone in all directions and I *did* still feel bad about how things had gone down on the day Dan died. The best lies are nearly all truth, so I was hoping this gambit sounded sincere.

I looked from one to the other, trying to gauge their response. Clarice looked puzzled. She tilted her head and seemed to be considering something. Warren leaned back in his chair and smiled.

"You've been worrying for nothing, Greer. Dan wasn't the kind who made big mistakes. If anything, he was too much of a Boy Scout. He was the one who worried unnecessarily. It would have been better if he'd let some things go," he said. "Wouldn't you agree, Clarice?"

"Well, I did appreciate his attention to detail," she said with a smile. "But I'd agree he could have let some of the smaller stuff go. That's why we agreed to let him hire—what was her name? Isabelle, I think. That one could have done an annual report in her head before breakfast, without even breaking out a calculator. But at least Dan was willing to delegate some things to her."

"Isabelle, yes, Isabelle Peterson. I met her recently, you know," I said.

"Oh?" Clarice replied without much interest, but Warren shifted in his seat. It was time for my second gambit.

"Yes, in Lake Placid. At a wedding," I said. "Last September. I saw Frank Benson there too. Oh, I forgot! I didn't mean to bring up a sad subject. He was still working here when he died, wasn't he?"

"He was. We were all devastated," said Clarice.

"I'm sure. He was a nice man. He remembered me, though we'd only met once or twice. He had some nice things to say about Dan."

I was lying again. I'd had to remind Frank who I was, and he'd been pretty tight-lipped. But they didn't need to know that.

"Anyway, it was shortly after that he keeled over. Heart attack, wasn't it?" I shook my head. "So sad. It was nice talking to him and hearing about the progress the company was making. So interesting, this move into CBD products and now cannabis dispensaries?"

"We feel there's a great opportunity in the wellness space," Clarice said. "There's a natural synergy with our current product line. We'd love to partner with small businesses to expand their offerings."

"In terms of products?" I asked.

"In terms of their business model," William said. "You know how gyms started adding juice bars? Picture exercise studios and meditation centers with an attached dispensary and lounge. People can consume the product on the spot. Of course, there are issues with banking and other legalities, but—"

"But we feel everything is moving in that direction," Clarice interjected smoothly. William looked annoyed, but he kept his mouth shut.

"Wow, that's fascinating," I said. "I've been so out of the loop since I changed careers and moved."

"Understandable, especially given everything you've been through," said Clarice. "But sometimes a change of scene is just what the doctor ordered, isn't it? Are you enjoying your work? You're a librarian, aren't you?"

"Yes. I've been working in a small library upstate. They had a fire, so I've taken a job here while they renovate the building.

And then we'll see. It's certainly interesting, and often gratifying, if not nearly as lucrative. But a nice change."

"I'm glad to hear it. And I'm glad we could put your mind at ease about Dan. Now, I have to get ready for a dinner meeting with some potential investors, but if there's anything else, I'm sure William—"

"No, nothing else. I don't want to take up any more of your time. This has been so helpful."

"No problem at all. Feel free to call if anything else comes up. I'll have Austin show you out." We all stood, and Clarice reached for the phone on the table.

Time to channel Columbo.

"Oh, there is just one more thing," I said. They both turned to look at me.

"I found this in Dan's desk at home," I said, reaching into my tote bag. I pulled out a red folder, and slipped out a piece of paper. "It's a spreadsheet. I don't recognize anything on it. It must be related to work. I doubt it's important, but I thought I'd check."

In fact, it was important. Important enough that Dan had mailed it, and three other pages like it, to our friend Ian Cameron. It came with no explanation, and it had been mailed the day he died. This was a copy of the last page, with only six lines of figures and a total.

Clarice took the paper from me and studied it. Then she passed it to Warren. Trying to maintain an expression of bland innocence myself, I watched them. Clarice raised an eyebrow and then frowned. Warren's whole body tensed. He looked over at Clarice, who shook her head.

"It looks like part of an old list of our vendors," she said. "Incomplete, of course. There were probably several more pages. Is this all you found?" Clarice asked.

"So far," I said. "I've only started going through the remaining boxes of things from the apartment. This is the only thing I've found that I couldn't identify. Is it important?"

"No, not really. We obviously don't want any confidential information floating around, but this is outdated and, as I said, incomplete," Clarice said. "Many of our early vendors have gone out of business. Regulatory environment, tax code—you know. Still, I'd like to shred this. And call if you find anything else?"

"Of course. Though Dan did anything work related on his laptop. He rarely printed things out, and when he did, he usually shredded them as soon as he was done. And the computer was taken during the robbery. But you know that."

"Yes," Warren said. "We froze his access the minute we heard."

"Well, then, another concern that amounted to nothing," I said with a smile. "I'm so glad I came to see you. Now I'll let you get ready for your meeting. Investors, you said?"

"Time for the old razzle-dazzle," Clarice said. "Yes, investors. I'll be glad when we have this latest round of financing in place and can take a break."

Warren hung onto the spreadsheet. Clarice summoned her assistant. We said polite farewells. I turned down the offer of a ride to take me home by volunteering the fact that I'd be walking a few blocks to warm up for the gym. Austin escorted me back through the office. Apparently, he was going to see me all the way to the street. I'd love to have been a fly on the wall in Clarice's office, or at least to have seen William Warren's face when he left it, but no chance of that now.

We'd reached reception when Austin patted his pocket and frowned.

"My phone," he said. "I must have left it on my desk."

"I'll wait right here while you get it," I said. Reception gave a good view into the offices, and I might see something interesting.

He hesitated, glancing back toward the executive offices.

"I'll only be a minute," he said, and disappeared down the hall.

The receptionist was not in sight. She might have left for the day, or she might not. I gave her desk a quick once-over. The surface was tidy, but not pristine, and there was a screensaver on her computer monitor. I hit a random key and a password field popped up. I stepped back and took a peek down the hall. No one to be seen. I spotted a box tucked under the desk to the left of the chair, with the logo of a well-known printing company on it. I moved closer and pulled my MetroCard out of my pocket, pretending to drop it. I bent and pushed the cardboard flap aside, revealing a stack of glossy folders with the company logo and the phrase "New Leaf, New Directions, New Opportunities" emblazoned across the front.

Not the most original, but it got the point across. This must be something they gave potential investors, or maybe it was a press kit. Not everyone wanted digital copies. Given the questions I'd asked, I was surprised they hadn't offered one to me. Since they'd been remiss, I took two for myself. I had them stowed away in my tote bag, my MetroCard back in my pocket, and was leaning against the front of the desk by the time Austin returned.

"Sorry about that," he said. "I forgot I'd put it on the charger."

He held the door and we left the office. When we reached the elevator bank, I saw him sneak a peek at the time. He probably had plans of his own since his boss was going to be tied up.

"You know, I think I'll just visit the restroom. It's right there, isn't it? No need to wait—I can find my way to the lobby. I'm sure you've got plans," I said.

"Oh, no worries," he said. "I need to make a quick call anyway."

Great. No chance of wandering back into the office for something I'd forgotten, and maybe chatting up an employee or eavesdropping outside Clarice's office. At that moment, the doors to New Leaf opened, and the guy who'd given me such a strange look earlier hurried out. He hesitated when he saw us, but then gave us a nod and punched the down button.

Options limited, I went and made use of the restroom, always a good idea when facing crosstown traffic. The trusty Austin was standing by the elevator, sending a text, when I returned. He pushed the button. Having exhausted the topic of the weather, I moved on to something else.

"So do those mail chutes get much use these days?" I asked as we waited.

"Not much, but they still manage to get clogged up regularly," he said.

"They always did," I said.

The elevator arrived. We rode down in silence, and Austin saw me out of the building before saying goodnight. I caught a crosstown bus to take me through the park and then switched to the subway. It was a walk of several blocks from the subway to the gym, but I arrived in plenty of time. Once I'd changed my clothes, I joined other early class members on the mats and did some yoga stretches. Our instructor, Yuri, appeared from the locker room, looked around and walked over to me.

"Greer. You have spent too much time at a desk. Your shoulders are tight. Come, I will show you a better way to loosen up."

I was surprised. Yuri was a man of few words. A soft-spoken Israeli, he shared little about himself in class. Rumor around the gym had it that he was a former Mossad agent, but I was not inclined to ask him directly, or even make veiled references to Daniel Silva novels. I knew only that his English was fluent and slightly accented; he had lived in New York for many years; and his wife played the clarinet for the Philharmonic. Those last two facts had come out when a few of us went out for drinks after class one night. Yuri was the type who listened more than he spoke.

Once we'd moved a little apart from the rest of the group, he demonstrated a move and then told me to do it in slow motion. With his back to the room, he said, "You were followed here tonight. Did you know?" When I stopped, surprised, he added, "Keep moving."

I continued the stretch.

"No," I said. "Are you sure? I didn't feel—I mean, see—"

He nodded. "I saw you get on the train. I was in the car behind you. A man got on right after you. He pushed on at the last minute. He was watching you. He got out when you did. He was trying to stay out of sight, I think, but he was obvious about it. He was behind you until you got here, then he went past and came back . . . Now the left side."

"What did he look like? I can't believe he followed me all that way and I didn't notice."

"You're not hard to spot. We've been on the train together before. You have a greater fondness for color than most New Yorkers," Yuri said, disapproval shading his tone. It sounded like he didn't think I had a future in undercover work.

"Ah," I said. "The tote bag."

"Today," he replied. "Usually, the scarf. Your follower had it easy. White male, twenty-five to thirty. About six feet tall, slender. Dark hair, black ski jacket, hat. I didn't get a good look at his face. Familiar?"

"No, not really." I thought of the guy from New Leaf. Had he been wearing a ski jacket? All I remembered was that his coat was dark. That description could fit any number of people, including my new friend, Grim. But somehow I didn't think Grim would be obvious.

"Back to the right," Yuri said. "You have been followed before?"

"I'm not sure," I said. "Once or twice, I've thought so. Just a feeling. Ow, this is starting to hurt."

"Yes, you will need to do it every day for a while." The man was merciless. "So—a feeling? Trust it. And tonight after class, walk with Larry to the train. He goes the same way, and he won't mind."

I must have looked skeptical because Yuri added, "He will be happy to. He's been trying to get your attention since you started here."

"Really? I've never noticed that."

Yuri muttered something that sounded like, "How does she survive?" then added "I will speak to him."

He then called the class to order. It progressed without incident, though I was chosen to help demo some new self-defense moves. So much for the days of hanging toward the back. To my surprise, I successfully disarmed my classmate, knocking him to the floor in the process. I looked over at Yuri, hoping for a word of praise. He only gave me a considering look and raised an eyebrow.

"Reacher said nothing," I muttered as I turned back to my sparring partner.

"I prefer the *Gray Man*," said Yuri. "Here, let's see if you can do the same to me."

I wondered if I would ever learn to keep my mouth shut. It seemed unlikely.

We ran through the sequence of moves. Yuri managed to stay on his feet but pronounced my effort "not bad." We then broke into pairs and spent the rest of the class knocking each other down, which was more fun than I would have thought. As promised, Yuri had a quick word with Larry, who then waited for me.

Larry didn't look too bright, but he was large and solid. He was also a real estate agent, which I hadn't known. Since native New Yorkers define birth as their first search for a larger apartment, we had an interesting conversation about rent stabilization until I left the train at my stop. He offered to walk me to my door, or even grab a coffee, but I declined, citing an early meeting the next day. I was vigilant on the way to my building, amped up as I was from my meeting, Yuri's belief that I was being followed, and my stellar performance in class. But tonight there were no shadows, no footsteps, not even a rat.

I was almost disappointed.

Chapter Eight

～

Grim arrived promptly at noon. I had the spare laptop ready to go and had placed it, along with some office supplies, on a table in the library. I walked him through the areas of the collection I needed help with, including the closet full of "miscellaneous magical supplies," and showed him how we were recording and tracking everything. He caught on quickly and seemed unfazed by any aspect of the project.

"Nothing too exotic here," he said after poking through the boxes in the closet. "Just an inventory, right? Shouldn't take long to get through this." He was excited when he saw the library. "Quite a bit more than the last time I saw it," he said. He pulled out some of the volumes in Italian. "I recognize a lot of these," he said. "Some of the language is archaic, but I should be able to get the information you need, presuming I don't get distracted and start studying a few of these books."

"Job-related hazard," I said. "So you're fluent in Italian?"

"Fairly," he said. "My mother was from Milan. Do you mind if I take a look around the house before I get started?"

"Sure, go ahead. I'm going to go have my lunch now anyway. I'll be in the kitchen if you need anything."

"Is there a coffeemaker?" he asked.

"State of the art," I replied. "Ava takes caffeine seriously. No food outside the kitchen, but you can bring your coffee up here as long as it's in a covered container. We've got quite a collection of thermal mugs. I'll show you when you come downstairs."

I left him to his exploring. I took my lunch outside—it was overcast, but pleasant. The forecast was for rain and wind starting that night, so I'd be stuck inside for the next couple of days. The crows appeared as I was finishing my sandwich, hopping and cawing on the ground in front of me, apparently annoyed they'd had to fend for themselves the day before. Grim came out as I was tossing them the last few crumbs. They gave him a quick glance and went back to the food.

"Friends of yours?" he said.

"Yes. We have a regular lunch date."

"Ah," he said as Mabel landed on the windowsill, cocked her head at him, then cawed and took off.

"I've fired up the coffee machine. Cappuccino?"

"Sure." I cleaned up and followed him in. We spent a quiet afternoon working in the library. The sky grew darker as the afternoon wore on, and the wind gusts grew louder and more frequent. Shortly before six, rain spattered against the windows.

"I think it's time to call it a day," I said. "I've got to pick up a few things, and I'd like to do it before the rain gets any worse. Are you at a good stopping point?"

"Just finished this shelf."

"Great. I need to back everything up. I'll be a few minutes, so if you want to head out, feel free."

"I'll wait for you. I'd like to pull out some of those boxes so I can go through them on the dining room table, if that's okay."

"Sure. Has Ava gotten you keys and an alarm code yet?"

"Not yet. She said she should have them tonight or tomorrow. I'll check with her."

I finished what I was doing and then went downstairs to make sure that everything in the kitchen was turned off and the back door was locked. When I came back up, Grim was still carrying boxes down the hall. I put on my coat and walked into the dining room. Grim was standing in front of the fortune teller.

"Glad to see Alexei is still here," he said, peering into the glass case. He turned to me and grinned. "Have you asked him to tell your fortune yet?"

"Nope. I'm not sure I want to know what the future holds. Besides, I don't think he works."

"Really?" Grim looked behind the machine. "Hmm. Well, maybe I can do something about that."

"If it's okay with Ava, it's fine with me," I said.

Once the alarm was set and everything was locked up, I said, "I'll be here at ten tomorrow, in case you don't have keys. Should I look for you around noon?"

"That should work. See you then."

We headed in different directions. I managed to pick up what I needed for dinner and make it back to my building just after the rain started to pelt down. I was cold and wet, so I took a hot shower, put on sweats, and settled in front of the television with my meal. After a long day and a dash through the rain, I was in no mood to play detective or even to read. I'd paid for some subscription channels but was happy to find the apartment came with an older but functional DVD player, and an assortment of videos. The subject matter ran heavily to magicians, assassins, and art forgery, which was fine with me. Warm and full of tortellini alfredo, I began to doze. I slid down on the couch and put up my feet, telling myself I'd go to bed as soon as this episode of *Lovejoy* was over.

My phone rang. Still swimming upward toward consciousness, I reached for it, then realized I wasn't in bed. I sat up and found the phone on the coffee table. I looked at the screen—it was the security company for the brownstone. The time was just after midnight. I said hello and was immediately greeted by a calm woman who identified herself, informed me there was an alarm going off at the Christopher residence, and gave me the details. Front downstairs door—the apartment.

I went to the window and looked out. I couldn't see anything through the wind and rain. After confirming that I wasn't at the location but would be there shortly, she let me know that law enforcement had been dispatched and that I should meet them there, but under no circumstances should I enter the house.

No worries, I thought as I pulled on a sweatshirt, thankful I was still mostly dressed. The phone rang again while I was putting on my shoes. Ava this time.

"I'm on my way over," I said.

"Good, thank you. Wait for the cops. And let me know what's going on. I can come down there if you need me. It's probably to do with the wind, though. This has happened before."

I hung up, grabbed my coat, and headed out. Finally fully awake, I texted Grim from the elevator. He might have gotten a code and keys, and being a night owl, decided to see if they worked. Unlikely, but you never knew, and it hadn't occurred to me to ask Ava.

Are you at brownstone?

No, downtown. Why?

Alarm going off. Probably the wind, per Ava. Meeting the cops now.

There was a brief delay before he responded.

Okay, keep me posted.

I saw the police car as I rounded the corner. Mindful of what had happened to Fritz, I crossed carefully. I could see a flashlight moving around in the area beneath the front stairs of the brownstone. I leaned over the rail and introduced myself to the officer, who motioned me down.

"You live here?" he said.

"No. I work here. The house is unoccupied. I live in the building across the street. The security company said something about this door setting off the alarm?"

He shrugged. "The door or the window. They're probably on the same zone in the system. Has this light been out long?" He pointed at the fixture above the door.

"No. I'm pretty sure it was on when I left tonight. It's not big, but it lights this whole area. I think I would have noticed— it was getting dark when I left."

He nodded. "You'll want to check the bulb tomorrow. Probably just burned out. No obvious signs anyone tried to break in here. Back door?"

"Yes, but we'll have to go through the house. The back door is alarmed too."

"Might as well check as long as we're here," he said. He had a brief word with his partner and followed me up the steps. Once inside, I keyed in the alarm code and checked the panel. It gave a message to check zone two, the downstairs door, but everything else looked fine. I flipped on a few more lights, then led the officer to the kitchen and unlocked the back door. He took a look around outside, going the full length of the yard, then came back in and checked the downstairs door from the inside.

"Notice anything strange?" he asked. I shook my head. "Good. Everything looks fine. Probably the wind—a hard gust against these old windows will disconnect the contact points between the pane and the frame. Happens a lot."

He waited while I reset the alarm and locked up. The patrol car did a slow crawl down the block, only turning onto the avenue and speeding up once I'd gotten to the door of my building and waved. I sent Ava a text with an update, letting her know that the police had done a thorough check. I got back a thumbs-up and a message: *Nice when one of our big donors is friendly with the commissioner.*😊 I sent a shorter text to Grim, saying it was a false alarm. Then I changed into my pajamas and fell into bed.

My phone rang. This time I came awake more quickly. It was 4:48 AM and the call was from Gus Skelly, my father's business partner of decades and an honorary uncle to me.

"Gus? Is something wrong? My parents?"

"They're fine, hon. But I do have some bad news. There's been a break-in."

I sat up. "At the pub?"

"No, at your parents' house. Old Mrs. Golumbeski called me. Your mom always gives her my number when they go out of town. She said she was awake and she heard some noise, like someone yelling and then a crash. It got quiet, but she figured as long as she was awake she'd get up and get a glass of water. She took a look out the window and didn't see anything, but then she heard glass breaking, and a minute later the door to the screened porch flew open, and someone ran out and took off through the backyards. So she called the police and then me. I'm at the house now."

"Did someone get into the house?" I asked.

"No, but not for want of trying," Gus said. "But that's not the worst of it, Greer." He paused, then cleared his throat. "You know Jackson, of course," he said.

"Yes." Jackson was a homeless man, a veteran of the Gulf War who was probably in his late fifties, but looked older from decades of living rough. No one knew much of his story or even his first name. The general consensus was that he had PTSD, and he had once mentioned a head injury. My parents hired him to do odd jobs around the pub and the house. So did some of the neighbors. Sometimes he'd stay in shelters or temporary housing, but mostly he'd camp out wherever he could. Jackson startled easily and talked to voices only he could hear, but he was a decent man.

"He would never try to break in," I said. "The police don't think that, do they?"

"No, honey, they don't," Gus said. "It's worse than that. Jackson's been hurt. You know your parents let him sleep on the porch when they're away—he was there last night. He was badly beaten by whoever tried to get in. They took him to the hospital, but the police told me it doesn't look good." Gus gave a heavy sigh. "I've let your parents know. Your dad's making noises about coming home, but I've told him it's not necessary."

"Of course not. Listen, I can be there in a couple of hours. Can you stay until I arrive?"

"I was planning on it. The police are still here. They've said we can clean up once they're done. I'll call the locksmith and the window guy we use. They won't be open yet, but they'll get the message as soon as they get in."

"Thanks, Gus. I'll text when I'm on my way."

I hung up and sat for a minute, trying to steady my breathing and order my thoughts. This was not a time to go off half-cocked. It was possible there were two random break-ins at locations connected to me within forty-eight hours of my showing that spreadsheet to the New Leaf crowd, but it was unlikely. I was with Nero Wolfe on this one: in a world full of random events, I expected coincidences, but I didn't trust them.

Chapter Nine

I decided to splurge for an Uber to get me to Riverdale. There wasn't a lot of traffic going in that direction early in the morning, and for the promise of a big tip and a free breakfast sandwich, I was able to make a stop on the way. Gus deserved to be fed, and I was not one of those people who reacted to stress by losing her appetite. Rather the opposite. In addition to the sandwiches, I picked up a box of paczki, the Polish donuts I knew my neighbor loved. I got a dozen in case there were still any cops around, because that's never a bad idea.

When I arrived there were still law enforcement vehicles parked on the street. Gus was in the kitchen, talking to a woman about my age, who introduced herself as Detective Haynes. He had provided her with a cup of coffee and most of the information she needed. I offered a donut, which, after brief hesitation, she declined. More for me. I got my own cup of coffee while she explained that because of what had happened to Jackson, they were treating this as more than just an attempted break-in, though it looked like a case of Jackson being in the wrong place at the wrong time. Mr. Skelly had been very helpful, she said, and asked if there was anything else I thought she should know.

"Yes," I said. "I agree about Jackson—he's bunked down on our back porch before, but it's not common. My dad would have told him to go ahead if the weather got bad, and last night was cold and rainy."

Gus nodded and added, "He'll often spend the night somewhere around the pub. He doesn't like the shelters. But he has an open invitation here when the family's away. Kind of an informal home watch."

Haynes nodded and made a note.

"The thing is, it's not common for him to be there, and my parents are away for longer than usual. A lot of people know that. And last night, there was also a break-in where I work. It's a brownstone in the city. There's a basement apartment. I think most people believe I live there, though I'm actually in a small co-op building across the street."

"And you think the two are related? You're the connection?" the detective asked. Her tone was neutral. She didn't seem convinced, but she was still listening.

"I think the connection is my husband's murder four years ago. Bear with me," I said when her eyebrows went up.

I gave her a condensed version of what I'd learned so far, emphasizing the meeting at New Leaf and the interest they'd shown in anything else I might find. I told her I thought I'd been followed a few times, and there was a witness to it on one occasion. Since telling one cop that another cop has blown it in a murder investigation will never win you points, I said that while the man who had been arrested was certainly implicated, I was sure he hadn't acted alone.

When I was done, Haynes sat tapping her pencil against the table.

"I can see why you might be concerned," she said. "But it's all very circumstantial."

"It's also very coincidental too, don't you think?" I asked.

Haynes frowned. Most police officers I know disliked coincidences as much they liked fresh baked goods.

"I see your point, Ms. Hogan, and I'll keep it in mind." She checked her phone, which had been chirping periodically while we spoke. "I need to go. If you could write down your contact information?" She ripped some paper from her notebook and slid it over to me.

I wrote down what she wanted and gave it to her. I saw her eye the bakery box and sigh. She'd taken me more seriously than I'd expected, so I felt she deserved a treat.

"Won't you please take a paczki?" I said. "I'm going to end up stress-eating my way through the box. You'd be doing me a favor. I can wrap it up."

Brief silence.

"Okay, thanks."

I packaged the paczki, gave her some extra napkins, and walked her to the door. When I came back, Gus and I settled in with coffee and donuts.

"I never knew all that about Danny's death," Gus said.

"Most of it has only come to light recently. My parents don't even know. I'd planned to tell them when they got back."

"I won't breathe a word. What'll you do now?"

"I'm not sure," I said, reaching for a second donut. "I want to talk to Mrs. Golumbeski. I'd like to know what she saw, hear it directly from her."

"Ah, herself next door is better than any security camera," Gus said with a grin. "And I'm sure she'll be glad of a visitor, especially one bearing gifts." He nodded at the donuts.

"Exactly," I said. "Speaking of security, do any of the neighbors have those doorbell cameras?"

"I don't know for certain, but some of them must," he said. "I'm sure the police will check if it comes to that."

"Are you? For a homeless man?"

"Yes, I think so, for the same reason you had such a crowd of them here this morning. Most of the local force has been in your dad's pub for a darts tourney or a quiz night or a stiff drink after a long shift. It's one of the last real neighborhood places around. And Jackson was known to them and has never given them trouble."

"Hmm," I said. "I hope so. Will the hospital tell us anything if we call, do you think?"

"I told the ambulance crew I was his next of kin, so it's worth a try."

"And they believed you?"

"Didn't even blink. They were moving fast. I'll call now."

Gus got on the phone while I cleaned up. Jackson was in critical condition in the ICU.

"Doesn't sound good, does it?" I said.

"No," Gus replied. "I was hoping they'd get him stable and he'd come to. He's a tough one. Well, nothing to do but wait and hope."

"Guess so. I know you didn't get much sleep—why don't you go home? I'll take care of things here."

"Nah, I'm fine. I plan to test-drive your dad's new recliner while I wait for the repairmen. You do what you need to do."

Gus ambled off into the living room. I put a couple of donuts in a fancy plastic container and went next door. Mrs. Golumbeski must have been watching from the window, because she opened the door before I'd finished knocking. After I'd been greeted, scolded for staying away so long, offered tea, and seated at the kitchen table, she demanded and received an update on "that poor man Jackson."

"And I hope they're not saying he was drunk," she said. "I've never smelled liquor on him, and he's done yardwork for me for years."

"No, they're not. You're right, Jackson doesn't drink." I told her he was in critical condition, and said, "I was hoping you could tell me what happened, what you saw. I'm afraid we might not ever get an answer from Jackson."

Mrs. Golumbeski tsked. "Now that's a shame. I'll say a prayer for him." She brought the kettle over and poured. "As for what happened, I'll tell you what I heard and saw, though it was dark out, so it's not much, really."

This seemed unlikely. The woman was in her eighties, but spry. She still had ears like a bat, and her eyesight wasn't bad either. Our neighborhood was one of older, smaller homes built sometime between the area's mansion age and its mid-rise phase. Mrs. G always knew what was happening on our block and on the surrounding streets. Of course, some of this was due to the fact that she slept with her window cracked open in all but the most frigid weather. She said she was afraid of carbon monoxide poisoning, but the general consensus was that she was more afraid of missing something.

"I'm sure you're a great witness," I said.

"I'm not sure the police thought so, though the officer was polite enough. Very much a 'just the facts' type. Not at all interested in what I thought."

"But I certainly am. Tell me everything, from the beginning. I'm all ears."

She looked pleased. She stirred some sugar into her tea and then settled back in her chair and began to speak.

"Well, I don't sleep as soundly as I once did, you know. For years now, I've woken up around three in the morning most nights, and I did the same last night. I know I wasn't dozing—that happens sometimes, you know, when you're kind of in and out—because I remember noticing the wind had died down, and I couldn't hear it raining. So I was listening."

I nodded.

"After a couple of minutes I decided the rain must have stopped, and was thinking maybe I'd be able to get out and do a few things in the morning. That's when I heard people yelling, and then a thumping noise."

That was a little bit different from what Gus had said, but I didn't want to interrupt her. She continued.

"Then it got quiet, but I felt like I could still sort of hear something. I thought it must be cats or a raccoon getting into the trash, but I decided I'd get up and take a look. I wanted a glass of water anyway."

Of course she did.

"So I went to the window. I didn't turn on a light—it was only a few steps from the bed. I looked out for a minute, and I didn't see anything in your yard or the one next door, so I figured it really was an animal. I was about to turn around, when I heard glass breaking and another yell. I kind of froze in place. A couple of seconds later, your screen door banged open. It made such a noise! Then someone ran down the steps and took off through the yard. They were out of sight quick, though, so I hurried and called 911."

"Wow. That must have been frightening," I said.

"It was, a little. I stayed upstairs until the police car showed up. Then I came down here and watched through the window. You know, just to keep an eye on things."

"Of course. I'd have done the same. I was wondering though—the yelling you heard at first—was it a man or a woman? Just one person?"

"I'm glad you asked because I've been trying to remember. I told the officer it was Jackson, but after I said it, I thought it didn't seem right. I know I heard Jackson—he has such a deep voice. You know how he used to sing as he worked sometimes—I loved to listen to him. But tonight, as I think about it, it seemed more like there were two different voices. One sounded kind of surprised, maybe a little higher? Though I wouldn't swear to it."

"And the second time? Was it Jackson you heard or the other person?"

She shook her head. "I'm not sure. It was the same time as the glass breaking."

"Then someone ran out?"

"Not right after. It was a couple of seconds. Now I know that doesn't sound long, but I was startled, and it seemed to go real slow at the time. Then the door banged open, and the person ran out."

"Did they stop at all? Any hesitation about the direction or anything?"

"No. Just down the steps and off. I lost sight of them for a second. Your back light wasn't on, but mine was, and so was the one at the Quinns' house. So I got a glimpse, then they sort of disappeared, and then I saw a dark shape running. Past the Quinns' yard I couldn't see."

I wasn't hopeful but I had to ask.

"Could you see anything of what they looked like? Male or female, how tall?"

"I'd say medium height and probably medium build, but it could be what they were wearing. All dark clothes, kind of bundled up, it seemed. Some kind of cap, like those knit ski caps. I'd say a man, pretty strong and fast, but again, I can't swear to it. It happened fast."

"You still did pretty well," I said. "Now, what is it the police weren't interested in?"

"Well, it's only speculation of course, which I'm sure is why the young officer cut me off."

Her words offered the benefit of the doubt, her tone implied abject stupidity.

I made a sympathetic noise. Satisfied, she went on.

"How is it," she said, "that whoever it was that tried to break into your house picked the only one on the block where no one was home, and knew to come and go through the backyards? And also knew to go through the Quinns' yard, where the back fence ends and you can get to the next street?"

"Good point," I said. I meant it—I didn't think for a minute it was luck.

"They'd cased the neighborhood, is what I think," Mrs. G said with relish. "Not a second's hesitation when they came off your porch—just down the steps and off like a shot."

"Have you seen any strangers around lately?" I asked.

"There's been more joggers than usual, mostly men, though I can't say I'd recognize the ones I don't already know," she said. "But I'll be watching."

"Good. I feel better knowing that. Will you call me if you think of anything else or see anything you think I should know about?"

She said she would. We visited for a little while longer, and then I left, promising to pass along any updates on Jackson.

Back in my parents' house, I tiptoed past Gus snoring in the living room, and went to take a look at the crime scene. I stood on the porch and tried to figure out the sequence of events. There was an old sleeping bag on the floor, half under a glider on one side of the porch. Jackson's. There was a pile of folded lawn chairs along the wall. In the dark, he wouldn't have been visible unless you were looking for him.

I went into the backyard and up the porch steps. I pushed open the screen door. The hinges didn't squeak at all—this was my mother's house, after all—but I thought the spring would need to be replaced. Coming in, the door and the lawn chairs were between me and Jackson's sleeping bag. I had to walk all the way in and up to the back door before I could see it. In the dark, expecting the house to be empty, I wouldn't even have looked over.

The back door had panes of glass in the top half, rectangles that started above the knob. One of them had duct tape completely covering it. I'd noticed that when I came out. The pane had a spiderweb of cracks, and there was one piece of broken glass on the floor inside. It looked like someone had hit it with a hammer. That would have made enough noise to get Jackson's attention. So then what? He yells, the burglar turns and beans him with the hammer? Maybe lets out an exclamation of surprise first? It would fit with what Mrs. G heard.

But what about the time between the two yells? Could be Jackson startled the burglar during the duct-tape phase, got knocked out briefly, then started to get up and was knocked out again. The window could have been broken during a struggle, and the noise convinced whoever broke in that they should bolt, even if Jackson was already down. Would he have gotten a good look at his assailant? Maybe, but it had been dark.

I took out my phone and got some pictures. The back door swung open, and Gus appeared, broom and dustpan in hand.

"Any theories?" he said.

I told him what I'd come up with.

"I like the second one," he said. "I had a good look at him, waiting for the ambulance. He looked like someone clocked him hard and then gave him a few more whacks to finish the job."

"Ugh, that's awful. Poor Jackson."

"Where there's life there's hope, Greer."

"Hmm. Here, give me those. I'll clean this up." I took the broom and dustpan. "I'll probably need the wet/dry vac. It's in the laundry room."

"I'll get it. I've heard from the locksmith and the glazier. They'll both be here sometime this afternoon. I was going to order a sandwich. Are you up for lunch? Do you have to get back to your job?"

"I'm up for a turkey club with fries. Extra bacon. And my boss doesn't expect me back today." I'd texted both Ava and Grim from the Uber. "What happened to the hammer, do you think? Mrs. Golumbeski didn't mention seeing the burglar carrying anything, and I think she would have."

"It's a good question. I know the police didn't take anything away. We'll have a look around after lunch."

And that was the rest of my day. Cleaning up, lunch, hunting for the weapon, talking to neighbors about what had happened and asking them to keep their eyes open. Gus was going to spend the night in the guest room. With all the outside lights on, the neighborhood watch was on high alert, and Detective Haynes had called to say a patrol car would go by regularly. I wondered if that meant she'd taken me seriously or if a bunch of neighbors had called the precinct in a panic, but I was happy to hear it regardless.

I went back to my apartment and called my parents with an update. In lieu of dinner, I made myself a martini. Then I got a call from Gus and did something I never do on an empty stomach—I made a second one.

Jackson was dead.

Chapter Ten

The next morning I woke up groggy, sad, and a little hungover. I'd had a long talk with my parents the night before, and we'd concluded there was nothing I could do at the house at this point. I'd come clean on the Danny angle, though I didn't use the term "murder investigation." They were supportive, which surprised me, and warned me to be careful, which did not, and told me that I was in no way to blame for what had happened to Jackson, which I didn't completely believe but which made me feel better anyway. After fortifying myself with toast and a cup of Irish Breakfast tea, about all my stomach could handle at the moment, I showered, dressed, and trudged across the street to work.

I walked into the brownstone and was greeted by an operatic aria, accompanied by intermittent sharp knocks. The music reminded me of Jackson, singing as he raked our yard. My eyes filled. I blinked the tears away. Enough. I slammed the door shut. A second later the music stopped, and Grim appeared in the hallway.

"You're bright and early today," I said.

"Greer, hi. Wasn't sure you'd be here," he said. "Everything okay at your parents' house?"

"Not really, but there's nothing I can do at this point."

"Sorry to hear that," he said. "So, long day for you then yesterday. You must be tired."

"Yes."

"Coffee?"

"Yes."

Slight pause.

"I'll just go make some then," Grim said.

"Yes. Please."

"Right." Off he went.

I dumped my stuff at the desk in the front room and looked around while Grim made coffee. He had obviously been busy the day before. The hall closet had been completely emptied and the boxes spread on and under the dining room table. The case housing Alexei had been pulled away from the wall. He'd shifted some books around too, piling quite a few on his desk and leaving bare spots on the shelves. It looked like he'd devoted himself to inventorying and organizing in my absence. The knocking I'd heard begged a question, but I'd leave that for now.

I went to fire up my computer and found a second lock and set of picks on my desk. Everything there seemed slightly off from where I'd left it, including the box of keys, but I couldn't be sure. It had happened before, a few days after I started, but I'd decided I was spending too much time working alone and had started to imagine things. I might still be imagining things, or Grim could have been looking for something. Whatever. I collected a cartload of books on card magic and settled down to try and get some work done.

My trusty assistant walked in a few minutes later and slid a mug onto my desk. He offered a bottle of ibuprofen. I took it, washed two pills down with my coffee, and handed it back.

He studied me briefly, then said, "I've got a few questions, but they can wait until you've finished your coffee. Just let me know when you're ready to talk."

I had a few questions myself, but he disappeared into the other room before I could reply. The man obviously had a good sense of self-preservation. I turned to my book cart and got to work.

About an hour later I admitted my concentration was non-existent. My headache had subsided but I was still tired, and had gone from sad to mad. I pushed my computer aside and picked up the original lock and picks I'd pulled out. Opening up one of the books I'd found on the subject, I located a likely-looking diagram and went to work. I turned over the events of the last couple of days in my head while I fiddled with the lock. I got nowhere with either and decided to go see what Grim was up to.

He had an array of items spread out before him on the table and was tapping away at his keyboard.

"I can answer your questions anytime," I said. "How's the inventory going?"

"Good. Let me finish this item, and I'll get my list."

"Take your time," I said. I walked over to inspect the fortune teller. There was a small toolbox on the floor next to it. The case that housed it was intact, and though the paint had faded, it was otherwise in good condition. The gentleman himself had aged well. With his dark curly hair and green eyes, he could have been related to Grim, though the brocaded clothes he wore spoke of an earlier age. None of the lights were on, though I could see that it was plugged in.

"Any luck with Alexei?" I asked when Grim spun around in his chair.

"Some. I can get the head and arm to move, but the voice isn't working right, and I think something's stuck in the card dispenser. I thought I had it fixed and put the panel back on, but it still needs some work. Ava said to go ahead and tinker when I have time, and if I can't get it going, she'll hire an expert."

"It's cool. I haven't seen one like it before. There's a definite resemblance between you, though. One of your ancestors?"

Grim laughed. "Not as far as I know, but I'm sure this was custom. That's not just any old Zoltar. Be interesting to know who had it made and where Lars got it."

"There may be records somewhere. He seems to have been a meticulous guy. Anyway, what did you need my help with?"

We went back to the library and went through the pile of books on his desk. I answered what questions I could and put aside a few things requiring more research.

"Anything else?" I asked.

"Not here, but I wanted to let you know I did some looking around. Because of the break-in."

I was confused, then realized he was talking about the alarm that had gone off here. The news about Jackson had driven it right out of my mind.

"Oh, right. I lost track of that. The police thought it was the wind. Something about contact points."

He looked skeptical. "Maybe, but I doubt it. I took a look at the window and the door downstairs, inside and out. They're more solid than they look, even if they are pretty old. It would have had to be a pretty strong gust. Plenty of marks on the frames of both, though none that are obviously new."

"So you definitely think someone was trying to get in?"

"I think so."

"And now they have a good idea of what kind of alarm system we have," I said.

Grim smiled. "I like the way your mind works. Twisty. I agree, although I don't think it was a test. But regardless, did you notice anyone on the street or in a parked car?"

"No. I did a quick look around before I crossed, and the police car was outside for a while. But someone could have been out of sight and watching. It would take steady nerves, though."

"Agreed. I took a look around in the back too. The lock on the gate is new and in good condition, and there's no way out through the yard behind. Going over any of the fences is risky, but you could get to the next street if you worked at it."

"You'd need to be pretty athletic. I couldn't do it. You could."

"Maybe," he said.

Almost certainly, I thought.

"I'll talk to Ava. I don't know what they can do about upgrading the system, but maybe cameras would help."

"Worth a try," Grim said.

"Thanks for your efforts. I know this is beyond your job description."

"No worries. I'm attached to the place. And I'm enjoying the work."

At which point we both got back to it. I called Ava and told her what Grim and I had discussed, and she said she'd look into it. "I think it's possible Lars had cameras at some point. When we had the security company in, the guy said there were bits and pieces of old systems tucked all over the place. I'm sure we can upgrade."

I got a few things done and then went downstairs to see if I could find anything to eat. True to form, my appetite had bounced back, I was now ravenous, and I hadn't brought lunch with me. I'd found half a package of digestive biscuits and a tired apple, and settled on the bench in the backyard, when my phone rang. A homicide detective from the NYPD had been speaking to Detective Haynes and would like to meet. He could be at my location in twenty minutes. I agreed.

I scarfed down several biscuits and half the apple and tossed some crumbs to the crows. Then I put on a fresh pot of coffee and went upstairs to tell Grim about our expected company. I found him in the hall closet, tugging at one of the shelves in the back. He hadn't heard me coming.

I cleared my throat and he turned. I raised an eyebrow.

"Checking to see how solid these are. I'd like to fit everything back in without cluttering up the floor. Easier access."

"Right," I said. "Well, I'm about to be visited by the police. I'll talk to them in the kitchen."

Grim looked surprised. "Following up on an attempted burglary?"

"Not exactly. It's complicated."

"Okay, well, I'll be busy up here. Yell if you need me."

I'd turned to go, when he added, "Oh, Greer? You might want to stash those lockpicks. That kind of thing tends to be frowned upon by law enforcement."

"Thanks for the tip," I said. I'd just finished putting away anything that might look sketchy to a cop when the doorbell rang.

An Inspector Calls, I said under my breath as I went to answer the bell. Not a good omen—that one didn't have a happy ending for anyone.

I opened the door and was greeted by two plainclothes officers, Detective Stewart and Sergeant Kopp. I refrained from making the obvious joke and, after being presented with their official identification, led them to the kitchen. Grim had made himself scarce. Coffee was offered and accepted. Once we were all seated, I waited. They'd asked for the meeting, let them make the first move. I wanted to know what they wanted to know, and gauge their attitude so I could decide how to present my theories. After a brief silence, Stewart cleared his throat and spoke.

"I've had a call from Detective Haynes out in the Bronx. She told me what happened at your family home and that you believe it's related to your husband's death here in the city four years ago. Now the officer who worked that case has retired. He's fishing in the Keys right now. So I'd appreciate it if you would tell me what happened and why you believe these two deaths are related."

Fair enough. His tone was respectful, he'd taken the time to check some details, and he'd come to me. Kopp pulled out a notebook. Worst-case scenario: Stewart heard me out and didn't believe me, but we could both say we'd tried.

"It started a few weeks before my husband was murdered," I said, and went from there. I told them everything I'd told Haynes. I even mentioned Frank Benson's untimely death. I finished up with the attempted break-in at the brownstone and how in the light of day it seemed less likely to have been the wind. Stewart asked a few questions but otherwise listened attentively, his face expressionless. Kopp took notes and said nothing, but his face spoke volumes. I hoped, for his sake, that he didn't play poker. I could easily tell when he thought I was making sense and when he thought I'd made a real leap of logic—his eyebrows went all over the place.

When I was done, Stewart pursed his lips. "Well, that was a very organized summary," he said, "and I can see why you think there may be a connection. But everything is circumstantial at best. I'll take a closer look at the file on your husband's death, and I'll keep in touch with Detective Haynes. However, unless we get something concrete to tie all this together . . ." He shrugged.

"I understand," I said. I pocketed their business cards. Stewart promised to be in touch if there were any developments. He also asked that I call him directly if anything else happened at the brownstone or if I thought I was followed again. Then I showed them out.

Once the door was closed behind them, I returned to my desk and looked out the front window. The two officers had gone down the steps and were taking a look at the entrance to the basement apartment. A few minutes later they disappeared toward the avenue. I retrieved my lockpicks. I couldn't even pretend to work. I couldn't figure out if I'd made my case or just convinced another cop I was crazy. And now I was worried. I'd wanted to keep my family and friends at a distance from this, try to keep them safe, do most of it myself, but I realized that might not be possible. I needed hard evidence. I needed help.

I looked up to see Grim watching me from the library. He came over, perched on the desk, and adjusted the angle of my hand.

"You need to keep steady pressure on the lower pick," he said. "Now move the top one gently. There you go," he said as the lock popped open.

"Oh, thanks," I said.

"I have an idea," Grim said as I stretched my fingers and flexed my wrists. "How about I go pick up an early dinner for both of us, and then you tell me about this series of highly coincidental crimes going on around you? Maybe I can help."

I wasn't surprised that he'd put things together. Grim wasn't stupid, and he'd probably listened in on at least some of my conversation with New York's finest. In his place, I'd have done the same.

"How much did you overhear?" I asked.

"Enough. That cop's voice carried up the stairs. Another break-in, same night. Somebody died?"

"Yeah, somebody died." I decided to be honest with him. He was in close physical proximity to me, and I didn't want any more collateral damage. As far as his offer to help went, I was pretty sure there was something in it for him, but I'd deal with that later. If I was going to come clean, so was he. He was clever and well able to look after himself, and I needed help. A dinner meeting was a reasonable start. Also, I was hungry. Decision made.

"Okay, dinner it is. Thanks."

Grim set off and I got my work organized for the next day. Then I went downstairs and verified everything Grim had said about the backyards and the construction of the window and door in the basement apartment, and figured out where we'd be able to mount cameras, should it come to that. I'd gotten back to the kitchen and was cleaning the coffeepot when my phone started to trill "When Irish Eyes Are Smiling"—my father's ringtone.

"Greer, love, listen. I've only got a few minutes. I need to tell you something without your mother hearing. Can you talk?"

This wasn't unusual—there were plenty of things that my dad and I agreed my mother and my sister didn't need to know. But this time I could hear tension and urgency in his voice. I left the coffeepot in the sink and sat down.

"Sure, go on."

"All right then. You remember after Dan died and you were getting ready to sell your place, you and your friends packed up some boxes and brought them out to the house?"

"Yes. Beau and Ben and I put them in the basement, back in the corner. Mom's been after me to go through them. I was going to do it this weekend."

"Well, they're not there now, and this is why. A couple of weeks after you dropped them off I found one of the basement windows broken. Not just cracked, but all the glass knocked out. So I looked around and there were some marks on the Bilco doors."

"Did someone get in?"

"No. The lock on the Bilco was fine, and no signs of an attempt anywhere else. And everything in the basement was right where I'd left it. But it made me wonder—it didn't look like something kids would do. Mrs. Golumbeski was out of town—new grandbaby—but I went to Jimmy Quinn next door, and he had a tale to tell."

The Quinns had lived next door to us for years, but they both worked, and their kids were grown and flown. Mr. Quinn was always puttering around outside, and Mrs. Quinn power walked around the neighborhood daily, but they had nothing on Mrs. Golumbeski in terms of surveillance skills. I said as much to my father.

"True, but when this happened they still had their big German shepherd. Otto had some arthritis, but there was nothing wrong with his hearing. Well, one Sunday morning when your mother and I were at church and Carol was out doing her walk, the dog started to go berserk. Jimmy was watching a hockey game he'd recorded the night before, so he tried to shush the dog, but Otto wasn't having it. Kept hurling himself at the back door and then running to the window that faces our yard. Jimmy finally got up and went to go check what was going on."

"Did he see anything?"

"No, but the dog was still agitated, so he leashed him up and took him out. Otto went right for our yard, nose to the ground. Then he circled back to his own yard, sniffed the air for a bit, then calmed down. Jimmy didn't notice the window—all the glass was inside and we were due for a mow—so he thought it must have been an animal. Raccoons had been getting in the trash. He took the dog inside and that was that until I came around and asked."

"Good boy, Otto," I said. "So what happened to my boxes? You said they weren't in the basement anymore."

"Well, I'd thought Dan was worrying over something when we saw the two of you for dinner the last time, about two weeks before he was killed. And then after, you were grieving but distracted—something wasn't right. I wasn't sold on the man they'd arrested having done it alone either. Then this happened, and I had a bad feeling."

That was all he needed to say. In all of my Irish Catholic family, out to the most distant cousins, having a bad feeling was treated as a subtle nudge from the Almighty. Attention was paid, intuition was honored, plans were changed, no further questions were asked.

"So where'd you move them?" I asked.

"I moved some of them to the pub. The ones with papers and personal items. There weren't as many of those. And I added any of the mail that you'd had forwarded once you sold the apartment— couple of cards and the like. The boxes full of extra pots and pans, and the set of dishes Dan's aunt gave you that you never liked—I left those. Didn't want your mother to notice and worry."

"If you put the stuff you moved in those crates where you hide our Christmas presents and your expensive whiskey, Mom knows about that spot. We all do."

"I know that, love. That's why they're in a different spot. Your old man's got a few tricks up his sleeve yet. There's a hidey-hole that goes back to Prohibition. It's an old building, remember."

"I can't believe I never found it. I used to hunt around when I was a kid. I'll get the boxes out as soon as I can. You'll have to tell me where it is."

"Gus knows. Give him a call and he'll show you. Take the car if you need it. You'll probably need some help at the other end though."

Grim walked through the door, takeout bags and a bottle of wine in hand.

"I've got someone in mind," I said.

"Good. And remember, whatever you find, whatever you decide, we're behind you." I heard something in the background, and his tone changed. My mother must be back. "Well, thanks for checking in. Got any plans for tonight?"

"Dinner with a friend. Looks like Vietnamese."

"Sounds grand. I'll let you go then. Bye, love."

I hung up.

"That was my dad," I said as I looked for a corkscrew. "There's some new information. I'll explain while we eat."

"Fine. Hope you like pho." He began unpacking the food.

"Love it. That smells delicious. Here you go." I handed him the corkscrew and wineglasses and got out bowls. Once we were seated with our dinner, I took a sip of my wine and said, "I'm ready to tell you my whole story, but before I start, I have one question for you."

"Sure," he said. "Ask me anything."

"Why are you really here?"

Chapter Eleven

❧

Grim stopped, his chopsticks in midair. He looked surprised. Then he shrugged.

"Because Ava asked me," he said. "And I was fond of Lars and thought what he was doing was important. I have some free time, so why not?" He went back to his pho, his face a study in bland innocence.

"I believe all of that is true," I said. "I also think you're looking for something. And honestly, as long as the work gets done and you don't walk off with anything that belongs to the Archive, I really don't care. But I'd like to know. Besides," I said, picking up my own chopsticks, "I might come across whatever it is when you're not here. It would save time if you told me. Librarians and archivists are known for our discretion."

I gave him an innocent look of my own and dug into my dish. He thought for a minute, then came to a decision.

"You're right. I am looking for something."

"Yes, but what?"

"That's the problem. I don't know."

"Then how do you know there's something to find?" I asked.

"Lars told me, but not in detail," Grim said. "It was right before Fritz died. He said he'd found something, or part of something, that might be really important. He was very excited, but he didn't want to give too much away. 'It could just be an old man's wishful thinking' is what he said. I wasn't going to be back in the country for a few months—he said he'd show me then. So I was curious but didn't give it much more thought."

"And then Fritz died?" I asked.

Grim nodded. "I got a call from Lars right after. He'd been out of town when Fritz was killed—I think he felt guilty about that. He got kind of paranoid. He asked me if I'd mentioned what he told me to anyone. I said no, and he apologized for even suggesting it, then he swore me to secrecy."

"So no further information?"

"I only spoke to him once more before he disappeared. He told me he wanted me to see what he'd found, that I would know what to do with it, but that I'd need the key. When I got back, he was gone. He'd disappeared right after we talked, and the house was sealed up by the lawyers. Per his instructions, they said. That was over seven years ago. He was declared dead after three, but the Archive didn't get access for some reason."

"I think that's because once you start handing out bequests, it's hard to undo," I said. "Ava said the lawyers on all sides were being very careful. She only got in here about a year ago. It's taken a while to figure out what's what."

Grim nodded. "I've checked in with Ava periodically. I told her Lars had been a mentor to me, which is true, and so if she needed any help with anything, to give me a call. I also told her I'd like to see the place again sometime, if that was ever okay."

"And you kept an eye on it, didn't you?"

"I admit to strolling by a few times whenever I was in town," he said. "But I never tried to get in. I'm not sure anyone else did either, but I wouldn't swear to it."

"Were you taking a look around the other night? Or any time before the first day you came to work?"

He shook his head. "I was in Spain until about twelve hours before we met for coffee."

"So in the last month, you were never here late at night? And you've never followed me?"

He looked offended. "I would never do that, Greer. And as far as coming here—I knew I had a way in before my plane landed, so no. Wait—has someone been following you?"

"I think so, and I've got a witness to it at least once. I also saw someone loitering around here very late one night, but they were closer to the house next door, so I don't know." I paused. "If anyone was here, it probably has to do with what's going on with me rather than with whatever Lars found."

"I agree. As far as I know, there haven't been any issues here since Lars died."

"I'll check with Ava. I'll make it a general inquiry that has something to do with the alarm going off," I added when he started to protest. "But no, I think things were quiet until I showed up."

"So maybe you should tell me what that's all about," Grim said.

"I will as long as you promise to stop the clandestine searches." I held up my hand before Grim could speak. "Whenever I have time, I'll help you. I'm sure Lars had more than one hiding place in this house, and knocking on walls is not the answer. We're going to have to go about it in an organized fashion."

"Said like a true librarian. So you have a lot of experience with this sort of thing? Goes with the job?"

I gave a brief, fond thought to the hidden nooks and crannies of Raven Hill Manor and then considered the happy surprises I'd found in Fritz's apartment.

"You've no idea," I said. "But those are tales for another time. Right now I have more pressing issues."

"You're right," he said. "Why don't you tell me the whole story? I know it's got to be painful, at least some of it, but try not to leave anything out."

He poured us each some more wine and sat quietly. I took a deep breath and began.

"My husband was murdered four years ago," I said. Grim nodded—he'd overheard some of this already, but I went through the story again. Maybe it was the wine, maybe it was his attentive listening, maybe it was that I had a good feeling about it—I told him everything. I left nothing out—not my impatience with Dan, not the drunken flirtation with Ian, not the three years of ignoring my suspicions about the murder while I reinvented my life elsewhere. The beginning of the nightmares and then the murder of an old friend, something that left me unable to pretend anymore. Carefully starting to ask questions, and then the deaths in Lake Placid. My plans to come back at Christmas time and start digging, changed by the fire at the Manor; and seeing how old secrets, held too close for too long, warped every life they touched.

I told him about Millicent and the task she had charged me with, along with the help she had given. Officer Jennie Webber, my unlikely friend, getting the police report. Beau and Ben, who had taken me in and helped me pack after Dan died, and who had wondered about a few things themselves, and quietly gathered some information. I talked and talked, cocooned in the warm, bright kitchen. Outside, darkness fell, the March wind began to moan, and the crows gave an occasional caw of annoyance. Inside, there was only Grim's unjudging silence, and the old house, full of magical secrets, that seemed to listen with a quiet sympathy of its own.

Then I got to Jackson.

"No one knows much about him," I said. "He came and went, in and out of the human services system. He'd become kind of a fixture in the area, though, doing odd jobs when he could. He had a beautiful singing voice. My mother gave piano lessons—did I tell you? When the weather was nice, she'd leave the window open. One day, Jackson was raking leaves and started to sing—it was an old hymn, I think. From then on, she would play whenever he was working—carols, hymns, show tunes. I suspect she started coming up with little jobs so she could listen to him."

"And he just happened to be there the other night?" Grim asked.

"He was welcome to sleep on the porch when my parents were away, but he didn't unless the weather was bad. He liked to be outside. Sometimes he'd sleep by the garage, just to keep an eye on the place. My parents don't have an alarm system at home, though they do at the pub. I guess you could say Jackson was an informal home watch."

"The neighbors—they knew that, I suppose?"

"Yes. But as I said—he came and went. He'd done work for most of them, so they knew his habits. They wouldn't think twice about seeing him at the house, but they wouldn't worry if they didn't."

"And beyond your immediate neighbors?"

"If anyone was paying attention, and I think someone was, they'd expect the house to be empty." I told him what Mrs.

Golumbeski had said about seeing a couple of joggers she didn't recognize. "So it was similar to what happened to Dan. No one was supposed to be home in either case, but someone was. Dan came home unexpectedly—we were both supposed to be out after work. My parents were away, but the weather was bad, so Jackson was asleep on the porch. Both of them ended up dead."

"There's a couple of important differences though," Grim said.

"Yes, I think so too. Whoever broke into our apartment knew Dan and me well enough to know we'd be out. Whoever broke into my parents' house didn't know them well enough to factor in Jackson. Of course," I added, "that does reinforce the police theory of random break-ins, with Dan and Jackson both being in the wrong place at the wrong time."

"Quite a coincidence, nevertheless, especially when you add in the fact that someone tried to get in here," Grim said.

"I think so, and maybe the police are starting to think so too, but I don't have anything concrete to show them. Sometimes I think they're taking me seriously, and sometimes I think they think I'm crazy. Honestly, sometimes I wonder if I *am* crazy."

"No more than most," Grim said with a smile. "I believe you."

"Thank you."

"Now, how can I help?"

"I can give you a list. But first—why? You barely know me."

Grim smiled. "Well, I could say it's because you figured out I was searching the place, and not only did you not call Ava and toss me out, but you also offered to help me. That's a part of it. But . . ." He paused, and looked away for a moment before continuing. "Let's just say I've left some scales unbalanced at times. This is a chance for me to help you balance yours."

I raised an eyebrow.

"A tale for another time," Grim said.

"Fair enough," I replied. "Okay. Do you have a car?"

"I've got a van. I use it for hauling equipment around."

"Perfect. There are work vans and trucks coming and going around the pub all the time. We need to pick up some boxes—three or four, I think—and bring them to my apartment without anyone knowing what we're getting or where they're going."

"Piece of cake. Though it would be better if you went about your day as usual and I got them. Just in case someone's keeping tabs on you. It sounds like that's a distinct possibility."

"You're right. That would be better."

"I take it something in these boxes is what our amateur burglars have been looking for?"

"I think so. I hope so anyway."

"What is it?" Grim asked.

I shrugged. "I'm not sure exactly. But I'm hoping I'll know it when I see it."

He grinned at me. "Nice. I feel better now. First we'll find your mystery prize, then we'll find mine."

"As you said, piece of cake. But I have some ideas."

"Good. So what's the plan? I could head out to Riverdale tonight, but it would have to be later. I'm meeting a friend for a drink."

"No, I need to make sure my dad's partner, Gus, will be there. And it'll be crowded. The morning would be better. Fewer people around. That's when we get deliveries and have repairs done. Not too early," I added.

"I'm free tomorrow and Sunday," Grim said. "You want to set it up? I'll take care of the dishes. Oh, and tell whoever I'm meeting to look for a van that says 'Jacob Grimes Plumbing.' One of my aliases," he added with a wink.

I decided not to ask and got on the phone to Gus. I told him about the conversation with my father and what we needed to do. He agreed to meet Grim the following morning before opening. We worked out the details, and by the time I hung up, I was feeling more optimistic than I had in a while. I had the beginning of a plan. Grim poured the rest of the wine, and we clinked glasses.

"If this goes well, I'll make you an honorary Raven Hill Irregular," I said.

"Cool. Do I get a secret decoder ring?"

"Afraid not, but I'll buy dinner next time."

"Deal. And now, I have to go. I'll call you tomorrow when I'm on my way back to the city."

We went upstairs. Grim grabbed his things and headed out, and I went to my desk. I'd decided to come to work in the morning as part of my "acting casual and going about my business" cover, so I made a to-do list. I was seeing my former neighbors, the Ginsburgs, in the afternoon. I planned to spend tomorrow night going through the boxes Grim was retrieving in the morning. I added to that a more thorough review of the material I'd pocketed at New Leaf. I'd only had time to give it a quick once-over. I'd been preoccupied with the news about Jackson. With any luck, I'd find something in the boxes. Presuming I could get through them all. With that in mind, I called Beau, told him what was going on, and changed our Sunday plans from brunch out to brunch at my place.

Having done what I could for the day, I packed up my bag. I eyed the lock and picks—I had nothing more exciting planned than another date with *Lovejoy*, and I was tempted to borrow them and practice while watching TV. They belonged to the archive, though, so I left them. But I'd have to come up with something for future quiet nights at home, because picking locks was a useful skill to have.

Undoubtedly Grim had a set of picks I could borrow.

I sent a quick text with my request. Coat on and bag in hand, I stopped and tried to remember if I'd turned off the coffeepot and the lights in the kitchen. Deciding I'd better check, I walked to the back of the house. The timed lights upstairs had started to come on, and were casting shadows down the stairwell and into the hall. I'd only been in the house once before after dark, with Ava. I found the subtle differences in light and shadow a little eerie, but tame compared to Raven Hill Manor.

In the kitchen, I found the coffeepot off and only one extra light on. I was checking the back door when I heard a strange sound. Not a creak or a thump, but something moving. I couldn't tell where it came from. Upstairs? Behind me? The wind was whipping outside. That was the most likely source of the noise, but I checked the door and window to the apartment anyway. No sign of anyone.

I went back upstairs, stopped in the hall, and listened. The house was quiet. *Must have been the wind,* I thought. I turned off the lights in the library and went to the dining room. Once I'd said goodnight to Alexei and hit the light switch, I was done. I studied the figure in the case. Grim had said he'd made progress but that the fortune teller wasn't fully operational. Just for fun and to prove I wasn't really afraid of what the future held for me, I stepped up to the case.

"What now, Alexei?" I asked. I pushed the button and waited.

Nothing.

"All right then. Good night, Alexei."

I walked to the front of the room, turned off the light, and stepped into the hall. I was about to set the alarm when I heard the sound again. This time, I could tell where it was coming from—behind me. I turned. There was nothing in the hall or on the stairs. I flipped the switch in the dining room. The noise continued—a kind of mechanical grind. I walked in, and looked at the source.

Alexei.

He turned his head toward me and raised his arm. A light flashed in front of him, illuminating eyes that stared into mine. There was a whirring noise, and a metallic clank. Then the entire mechanism faded into silence and darkness, as something white fluttered from the front of it to the floor.

I took a deep breath and walked to the machine. Alexei was motionless, his face still turned toward me. I bent and picked up the scrap from the floor. It was a fortune card, torn in half, with only one word remaining.

Beware.

Chapter Twelve

The next morning I was back at the brownstone at my usual time. After my brief interaction with Alexei the night before, I'd pocketed the fortune card, thanked him for the tip, and unplugged him. Just to be on the safe side, I'd checked as soon as I got to work, and found the machine was still unplugged and had not spewed forth any more cryptic warnings. I'd let Grim know what had happened. He could deal with Alexei. I kept the ripped fortune card though. It never hurt to have a reminder to stay on your toes.

The morning was, for the most part, uneventful. I cataloged, shared a snack with the crows, and sent Ava my weekly update. Not a single strange noise to be heard. Nothing unusual until my phone rang. It was Clarice, inviting me to lunch the following Tuesday.

"I'm desperate for an afternoon out of the office," she said. "I know how much you've had to deal with lately—let me treat you to a nice lunch. And I'd love to have an intelligent conversation with someone about something other than work!"

This was an unexpected opportunity.

"I'd love to," I said. "A good meal and a good chat sound like just what I need. Name the time and the place, and I'll be there."

She did and I wrote it down. We both said how much we were looking forward to it and then hung up. Interesting. As I entered the information into my calendar, I wondered what her game was. It was always possible she was sincere, and I was too cynical. Unlikely, but possible. I'd have to figure out how to play it.

Once I'd completed my planned tasks for the day, I pulled out one of the folders I'd liberated from the New Leaf office. I'd read through it the night before, concluded I must be too tired to truly understand the proposed business model, and decided to review it when I was more alert. I went over it again, from beginning to end. I had, in fact, understood the business model. I just couldn't quite believe it.

Clarice hadn't been kidding about moving into what she called "the wellness space." The New Leaf product line had always focused on natural products in general, with a small assortment of items that would fall into a holistic remedy category. This was where all the CBD oil products had landed. The goal now was to take what had been a mostly online business and expand it with select product placements into retail outlets like yoga studios, gyms, and anyplace else where they might find a receptive audience. This required more complex logistics in terms of inventory and shipping, but I could see the benefit, especially in light of what came next.

New Leaf envisioned cannabis dispensaries and what they called "lounges" sharing space with or adjacent to these same yoga studios and exercise centers. William's juice bar analogy was apt. After stretching, meditating, or engaging in your workout of choice, you could loosen up a little more by consuming your preferred cannabis product on the premises in the company of your friends. Pilates and pot? Yummy gummy yoga? Breathe in, breathe out, inhale?

The mind boggled. None of this had ever occurred to me, no matter how many news stories I'd seen about legal cannabis. I envisioned the yoga pants crowd trading in their decaf oat milk lattes for a cannabis consumable after a stressful morning in the carpool line. Or the after-work crowd exchanging their craft cocktails for something that wouldn't give them a hangover, at least according to the literature. I hadn't thought of any of this, but I could see how it could work. Once all those pesky regulations had been dealt with. No telling when that would happen, though William and Clarice thought they wouldn't be an issue for long. Hmm.

I put the folder back in my bag. I'd definitely bring this to my meeting with April's expert. I went back to my lock-picking practice until my phone buzzed. It was Grim, texting that he was on his way, so I closed up shop and went back to my apartment, once again following my usual routine As far as I could tell, no one was loitering in the area outside. If someone was keeping an eye on me, they were doing a good job of staying out of sight. I said as much to Grim when he got upstairs and rolled a dolly full of boxes into my apartment.

"Given how inept they are at burglary, I think you'd spot them watching you," he said. "You already have, a couple of times. These are not pros. Anything else? I'm double parked."

"I've called a meeting of the Irregulars for tomorrow morning. Brunch. Are you still free?"

"I'll be here," he said.

"If you want to come early and see if you can find anything Lars might have stashed here, you're welcome to. I've found a few things that might interest you."

His eyes lit up. "What time?"

"Ten? I know you consider anything before noon the middle of the night . . ."

"I managed today, didn't I? Want me to bring anything?"

"Got it covered. See you then."

Once Grim was out the door, I took a look at what he'd dropped off. My father had transferred the contents of the moving boxes I'd left into some sturdier ones that had once held bottles of whisky and were less likely to be noticed in the basement of a bar. I didn't have time to dig into them, so I shoved them into the bedroom. I'd start sorting when I got back. The problem, as I'd admitted to Grim, was that I wasn't entirely sure what I was looking for. Anything to do with New Leaf, of course, but would I know it when I saw it? I had a six-page spreadsheet that Dan had sent to Ian, but neither one of us had been able to figure out what it meant. Would I have better luck with anything else? If I didn't, who might?

Isabelle Peterson.

I sat on my bed and pulled out my phone. I'd met Isabelle during the brief period she'd worked for Dan, right before he died. She was a bona fide mathematical genius who'd left her PhD program due to disgust with academic politics. I'd bumped into her again at the wedding of a friend the previous September. She'd expressed a willingness to help when I told her I had some questions about what had been going on at New Leaf, but an untimely death among the wedding guests had derailed my investigation plans. We'd forged a friendship during the long wedding weekend and had kept in touch since, but I'd never asked her to look at the information Ian had received. I thought she'd be willing to look at that and anything else I found—I could scan and send it to her. Worth a try.

She answered on the first ring, sounding somewhat breathless.

"Greer! I was just thinking of you. I'm in the city with Great-Aunt Caro and she took me to her favorite Irish pub last night. Now she's trying to figure out where to go tonight."

That explained the breathlessness. Pub crawling with Carolynn Quinn was not for the faint of heart, even though the lady was in her eighties. Just trying to keep up with her thought process would wear anybody out. But the good news was that Isabelle was in town, and I could offer her a temporary reprieve.

"I'm here too, and I could use your help with something, if you have time."

I gave her a brief rundown of what was going on and invited her to brunch the next day. She accepted immediately.

"Caro's meeting some friends tomorrow. I'd love to help. What time?"

I gave her the time and my address. After we hung up, I took a look in the alcove and tried to figure out where I'd fit everyone. It would be tight, but we'd manage.

This afternoon, I had a couple of potential witnesses to interview.

* * *

I'd been back to the building Dan and I had lived in a few times. My friends Beau and Ben still lived there, a few floors above my old apartment, and I'd visited them. But this was the first time since I'd moved out and sold the place that I actually took the elevator to my old floor, and walked down the hall to my old front door. The Ginsburgs lived in the unit at the end, their door about ten feet away. I'd only visited in my dreams, when I'd walk down the hall and find the door ajar, as I had the night Dan had died. Sometimes, I pushed the door open, and saw him there, on the floor, the whole scene rendered in shades of black and white and gray, lit only by the purpling sky outside the window, the way it had looked on the night of the murder. Other times, he was there, alive, standing close enough to touch, yet I couldn't reach him, or else I would open the door, step in, and be somewhere else, some other place entirely.

Today, on a bright afternoon, the door was closed. I reached out, put my fingertips against it, and pushed gently. It didn't budge. All was silent inside. I let my breath out in a whoosh. I'm not sure what I expected, but I was relieved, nonetheless. I let my arm drop and turned away, heading down the hall to the Ginsburgs'.

I knocked on their door. The sound of quick footsteps was followed by that of the peephole cover sliding up, and then dropping back into place. The door opened wide, and I was enveloped in a warm hug and the scent of L'Air du Temps.

"Greer! It's so nice to see you! Come in, come in. Let me take your jacket." Goldie Ginsburg beamed at me, hung up my coat, and led me into the living room. "Herb, Greer's arrived," she yelled down the hall. "Don't you look pretty! I love your hair. Shorter, isn't it? Have a seat. The coffee's on, and I got rugelach from the kosher deli down the block. The doctor says I shouldn't have it because of my cholesterol, but I know how much you like it. Besides, this is a special occasion. Herbie!"

"What?"

"Our guest is here," Goldie yelled, this time more loudly. "He's got new hearing aids, but I swear he never has them in," she said to me. "Herb!"

"All right, all right, no need to yell, I'm not deaf you know." Herb Ginsburg appeared in the hallway to the bedroom. "Greer! You look wonderful, a sight for sore eyes. Sit, sit, you girls visit. I'll get the coffee."

Herb went into the kitchen.

"Not deaf, he says," Goldie muttered. "Like we don't have every conversation at the top of our lungs."

"I heard that." There was a rattle of crockery from the kitchen. Herb poked his head back out. "Cream and sugar all around? Just cream for you, Greer? And I'll just add some more pastry to this little plate. There's hardly enough for the three of us."

True to his word, Herb came back with a plate heaped with rugelach, and then a tray with the coffee. We ate and chatted. I brought them up to date on my temporary job and my life in Raven Hill, and they filled me in on current building gossip— who had moved, who was renovating, the outrageous schemes of the new HOA president. When the subject came around to births, marriages, and deaths, I saw the chance to gently introduce the topic I wanted to discuss.

"So how is your new neighbor working out?" I said. "Still the same guy I sold the place to?"

"Well, he's turned out to be very nice," Goldie said. "Quiet. Never has loud parties. We were a little concerned at first. The incense made me nervous. And the bells. But they didn't last long."

"Incense?" I asked.

"That was the mother," Herb said. "Cleansing the energy of the space." He put the phrase in air quotes. "Or something like that. Middle-aged hippie. Long wavy silvery-blonde hair, floaty clothes, strange jewelry, and those ugly sandals. She's from California. Berkeley," he added, as though that explained everything.

"It's called feng shui, she said. Apparently, it's what she does for a living." Goldie sounded skeptical. "Anyway, she came to apologize for the incense, said it would clear soon. She brought us a plant, which was very nice of her. Explained she was getting rid of negative energy because of what had happened."

Goldie gave me a nervous glance. I smiled at her.

"I think that was a good idea," I said. "It certainly couldn't hurt."

Goldie relaxed. "I guess not. And the bells made a nice noise, sort of like a wind chime, but Scott—the son—took them off the door handle as soon as his mother left town. Anyway, if you don't mind talking about it, there was something I wanted to tell you. About that night."

"Go on," I said.

"Well, you know Herb had a bad cold, and I was starting to feel a little under the weather myself, so we'd ordered from the deli. A big container of chicken soup and a couple of sandwiches. A little while after we'd ordered, I heard something. Through the wall. Sort of a bang or thump. I thought it was from your apartment, and it was strange. I peeked out and didn't see anyone, so I opened the door. I thought maybe I should check with you. Then I heard the fire door slam, so I figured someone had slammed their own door and didn't want to wait for the elevator. I closed the door and went back inside. Herb asked if dinner had come, and I said no."

"It took an awfully long time that night, the delivery," Herb said. "I dozed off in my chair, waiting."

"And I went and tidied the kitchen, and then sat down to make a list of things we needed from the drugstore. Well, I started to get a little impatient, I tell you. So I called Koch's to check on the order. They apologized, said their usual delivery guy was sick, so they had to send someone else, but the order was on its way. Right as I hung up I heard something in the hall so I thought the food was here. I peeked out again and saw someone going into your apartment. Just the back of them. I thought it was you."

Goldie stopped. Herb patted her hand.

"That would've made sense," I said. "It was about the right time, wasn't it? The time I usually got home?"

I wasn't sure about that, but I was hoping it would prompt Goldie to remember. She frowned.

"I think so. A little past our dinnertime, but then we eat early. I get heartburn at bedtime if we don't. Anyway, I sat back down with my list—I was on to groceries by this time—and then I heard another noise. This was more like a crash, like something broke, and it definitely seemed to be on the other side of the wall, right in your place. Well, I hopped right up, but then the phone rang. I picked it up and carried it over to the door and looked out while I was talking. It was the doorman—on the phone, I mean—asking could he send the deli guy up, and I said sure. But I was looking out the whole time, and I saw someone walk out of your apartment and down the hall."

"Could you see them at all? Man, woman?" I asked.

"Well, at first I thought it was you, Greer, but then I realized whoever it was didn't have long hair, at least that I could see, and was taller. Seemed a little more broad-shouldered too. So it could have been a woman, but then again, maybe a man, one with a slighter build?"

"What were they wearing?" I asked.

"A raincoat—more like a trench coat. You have one like it. And a hat of some sort. Flat shoes, pants. Their hands were in their pockets. I'm sorry I can't be more specific, but I was looking through the peephole. You know how it makes things look."

I nodded. "Distorted," I said. "What happened then? Anything?"

"I heard the elevator, so I opened the door. Right as the delivery guy got off it, I heard the fire door close. That always makes a noise. So I walked out into the hall to get our order and to tip the man. I looked at the door to your apartment, Greer, but it was closed. I didn't hear anything else, so I went back inside. I felt like something wasn't right, but then Herb woke up, and we ate. I really wasn't feeling too well. I wish I'd gone and knocked on your door. Maybe I could have done something."

"I don't think so, Goldie," I said. She didn't need to know the door wasn't completely closed. She wouldn't have been able to tell unless she'd walked right up to it—the doors were set in a bit, with an area deep enough for a doormat and a little wider than the door itself outside. "I'm glad you stayed in your apartment until the delivery man came. You could have been in danger otherwise."

"Do you think so?" Goldie asked.

"I do," I said. Herb was nodding.

"We told all this to the police," he said. "They wrote everything down, but they were most interested in the noise Goldie heard earlier, not the person she saw leaving."

Because the first noise coincided with Pete Perry coming in and then leaving through the back, I thought. Beyond that, they weren't really interested. I couldn't fault the cops for that—this second person, glimpsed only through a peephole, didn't obviously tie into the murder. My septuagenarian neighbors were still very much on top of things, but Herb didn't hear well and Goldie's communication style wasn't what you'd call linear. Two older people who admitted they weren't feeling well and had been hearing strange noises all evening—it would have been easy to write off anything they said that didn't fit.

"I think it's great that you told them everything, and I'm glad to hear they wrote it down. Do you happen to remember the times you heard all these things? I'd like to write it down myself."

"I'm glad you asked, Greer. I've already done it!" Goldie set her coffee cup on the table and stood. "You know, when the police and the ambulance showed up at your door, I thought those comings and goings might be important. I asked myself, 'What would Jessica Fletcher do?' and I thought she'd make some notes, and so that's what I did. I offered them to the detective who came, but he just wrote everything down in his notebook. Give me a minute."

Goldie took off down the hallway, and returned a minute later, waving a sheet of paper.

"Here you go. I made a copy so you can keep this one."

I looked at what she'd written. Jessica Fletcher would be proud. Approximate times; descriptions; and at the bottom, a few thoughtful questions. I was glad Goldie was so fond of mysteries.

"This is wonderful, Goldie. Thank you."

"You really believe they got the wrong guy?" Herb asked.

"I'm afraid so. I don't know if I can prove it though," I admitted.

"I gotta say, when Goldie first came home and said she'd been talking to your friend Ben, and they were wondering about what really happened, I thought maybe they'd been watching too many crime shows. But then she started going through it, and I decided maybe they were right. There were a lot of strange things happening in the building that night."

"You're not the only one to say so, Herb. I'm grateful so many people are taking me seriously."

"But will the police take you seriously, is what I want to know," he said.

"That's the million-dollar question," I said. "But I have to try."

They both nodded. Then Goldie, ever the optimist, said, "I'm sure you'll get to the truth, Greer, and when you do, you'll convince them." She picked up the coffee carafe and poured us each a fresh cup. "Now," she said, settling back with a pastry in hand, "on a happier subject—isn't it time Beau and Ben got married? It would be nice to have a wedding in the building. It's been a while."

We visited a while longer, and after promising to meet them for brunch before I went back to Raven Hill, I said goodbye. While I waited for the elevator, I looked down the hall at the Ginsburgs' door, then at my old apartment, and then in the other direction to the fire door that led to the stairs.

He was alive when I left him.

Pete Perry had said it, over and over. I'd always suspected he was telling the truth.

Now I was sure of it.

Chapter Thirteen

~

I was up and out early the next morning, to pick up fresh bagels, in spite of a late night sorting through the detritus of my previous life. I'd found plenty to throw out, a number of things to put aside and make decisions about later, and nothing related to New Leaf. There were still two boxes to investigate, but they were smaller, so at least I'd managed to free up some space.

I was reading the heating instructions on a prepared quiche when Grim arrived, bearing gifts. He handed me a bottle of the same wine we'd had with dinner, and a box containing a set of picks, two different locks, and a pair of handcuffs.

"The cuffs are a little advanced," he said. "I taped the key inside the box, but you'll want to use a paperclip to practice. I'd start with the big lock and go from there. Now, can I take a look around?"

"Sure," I said. I left the box on the kitchen counter and showed him what I'd discovered so far. "I've pulled apart the dresser, so you can skip it. When I moved in, everything was empty except for the bookcases. The bed's new, but Ava said all the other furniture belonged to Fritz. He seems to have customized a few things. Check out the bedside tables, the screen in the alcove, and the built-in cabinets beneath the bookshelf. It's impressive."

"He started out as a carpenter. Set design, that sort of thing. He was very skilled with cabinetry."

I left Grim to his search and went back to brunch preparations. The galley-style kitchen was small and shared a wall with the living room. There was no door, so I expected to hear Grim moving around. Instead, it was so quiet I might as well have been alone in the apartment. Finally I poked my head around the corner to see what he was up to. He was lying on his back on the floor, shining a small flashlight at the underside of the couch. While I watched, he turned off the light and rolled up onto his feet in one smooth, soundless motion.

"Almost done in here," he said when he saw me watching. "Only the bookcase is left."

I looked around the room. I had tidied up since I was expecting company. I still had plenty of things in what looked like random piles, but there was a system to it. I knew where everything was, and as far as I could tell nothing had been touched.

"Impressive," I said. "I'd never know you'd been here. Tell me, is this all part of your magician's bag of tricks?"

"Some of it. The rest—well, let's just say I had some interesting jobs when I was younger. Also some interesting relatives," he added with a grin.

"I see. Well, if you're done with the coffee table, I'll start putting out food."

"All yours," he said. He began a meticulous examination of the bookcase. I went back to plating food. Beau and Ben arrived a few minutes later, loaded down with Zabar's bags.

"We've got lots of goodies," Ben said. "Here, give me a plate for these pastries and then I'll make some mimosas."

"Ben, we're here to solve a murder, not indulge in bottomless bubbles," I said.

"I know," he replied. "That's why I only brought one bottle of champagne. See if you can find the orange juice, Beau. Where do you want these, Greer?"

"Living room—there's space on the coffee table. Then you can make me a drink," I said. Resistance was futile.

Ben took the plate of pastries and went into the living room. A moment later he was back, giving me a pointed look and saying, "Greer, there's a tall, dark, handsome stranger going through your underwear drawer!"

"Bookcase," Grim yelled from the other room. "I'm still working on the bookcase."

"That's my colleague. He's going to be helping us out. You can call him Grim," I said.

"I'd call him hot," Ben said, sotto voce, then went into the other room. I could hear him introducing himself and getting Grim's drink order.

"New recruit?" Beau asked as he handed me some bags and tried to find space on the counter.

"He got pulled in through proximity to me," I said. "But he offered to help and I accepted. He's got an unusual skill set."

"It's certainly looking that way," Beau replied, dangling the handcuffs.

"Put those back. He's teaching me to pick locks," I said, grabbing the box and stuffing it in a cabinet.

"Ben has a cousin in Newark who could've helped you with that," Beau said with a grin. "But the more, the merrier."

"Glad you think so," I said as the downstairs door buzzed. I hit the button to let Isabelle in. "Here's our last guest. She was working for Dan at the time of the murder."

Once Isabelle was introduced, we all filled our plates, and Ben handed out mimosas. I brought everyone up to speed while we ate. Then I sat back, took a deep breath, and finished my drink while the group debated a few points.

"Pretty inept burglars," Ben said. "They obviously haven't ever gotten what they wanted, and they've left two people dead."

"Amateurs," Grim said. "If they knew what they were doing, they wouldn't have gone in with anyone there. Okay, I know the first guy, Perry, was interrupted. He said he knocked Dan out and left, which makes sense. He'd had some experience with the breaking and entering. Whoever tried to get into your parents' house waited until they were away, but then moved too fast. It would have been easy enough to shine a light around the porch before going in. Sloppy."

I saw Beau raise his eyebrows, but all he said was "I agree. Sloppy. My question is, why did someone come back to Greer's apartment? Did they know Perry didn't get what they were after?"

"I think they couldn't be sure. Based on what he told the police, he called his contact and said he'd been interrupted, but he thought he'd gotten all the electronics. So whoever it was went back just in case?" I said. "And this week, I went to the New Leaf offices and said I was going through some things of Dan's and I'd found part of a spreadsheet I thought might be work-related. That's what I wanted you to look at," I said to Isabelle.

She nodded and said, "But it wasn't the first time someone tried to break into your parents' house. It happened right after you moved too. So someone had to be watching, to know you left things there."

"Someone has been watching," I said. "I've been followed at least twice that I know of since I got back. I think once I left the city and nothing happened, they relaxed. Then I turned up again, and they got nervous."

"So what's the plan?" Beau asked.

"I want Isabelle to look at the spreadsheet. We've got two more boxes to go through, and I think we need a timeline—who was where, doing what, on the night Dan was murdered."

"Do you have a list of suspects?" Isabelle asked.

"Yes. I've actually made an evidence board."

"Perfect," said Ben. "I'm a very visual person. Where is it?"

"I'll show you. It's going to be tight, with all of us," I said.

"Honey, think about where you are. People in the city throw parties for a hundred in smaller spaces than this," Beau said.

"True," I said. "All right then—I'm going to put Isabelle and Grim in charge of those last two boxes because Isabelle is more likely to recognize something important, and Grim is very efficient at this sort of thing. Beau, you've got the best handwriting, so you're in charge of the timeline. Ben and I will sort out our witness statements. I've also got some New Leaf propaganda—you can pass it around and take a look."

We moved into the alcove. With Grim and Isabelle at the back with the boxes, there was just room for the rest of us at the evidence board. I handed Isabelle copies of the sheets Ian had received from Dan. She studied them and then set them aside, a thoughtful look on her face.

Everyone got to work. After some debate on how to best set up the timeline, Beau made a chart. Ben and I each took responsibility for different suspects. With the notes I had from Suleiman and the Ginsburgs, combined with the text string from

Dan and information from various conversations, we were able to create a decent timeline.

"We've got a good amount of information on the New Leaf management," Beau said, "but your question marks are trickier. 'The man who fell down' and 'person who came in the back' we can put in a certain place at a certain time, but that's all we've got."

"I know. We don't even know that they're not the same person," I said. "We'll concentrate on Frank Benson, William Warren, and Clarice Phillips. They've got the most to lose if Dan found something."

"Benson died, though, didn't he?" Ben asked. He flipped through the notes.

"Recently," I said. "So he could have been involved in Dan's death, but not Jackson's."

"Which would mean there was more than one person behind this," Beau said.

"It's possible. If there was any kind of fraud on a wide scale, I think there would have to be. But until we know what Dan found, we don't know what that is."

"Keeping tabs on you would take either a group effort or a good source of information on your schedule," Isabelle said. "Dan had everything on his Outlook calendar, but no one at New Leaf would know what you were doing and when, especially after Dan died. Before, he usually noted when the two of you were doing something together."

"Which is how someone knew both of us would be out that night—he would have had drinks and dinner on the calendar. He sent me a reminder—we used the same program at my job." I said. "Do you know who had access to it? No one keeps their calendar open to everyone."

"I'm not sure," Isabelle said. "I could see his, he could see mine, and I'm sure senior management had access to each other's, though you could put in private appointments. Tech support could get in."

"You've also got to consider that whoever is behind this was willing to hire someone to break into your apartment," Grim said. "They could have hired someone to keep an eye on you, both after Dan's death and now that you're back. Maybe even periodically while you were in Raven Hill. Otherwise, how would they know? Social media?"

I shook my head. "I've posted very little since the fire last fall—basically only updates on how the library is coming along. And I'm technically still on the payroll there. So someone had to be keeping tabs." Then it hit me. "Moira! My hairdresser. Clarice was a client until shortly after I left town, then came back a few months ago. Moira said she always asks about me."

"Clarice still had to know you were coming back to the city, or she wouldn't have gone back to the salon. She's been keeping tabs, or someone close to her has," Grim said.

I hadn't considered that before. Raven Hill had been my safe haven from all of this. The fact that it wasn't both creeped me out and made me angry.

"So what does this tell us?" Ben said. "That it wasn't a group effort? One person directing others?"

"Someone who can't disappear for lengths of time to indulge in surveillance," I said.

"Or someone who doesn't like to do their own dirty work," Grim added. "Anyone fit that profile?"

"William Warren never did anything for himself as far as I could see. He likes to have minions," Isabelle said. "But Frank Benson was in and out all the time, and if he was stopping for coffee, he'd always check with his assistant to see if she wanted anything. Clarice Phillips never made a move without her assistant knowing about it."

"Austin? He seemed very efficient," I said.

"No, it was someone else while I was there. It was an older woman. Gloria, I think. She was a holdover from the previous owners. I can't remember her last name. We would chat once in a while. I never had much to do with Clarice."

"All right. No definitive answers, but stuff to keep in mind," I said. "Did you have any luck with those last two boxes? Any insight on those spreadsheets?"

"It's a list of suppliers; that much is true. Some had been with New Leaf for a long time. A lot of the others were fairly new additions. It's a lot heavier on the add side." She frowned. "I know that was something that bothered Dan. New ones were added and old ones disappeared all the time. We were constantly adjusting the budget and projections. We had to prepare information for potential investors, and the numbers kept changing. I remember Dan and William had a pretty tense discussion about it once."

"Did you get any details?" Beau asked.

"No, not really. I was looking for Dan one afternoon. He was in a conference room with William. I heard him say, 'This doesn't make any sense,' and William started to answer, then saw me in the doorway and said they'd talk later." Then she added, "But if it's okay with you, I'd like to keep this. I feel like there's something I'm missing."

"Sure, it's a copy," I said.

"As for the boxes," Isabelle said. "There are two things that are strange. First, there's this." She held up a couple of neatly typed pages with the New Leaf logo. "It's a performance review."

"That is strange. Dan never did that stuff at home," I said.

"Stranger still, it's not for someone who worked for him," Isabelle said. "It's someone in tech support. He's got one or two penciled notes on it, though. Maybe you can read them—I can't." She passed the pages forward.

"Then there's this." Isabelle held up an aqua envelope, the type greeting cards come in. This one looked a little battered. "It's addressed to you, care of your parents. It's Dan's handwriting, with a date written in tiny print on the back. My mother does the same thing, when the card is for my birthday or something and she doesn't want me to open it before. But the date on this is the day he died. There's something else—the postmark is two weeks later."

I went cold. The information Ian had received had arrived a couple of weeks after Dan died. I hadn't really thought about it at the time. Now, looking at the rumpled envelope, I thought I understood.

"The mail chute," I said.

"I think so," Isabelle said, nodding. "It didn't get a lot of use, but things got stuck once or twice while I was working for Dan. The last time I saw the postal service trying to clear it was my last day, a couple weeks after he died." She passed the card forward as well.

"This could be what we're looking for," I said, studying the envelope.

"Or it could be something personal," Beau said. "Would you like some privacy while you open it?"

"It's all right," I said, looking at the tiny numbers Dan had written on the back of the envelope.

"Well, I'd like a little more coffee," Ben said. "So while you open that—anyone else for a refill? Yes? I'll just bring the pot then."

"Don't forget the cream," I said, turning the envelope over in my hands.

Ben left for the kitchen, and Grim and Isabelle busied themselves putting things back into the two whiskey boxes. Beau perched on the arm of the chair.

"Birthday? Anniversary?" he said. "Wrong time of year, though, wasn't it?"

"Right," I said. "No reason for a card that I can think of." I carefully opened the flap.

It was indeed a greeting card, but not one for any particular occasion. It was a beach scene—sand, seashells, a starfish—with a familiar lighthouse to one side. I flipped the card over. On the back it gave the photo credit, and said "Sanibel Island Light, Sanibel Island, Florida." I opened it up. There was a brief note from Dan inside. "Can't wait until our beach vacation! I'm ready to indulge in everything the place is known for. I'm sure our friend Ian will have something to say about that! XOXO Dan."

That was it. Nothing about New Leaf, nothing that made any sense at all. I handed it to Beau. Ben came back with the coffee and took a look.

"Were the two of you planning a trip?" he said, sounding sympathetic. "Your sister is near there, isn't she?"

"About an hour away," I said. "And no, we weren't planning a trip. We did go out to Sanibel once when we visited. Saw the lighthouse and spotted some manatees and porpoises. The day was cool and breezy, not great for the beach, so we walked through a preserve and ate at a restaurant that served lots of umbrella drinks. We went to a gift shop too. Dan would buy this kind of blank card whenever we went away, and keep them in his desk at work for birthdays or baby showers or whatever event he might have forgotten about. I know he got several while we were there."

I looked at the message again. "The reference to Ian must relate to the stuff Dan mailed to him. I'll get in touch and see if this means anything to him."

"Where does all this leave us?" Beau said.

"It leaves us without a motive," I said. "Although I have it on good authority that motive is overrated, it would still be helpful." Jennie Webber had repeated that to me more times than I could count. "And with no way I can think of to figure out where our three main suspects were the night of the murder."

"I may be able to help you there," Isabelle said. "I was in the office late. I left right before Dan. The place was practically deserted, which was unusual. It was because most of the senior people left early for one reason or another. Frank Benson left at around four thirty. I bumped into him on his way out. He said he had a thing at his daughter's school."

"He did. But it wasn't until seven thirty, and he was late," I said.

"Sketchy," said Beau, and updated the timeline.

"William was looking for Frank around five. He was walking around, asking people if they'd seen him. I told him I had and what he'd said. William looked annoyed. Checked his watch and went over to Frank's paralegal and told her he needed something from Frank first thing, so if Frank called in, to let him know. William said he had a law school alumni cocktail event, and he had to go. I remember because it was unusual—he never spoke to anyone about anything personal."

"Tough to check but I might have someone who could find out if there was such an event," I said.

"And then Clarice left. She was meeting an investor for dinner and then going to a Broadway show. *Phantom,* I think. I saw Gloria in the restroom. She was leaving too."

"Cat's away," Grim said. "So everyone left right after their boss?"

Isabelle nodded. "It was a Thursday. The staff was small. and everyone had been working long hours."

"I'd still like to find a motive," I said. "It would point us in the right direction. And then be able to verify alibis."

"I'll try to come up with Gloria's last name," said Isabelle. "And I'll keep working on this list. Something's not right, but I'm not sure what."

"And we'll follow up with John Norton. Maybe he saw something while he was out having his cigarette. His memory's getting worse, but you never know," Ben said.

After that, we threw around some more ideas and finished off the champagne. Grim volunteered to stay and help me clean up. Then the other three headed out. I figured Grim had said he'd stay so he could finish his search, but when I'd closed the door behind my other guests, I found him rinsing plates in the kitchen. He was looking thoughtful, so I kept quiet and brought in all the dishes.

"Penny for your thoughts," I said, when even the coffee-maker had been cleaned and every counter sparkled.

"Couple of things," he said. "You said you have the police file on your husband's murder. Do you mind if I take a look?"

"Not at all," I said. We went back into the alcove, and I handed it over. While he studied it, I made a list of my next steps. He put the folder down and looked at the timeline.

"I asked Gus some questions when I was picking up those boxes," he said. "He described the crime scene pretty thoroughly. Something he said stuck with me. It was something like 'Whoever hit Jackson knocked him out and then gave him a few whacks for good measure.'"

"Yes, he told me that too."

"Gus also said the window was smashed, and it looked like someone had used a hammer. So the question is, why?"

"I assumed Jackson came to, and there was a struggle. It would explain the short time between the sounds the neighbor heard," I said.

"Maybe, but from what Gus said, Jackson was beaten pretty badly, struck a few times after he was already down. And nowhere near the window. It's similar to what happened to your husband. I looked at the pictures. Big bruise along the jaw—that's Perry. Dan goes down, maybe hits his head. Looks like he definitely did, based on the file. I don't think he regained consciousness. I think someone hit him and then broke the glass vase you can see on the floor, because they were angry. They didn't get what they wanted. It wasn't extra blows for insurance. It was rage."

I didn't say anything. I was picturing the scenes, how it would have played out. It fit.

"Greer? Do you—"

"Yes. Yes, I understand rage." I'd been living with it coiling and hissing in my gut for a while. I'd watched myself think and do things I otherwise wouldn't because of it. I knew the danger.

"I think you're right." I looked at my evidence board. "We need to find them, whoever did this. Soon." Then I turned to Grim. "Go ahead and finish your search. Want some sparkling water?"

He looked at me for a minute, then nodded. I got him a drink and then sat in the living room, thinking, staring at the greeting card on the table in front of me. When he was done, he sat on the couch.

"Nothing here—at least nothing I'm looking for. It was a long shot, but thanks for letting me check. I'm going to go. Call if you need me. See you tomorrow?"

"Yeah, sure. Thanks, Grim."

I got up and locked the door behind him, then went back to the alcove and stared at the board.

No one ever really believes they're going to die.

April had said that, and so had Grim. And I thought they were right. But Dan had taken precautions—he'd sent things to two people he trusted in case he couldn't share the information himself. He'd sent it through the mail, so there was no electronic footprint leading from him to me or to Ian. He was worried, and not just for himself. This had to be big.

Chapter Fourteen

I spent the rest of the afternoon trying to get answers to some of the questions that had come up that morning. First, a call to Ian Cameron. Could he shed any light on the message Dan had left in the greeting card?

"I've got no idea. I've never even been to that part of Florida. Are you making any progress?" he said.

"Some. Have you ever met Clarice Phillips or William Warren?"

"Both. Friends of a friend kind of thing. They mentioned their finance guy decided to retire due to health issues. I recommended they talk to Dan. They wanted someone with a sterling reputation and an entrepreneurial mindset—traditional background, but ready for a big opportunity. Warren seems competent, but full of himself. Clarice Phillips struck me as very bright, but—I don't know . . . kind of brittle? I don't think she tolerates fools gladly. Very charming, though. She's a big theater buff. You know, she offered me a spare ticket to *Phantom of the Opera* the night Dan was killed. Said her uncle was in it for five years, early on, and she loved it."

"That's interesting. I've come across a few tidbits like that, actually," I said.

I filled him in on what I'd learned, verified the timing of his receipt of what Dan had sent him, and asked after his parents. He had recently moved back to Delaware to be near them, and was trying to convince them to move into an independent living facility. He was having about as much luck with that project as I was with mine. I hung up, feeling relieved that my mom and dad were younger than his and that I was not an only child. Maybe my parents would decide to retire to Florida, and my sister could have those fights with them.

There was an idea. I sent a text to my nephew.

Trivia question—what is Sanibel best known for?

The lighthouse. Seashells. Was just out there and found a whole Junonia. Nana's impressed.

Not helpful, but I smiled, nonetheless. He was at the age where he was still happy to spend time with the adults in his life, but mortified if any of his friends saw him doing it. I texted my thanks and moved on.

Next up—April Benson, and with any luck, she'd kill two birds with one stone. I sent an email asking if she could tell me exactly what time Frank had shown up for his daughter's play and where the performance was, and if she knew whether her law school had held an alumni cocktail the same night, since that was also William Warren's alibi.

She replied almost immediately. Frank had arrived at seven forty-five. The school was on the Upper East Side—she provided the address. It was about fifteen minutes from my old apartment. The timing was tight but possible. April also said she wasn't sure about the alumni event but knew who to call to find out. She'd check and see if there was a record of who came, but it might take a day or two.

Fine with me. At least there was some progress there.

I picked up the performance review Isabelle had found. It was for someone named Steven Malloy who worked in tech support. He seemed to have done an acceptable job—no dings, no effusive praise. Dan had three notes on it. One said "NDA" and the other "hacked." At the very bottom he'd written, "Where now?"

If this related to his death, I couldn't figure out how. I read through it again and still got nothing. I filed it away with the other evidence. With all my investigative avenues closed for the time being, and no further excuses, I did my laundry, ate leftover pastries for dinner, and went to bed.

* * *

When Grim arrived at the brownstone on Monday, I remembered to tell him about the incident with Alexei and made him promise never to leave the machine plugged in again. Then we both got to work, occasionally exchanging thoughts on the murder and our prime suspects. I was despairing of ever getting a break when one arrived in the form of call from April Benson.

"Listen to this," she said as soon as I picked up. "Our buddy William was a little loosey-goosey with the truth about where he was that night."

"No alumni event?" I asked.

"There was, and he did attend, briefly. Or better put, in two stages."

"What do you mean?" I asked.

"Well, I talked to a woman I know from law school. Her name is Sherry, and she's very involved with the alumni group and fundraising. In fact, fundraising is what she does for a living.

Anyway, she said William got there rather early that night. She made a point of chatting him up so she could hit him for a donation to something or another. She said he gulped down his drink and kept checking the time, then excused himself to make a call. She was talking to someone else, near a window, and she saw him coming out and walking up the street. He hadn't stepped out for the call—he had his briefcase in hand, but no phone. Looked like he was in a hurry. Then just when things were wrapping up, he found her again, apologized, and said he'd gotten tied up with someone he knew from work, but wanted to hear all about her current cause."

"I suppose she didn't call him out on the lie because he's a potential donor, and you can't check on who he was talking to, because it wasn't necessarily another alum," I said.

"Exactly," April said. "And he did make a small donation, which surprised her. He's not known for his generosity. But it gets better." April sounded positively gleeful. "Sherry said she thought maybe he was trying to cultivate a new image because, before his current job, he had started to get a certain reputation."

"Really? Did she elaborate?"

"Apparently, William Warren has left a few jobs with quiet encouragement to make himself scarce, and left someone holding the bag for his mistakes at others. All very discreet and civilized, of course, but people do talk."

"Of course they do. I thought he'd moved around a lot, but it always seemed to be a move up. What was he up to that got him into trouble?"

"He's landed on his feet, that's for sure. Sherry said it always had to do with money. The guy's just plain greedy. Sherry has no problem separating people from their money—it's a gift, really—but she doesn't do it to line her own pockets. She thinks that now that he's in a plum position, with a company planning to go public, he's trying to whitewash his past."

"Hmm. I can see that. Did she say what time she saw him coming and going?"

"She did, because they only had the function room until seven. After that, she was talking to him in the hotel bar. He arrived at five, left again at five fifteen, and got back a few minutes before seven." April then gave me the name and address of the place. It was a medium-sized hotel with a nice bar and restaurant only about ten minutes away from my old building.

"Thank you, April," I said. "I hope this information didn't cost you too much—I'm sure Sherry extracted a fee."

April laughed. "Two tickets to a charity auction, and you're coming with me if you're still in town!"

"Deal," I said. "This is well worth it."

April told me she hadn't found anything else in the stuff from Frank's office and asked me to keep her informed.

I hung up and pulled out my timeline. More empty space filled in, but still nothing definitive. Grim wandered in and looked over my shoulder. I told him what April had said.

"It's got to be one or all of these three," I said. "But why? And how do we prove it?"

"Keep poking until something gives," Grim said. "Any luck finding the guy in the performance review Dan had?"

"I checked social media—either he's not active or he's got his profiles hidden. On any of the networking sites, he lists himself as freelance, willing to work remote or on-site pretty much any-where. I sent a message, but no response."

"So he's disappeared?" Grim asked.

"Yes. Whether literally or figuratively, I don't know," I said.

We both went back to work. The day dragged on. Finally, Grim said he was wrapping up the library work for the day but wanted to go up and investigate the attic while there was still some daylight.

"Be my guest," I said. "And as long as you're there, check all the windows and locks and lightbulbs, will you?" I handed him a checklist, and off he went.

I was finishing up when my phone buzzed. Isabelle.

"Tell me you've solved the secret riddle of the spreadsheets," I said.

"Not yet, but I'm still digging. I remembered Gloria's last name and sent her a message. But that's not why I'm calling. There's been a—complication," Isabelle said.

"Is everything all right? Do you need to go back upstate?"

"No, everything's fine at home. It's Great-Aunt Caro. Well—we had dinner last night, and she was asking how you were. After a couple of Irish coffees, I ended up telling her about the murder investigation, and now she wants to help!"

"Ah, I see."

"Hang on—she just walked in." There was some muffled conversation, and then Isabelle was back. "She wants me to put you on speaker."

"Okay," I said, mind racing. Caro had led a colorful life and knew lots of people. *Was* there some way she could help? Someone she knew?

"Greer, darling, how are you?" Caro said. "Listen, Isabelle has been telling me all about your attempt to see justice done. I feel terrible that I was part of what derailed your investigation in Lake Placid. I want to help. Tell me, what can I do?"

"Oh, Caro, I really couldn't ask you to—"

"Nonsense! I insist!"

That's what I was afraid of.

Caro went on. "I'm only here to see a couple of doctors and go through mementos of my misspent youth. A friend asked for some things for a charity auction. It's time I started getting rid of this stuff anyway, but I'm boring poor Isabelle with all my stories."

Wait a minute. This might be something I could use.

"Caro, when you were modeling, you lived here full time, right? Did you know a lot of theater people?"

"Oh yes, quite a few. I met some of the big names at parties, but when I started out, several of my neighbors were actors and musicians. There were places that were affordable back then, even without a steady paycheck. I'm still in touch with a few people I knew. Why do you ask?"

"One of our chief suspects is a theater buff. She actually had tickets to a show the night of the murder. She's invited me to lunch on Wednesday. I'm not sure what she's up to, but I thought it would be a good chance to try to shake something loose. Want to help?"

"I'd love to! Sounds like it's right up my alley! I'll play the dotty-old-lady card—regale her with stories and ask nosy questions."

"Caro, I'm not sure anyone will believe you're a dotty old lady," I said. Isabelle seconded that.

"Oh, of course they will. I'll just be myself, only more so. I believe it's what you girls would call 'leaning in.' Or something like that. I'll ask all sorts of shrewd questions and be a detective too. So how shall we do this?"

The three of us tossed some ideas around. Caro sounded delighted, and Isabelle apprehensive. Once we had a workable plan, Caro said she had to go.

"You and Isabelle figure out the rest of the details. I've got to dash. See you Wednesday!"

Isabelle took me off speaker.

"I'm sorry you got dragged into this, Isabelle," I said.

"No, it's fine. I needed a break, and Caro provides quite a distraction. She has such confidence—I'm hoping some of it rubs off. Honestly, I'd like to be Great-Aunt Caro when I grow up."

I wanted to be DCI Vera Stanhope, or perhaps Professor Harry Wild, who was just as sharp, though better dressed. But I could see Isabelle's point.

"Can't blame you there," I said. "Okay, let's get this buttoned down."

We figured out timing, and I sent the restaurant info to Isabelle. She promised to call if she heard back from Gloria. By the time we hung up, I had just enough time to do all my backups before leaving for class. I sent a text to Grim, asking him to lock up, and once he replied, I raced out the door.

I made it to my class with seconds to spare. Before I went into the gym, I tried to take a good look around, without being obvious. I didn't think I'd been followed. I was wrong. Yuri came over the minute we started warming up.

"Your little friend from the subway was waiting for you," he said. "Pretty obvious—same jacket and cap, milling around outside."

I sighed in frustration. "I didn't think anyone followed me—I was trying to be aware. I didn't see him. I did look around when I got here. But how did he—ugh! The class schedule. It's online."

Yuri nodded. "He was near the shop next door. Now he's in the coffee shop across the street."

"How do you know?"

Yuri gave me a thin smile. "Because *I* was in the coffee shop across the street, watching the front of the gym."

"Why?"

"Because tailing someone is hard, but, as you said, looking up the schedule is easy. You are my student, and what this young man is doing bothers me." Yuri said. Then he shrugged. "Also, my wife has a performance tonight, and my mother-in-law has my kid."

"I see," I said. "Thank you for looking out for me."

"He's not gone yet, Greer. Whatever he wants, he seems determined. Larry isn't here tonight. We will talk when class is done."

For the next hour, I worked on a move designed to disable an opponent. Yuri had paired me with an older gentleman named Len who couldn't have weighed more than I did. Even when I was sure I had the move down, I was hesitant to go all out. Yuri noticed and yelled across the room.

"Greer, you have to decide you're willing to really hurt someone. That scrawny-assed old guy is tougher than he looks! That goes for all of you—no debating with yourself in the moment."

Len chuckled. "Go ahead, hon, give it your best shot. I used to be a jeweler. I've been mugged more times than I can count. I'll be all right. Or would you feel better if I knocked you down first? Yes? Okay, pretend we're in a dark parking lot and come at me."

Within seconds I was on my butt on the floor, rubbing my shoulder where Len had nearly wrenched it from the socket. He was chucking again.

"See? Now come on, your turn."

I was more successful the next time, and by the end of class, my reaction time had improved considerably. As instructed, I waited to speak to Yuri while the rest of the class headed for the locker rooms.

"Meet me in the hall by the lobby once you have your things," he said. "I'll need your cell number. I'm going to leave first and watch to see if he follows you when you come out."

"What if he sees you?"

"He won't see me. Now listen—if he does follow, I will call. Don't answer. Keep going down the block. There's an alley about halfway. It's used for deliveries, but no cameras. Turn in there and stay against the wall. If he follows, use the move we learned last week. Then make him tell you what he wants. I'll be there if you need me."

He was serious. I nodded my understanding and went to the locker room. This kind of thing was out of my comfort zone, but I found myself more excited than apprehensive. I wanted some answers. I put on my coat and moved my phone from my bag to my pocket as I went out into the hallway.

Once Yuri had my cell number, he told me to wait two minutes and then leave. Then he walked down the hall and handed something—a scarf, I thought—to the woman at the front desk. I watched the time, and at the two-minute mark, walked to the lobby and out the door. I turned and followed my usual route toward the subway. I hadn't gotten far when my phone vibrated. I took a quick look then shoved it back in my pocket. Yuri.

My adrenaline kicked up. It was hard not to look behind me, but I kept my pace steady. I could see the alley ahead. When I got there, I turned, stopped a few feet in, and stepped out of the light. I didn't put my back against the wall—no way was I touching anything I didn't have to. It was bad enough that I had to drop my bag so I could keep my hands free. Time seemed to crawl, and some rustling noises from a few feet away were making me antsy. I had decided I was both too impatient and too prissy to make a good spy when someone stopped in the mouth of the alley. Black jacket, black knit cap—this was the guy.

I waited in the shadows, staying as still as I could. *Come on,* I thought. Finally, he moved toward me, peering ahead. He stepped out of the light and stopped, waiting for his eyes to adjust to the darkness. He was less than a foot away. I shifted my weight.

"Who are you looking for?" I said in a low voice.

He flinched and turned. While he was off-balance, I moved. A second later he was face down on the ground, my knee on his back. He'd grunted when he went down but hadn't made another sound. I thought I'd knocked the wind out of him, but I didn't want to take any chances.

"Listen up, buddy. I have a gun, and I know how to use it. The only sounds you're going to make are answers to my questions—got it?"

It wasn't dialogue worthy of Jason Bourne, but it worked. The guy gasped out, "Okay." He seemed to be panting. Either that or crying.

"Who are you?"

"Carl Guenther."

"Why are you following me?"

"Because of New Leaf. Your husband."

"What about him?"

"He found something."

"What?"

Silence. I dug my knee into his back.

"What?" I hissed.

"I'm—I'm not sure. But I kept it. Please, can I get up? This is so gross."

True, but he might try to run.

"Please? I've been trying to find you, to tell you, but there was always someone around."

I sensed some movement to my right, where I had left my bag. I looked up. Yuri. He nodded his head and gestured, then faded back into the darkness.

"Okay. I have a lot of questions. There's a deli around the corner. We'll go there. Don't try anything," I warned as I stood. I grabbed my bag, ready to hurl it at him if necessary.

Guenther got up. He pulled off his hat and used it to wipe his face, then brushed at his jacket and jeans. He'd probably have to toss those, but since I planned to do the same with my gym bag, I didn't have much sympathy.

"Let's go," I said.

The two of us walked out of the alley, attracting no notice from other pedestrians. Though I heard and saw nothing, I was sure that, in the darkness, Yuri followed.

Chapter Fifteen

We got to the deli and slid into a booth. The waitress who came to take our order wrinkled her nose when she got near Guenther, who was still trying to wipe off the alleyway grime.

"My friend fell," I said. "Got any Wet-Naps? And two coffees. Thanks."

She left, shaking her head, but was back quickly with everything I'd asked for, and water and extra napkins for good measure. I took a good look at Carl Guenther while he cleaned his hands. I recognized him now—he was the guy I'd seen at New Leaf the day I'd met with Clarice and William. He might be telling the truth about trying to talk to me when no one was around.

I watched him as I sipped my coffee. He was nervous. Nervous about more than just me, I thought. He kept looking out the window and toward the door. I was sure he hadn't spotted Yuri, so it was something else. *Someone* else. I let the silence stretch. Finally, he took a big swig of his own coffee, made a face, and looked at me.

"I'm sorry I've been following you. I didn't know what else to do," he said.

Someone dropped a glass and swore at the ensuing crash. Guenther flinched and looked at the door.

"Expecting someone?" I asked.

"No. Maybe. I don't know," he said.

"You don't seem to know much, Carl. This isn't helpful. Why don't you tell me what you do know?"

He nodded.

"Okay, okay. So this is what happened, what I'm sure of, anyway. I started working at New Leaf right after college, like four years ago. I got the job because I knew this guy Steve from school, and he'd been working there a couple of years."

"Steve Malloy? In IT?" I said.

He looked surprised. "Yeah, that's right. That's what I do too. Anyway, I ran into him, and he told me he worked for this cool company that was getting ready to open all these cannabis dispensaries, like a drugstore, you know, except you go in and they figure out the right kind of weed for you. And he said that the company was going to go public soon, and everyone who worked there would make a ton of money. He said they were looking for someone else in IT, someone who could do desktop support and was a pretty good generalist."

"Which would be you?"

"Yeah, I'm good at all that stuff—it's easy. But I'm better at security." He looked embarrassed. "That's because I spent a lot of time in school hacking into things. Nothing big," he said, "nothing illegal, I don't think. Just for fun, because I could."

"And Steve knew about it?"

"Yeah, he did. He said I should keep it quiet, the hacking, but eventually they were going to need better security, and I could move up because I know a lot about ransomware and stuff—you know what I mean?" he asked.

Set a thief to catch a thief. Not a bad plan.

"I understand," I said. "Go on."

"So anyway I got the job. Entry level, but decent money and health insurance. A lot of these jobs are gig work, you know? No benefits. Everybody was pretty cool, and they liked me. I was willing to help anybody out—I don't like to be bored—and I'm good at explaining things."

I had yet to see evidence of this but gave him the benefit of the doubt. These were unusual circumstances.

"So then what happened?" I asked.

"Steve started to get antsy. I think he expected a bigger payoff sooner, you know? Then he started volunteering to do a lot of the late shifts, when we do backups and upgrades, the things you do when no one else is in the system. Only one of us needs to be there, and it would normally be me. But he started saying he'd do it."

"Why do you think that was?"

Carl hesitated. "I think he was looking for something. I mean, that's what I think now. At the time, he said he'd always been more of a night owl anyway."

"Do you know if he found whatever it was he was looking for?"

Carl looked miserable. "He didn't, but I think I did."

"Recreational hacking?" I asked.

"Not on purpose. Steve asked me to stay late one night to help him, said he wasn't feeling well. When everyone left, he told me Frank Benson had asked him to recover some encrypted files he'd lost the password for. Do you know how encrypted files work?" he asked me.

"Not really, other than that it's an additional layer of protection. Give me the short version. More passwords?"

"Yeah, and there are different access points, and the passwords are generated. If you can get into the operating system, you can get in, no matter what computer it's on." He stopped and looked at me, checking to see if I was with him,

"I'm following," I said.

"Yeah, well, that's the simple version. So Steve should've been able to get in, but I figured maybe because he had a fever he didn't feel like it. And Frank tended to mess around with things and forget how he'd done stuff."

"And he usually left his work laptop in the office," I said, remembering April's comments.

"That's right," Carl said. "Steve pointed me at Frank's office, told me what he was looking for, and then asked if I wanted anything. He was going to get something to eat and some cough drops or something. Then he gave me the name of two files to print out, because Frank wanted a hard copy. He left and I got to work." He looked sheepish. "It's not like it was tough. Frank used to write down all his passwords on those sticky notes. Anything generated he would never remember. He had a system for his own but it wasn't hard to figure out. Real old school."

Since I was also guilty of doing the very same thing from time to time, I said nothing. Carl continued.

"So I sent the first file to the printer. I thought it was weird, but like I said—old school. I heard someone moving around and figured it was Steve. I looked at the printout and it had a line down it. The printer needed a new drum. I put it aside and sent the file to the office printer. It's the only one that's consistently okay because it gets used the most. I mean—who prints stuff out anymore? I was pulling up the second file when Steve stuck his head in. He looked really nervous. He said Dan Sullivan had come back for something and asked if he had he seen me in Frank's office. I said no, and then he told me to hurry up. I explained about the printer and showed him and he said it didn't matter, it was legible. Then he said Frank didn't want anyone to know what happened, and Dan shouldn't see me in there, so he'd go distract him. Now I was nervous—I thought all this was strange. So I did what he asked, but I kept a copy of each file for myself. I don't even know why. So I got out of Frank's office and I left the files on Steve's desk and went to my own."

"What about the one you sent to the office printer?" I asked. "Did you get it? Did Steve?"

"I looked later, after your husband left. It wasn't there. I'm sure Steve didn't have it because he would have yelled at me for doing it."

"Dan found it," I said. That was the spreadsheet. But it was only one of the two.

Carl was nodding. "I think so."

"And he never saw you?"

"No. He left a few minutes after Steve came back."

"And then what happened?" I asked.

"Nothing, really. After that we did the system update. Steve was in a pretty good mood. He reminded me again not to say anything. That was it."

"But you still have those printouts?"

"Yeah, I kept them. Here's the thing, though. I guess when I picked up the first copy, the one I'd set aside, I grabbed some notes Frank had made. It was only one page from a legal pad. I saw it when I got home. Well, I couldn't figure out how to put it back. So I kept everything. At home, though, in a safe place. After what happened to your husband—I don't know, I got nervous. And another thing—I went looking for those files again. They're nowhere on the system. I checked Frank's laptop too. They're just gone."

That didn't surprise me. Even Frank would've been smart enough to get rid of the evidence once he figured out he had a problem. Or more likely, to get someone to do it for him.

"Where is Steve now? I know he's not with New Leaf. Are you still in touch?" I asked.

"No. We were for a while. Right after your husband died, Steve came in and said he got a new job. Hawaii. He kept in touch for a while, but then nothing. Not a big deal—we weren't that close. But then Frank Benson died. He was a decent guy. I liked him."

"Most people did," I said.

"Yeah, well, I felt bad. I started thinking about things, and I tried to get in touch with Steve, just to let him know."

"You can't find him," I said, a cold certainty settling over me.

"No. No one can. I checked with people we knew from school. He wasn't tight with anyone at work, and he wasn't close with his family. The last anyone heard he was moving to Bali to work, but that was a few years ago."

"He wouldn't be the first person who decided to disappear," I said. *Or who someone decided to make disappear,* I thought. It could go either way given what Carl had said about Steve.

"You think he was up to something, something that got him in trouble?" I said.

"Yeah, or got him enough money to disappear."

I detected a note of envy in Carl's voice. Time for a reality check.

"Let me make sure I've got the details straight: Steve started taking more late shifts, and you think he was looking for something. Then one day he asks you to stay and help him, which you do, so you're both still there when everyone leaves, and other people in the office know that. Then he has you sign into Frank's computer and find and print specific files while he's out getting something to eat. He gets a hard copy, so at that point, the only electronic fingerprints left are yours, yes?"

Carl swallowed and nodded.

"So," I continued, "Looks like Steve set you up to be the fall guy if his plan went south. But the two of you didn't get caught—though it was a near thing when Dan came in. You lucked out, and he only saw Steve. Now Dan is dead, and Steve is MIA. Which leaves you. Though to be honest," I said, thinking out loud, "I think if anyone knew you were involved in Steve's little information heist, you wouldn't be sitting here talking to me. But how did Dan tip his hand?"

"Steve could have said Dan had been there or that he's the one who asked him to get the files," Carl said. "It's the kind of thing he'd do."

What a charming fellow this Steve was. But those weren't the only possibilities.

"Or he could have told Dan that Frank asked him to do something or had a concern," I said. Probably the latter; then Dan would have gone to Frank, both because Frank was the general counsel and because Dan didn't think Frank was the type, or had the brains, for any kind of criminal enterprise.

"You still have those printouts, don't you?" I said to Carl.

"Not with me. Like I said, they're at home, in a safe place."

"You need to give them to me," I said.

"That's what I thought," Carl said. "You know, I almost forgot about them? Then when you showed up, everything got tense at the office. I kept them in case they were worth something. Now I want to get rid of them. I was going to shred them, but then I thought, maybe I need them. Insurance, right? But I've got a new job. I'm giving notice on Friday. I want to get out."

"Good move. I can come with you now," I said. "The sooner the better."

"No, my girlfriend's home. She doesn't know about any of this. Tomorrow. I'll meet you somewhere. But it has to be after work. And no more alleys," he said, wrinkling his nose.

"Do you live on the West Side?"

He nodded.

"The Hungarian. Do you know it? It'll be crowded, lots of people—no one will notice us." *And I have Grim for backup,* I thought.

"Okay," he said. We agreed on a time, and I pulled out my phone.

"Give me your number," I said. "In case something comes up. I'll call you now so you'll have mine."

He nodded, and to my surprise, pulled out two phones. One was a top-of-the-line smart phone, the other was a clunky-looking model with no screen. He saw the look on my face and waved the clunker at me.

"This one's mine. It's good for text and calls. You'll get a generic message on the voicemail."

"Cheaper?" I asked.

Carl nodded. "More secure too. The smart phone belongs to New Leaf. I don't want any connection to you on my work phone."

He sounded a little paranoid, but I couldn't blame him. I punched in his number as he gave it to me. His phone rang. Satisfied, I disconnected. Carl got up to go, with one more look out the window. Still nervous. He bit his lip and turned to me.

"Dan was a nice guy too. He was nice to all of us. We talked about sports and stuff—nothing major, but he made an effort. Not like some of the others. I'm sorry about what happened to him."

"Thank you. And Carl?" I said. "Don't say anything to any-one. You've been lucky so far. It might not last."

He nodded and left.

I signaled the waitress for a refill, and when it came, asked for a piece of chocolate cake and the check. Yuri arrived at the same time dessert did.

"He went to the uptown train and got on it," he said, sliding into the booth. "No limp, not even a bruise that I could see. We still have work to do, Greer."

"I'm getting the hang of it," I said as I dug into my cake. "I certainly worked up an appetite."

"Yes, you did well enough. For a beginner. Tell me, do you really have a gun?"

"Sure. It's at home, locked up, but he didn't need the details."

"Have you resolved the issue? Will he be leaving you alone?"

"He has some information for me. I'll have someone with me. After that, I won't be seeing him again."

"Good," Yuri said. "I will leave you then."

"Thanks for helping me," I told him. "I appreciate it more than I can say."

"No problem," he said, and then grinned. "This is the most fun I've had in years. Goodnight, Greer. Take a cab home."

"I planned on it," I said. "Goodnight."

He left with a wave. I finished my cake and paid the bill, hitting the sidewalk with a spring in my step.

I might not be ready for my junior secret agent badge, but I was closer to an answer than I'd ever been. The amount of enjoyment I took in knocking someone down and threatening them was a feeling I decided not to examine.

I stepped off the curb and hailed a cab.

Chapter Sixteen

I arrived a few minutes early for my lunch date with Clarice. Isabelle and Caro were somewhere in the vicinity, but I didn't look around for them. I'd taken a cab and was pretty sure I hadn't been followed, but to be on the safe side, I hopped out and walked right into the restaurant. Clarice walked in a minute later and gave me a big smile.

"I'm so glad we decided to do this, Greer. Honestly, I feel like I'm skipping school! It's so nice to be out of the office," she said.

"I'm sure," I replied, as the maître d' led us to our table. "It must be quite a pressure cooker, working on the IPO. Still lining up funding?"

"Yes, we are. Of course, it's a complicated business—the cannabis dispensary part. The laws are different everywhere. We'll start with the apothecary line and have everything in place to expand."

"It sounds so interesting—I'm reading about it everywhere. Tell me, do you have a lot of investors interested? I would think so. It's the newest game in town," I said.

"Exactly. Everyone wants in, and everyone's in a hurry. But there are a lot of technical details to work out."

"I would imagine. Losing Frank Benson at such a crucial point must have been a blow. Have you found someone for his job?"

"No, we're having trouble finding the right person. William knew someone who could step in quickly after Dan died, but right now he's has been handling his own work and Frank's." A tiny line appeared between her brows. *No Botox yet,* I thought. *Interesting.* She was very appearance conscious.

"That's a lot for one person, isn't it?" I asked.

"It is. We can outsource some, and he's hired another paralegal, but . . ." Her frown deepened. "I do wonder sometimes about William."

"In what way?" I asked.

"Well, about his . . . motivation, I guess you could say."

I tilted my head and pretended to consider what she'd said.

"From what Dan told me, he has moved around a lot, hasn't he? Not that there's anything wrong with making a change to move up or expand your horizons," I said, injecting a hint of doubt into my tone.

"No, of course, there isn't," Clarice said, "but he does seem to keep a tight hold of a lot of things. He seems tense, almost secretive. Jumpy."

"Hmm, I see. Some people get like that when there's a lot of money at stake," I said. "Some people stay cool, others can't. Probably not a good idea for William to play poker," I added with a smile.

Clarice laughed. "You're right. And why are we talking about this anyway? I need to leave work at the office. So tell me about your job. You're working for a magician's group? I loved magic shows as a kid. Have you learned any sleight-of-hand tricks or anything else fun?"

We chatted and ordered, and I fought the urge to look toward the door or check the time. Finally I heard it, the sound I'd been waiting for, the bugle call of my personal cavalry.

"Darling!"

Great-Aunt Caro had arrived.

I gasped.

"It can't be," I said. I looked up and shifted to get a better look at the front of the restaurant. "Oh, dear. It *is*!"

"Is what?" Clarice said, turning in her seat.

"Carolyn Quinn. She's—oh, wait, you know Isabelle Peterson, don't you? Caro is a relative of Isabelle's fiancé. *Quite* a character. I've known the family for ages. I'll have to say hello."

I smiled and waved.

"Maybe they're meeting someone and can't stop? Nope, here they come." I leaned forward and spoke to Clarice in a stage whisper. "Anyway, Caro was a famous model back in the day. Knew everyone, dated most of them. You name it—actors, playwrights, congressmen, spies. Amazing stories, and the older she gets, the more she's willing to share. Brace yourself!"

Caro descended, Isabelle right behind her. I stood and Caro greeted me with a kiss on both cheeks. Very continental—she was really working it, and she'd only just arrived. I made introductions. Clarice greeted Isabelle warmly, saying how nice it was to see her again and how delighted she was to meet Caro. She seemed to mean it.

"So are the two of you meeting someone?" I said. "We shouldn't keep you."

"Oh no, we're out window shopping. I'm tired of being cooped up, going through all my memorabilia. What are you girls up to?"

"Taking an afternoon off. Clarice invited me to lunch. I may do a little shopping this afternoon, and she has tickets to a matinee," I said.

"How lovely. What are you seeing? I love the theater. Greer, did I ever tell you about the time I met Stephen Sondheim? It was right after *A Little Night Music* opened. Lovely man, though a bit reserved, I thought."

And she was off and running. When she finally paused to take a breath, Clarice said, "Why don't you two join us? I'd love to hear more." She gestured at the hovering waiter, who quickly set two more places.

Success! This was the best-case scenario. Better still, Clarice seemed to be genuinely enjoying herself. Caro had a wealth of stories, ninety-nine percent of them true. She entertained us until our entrees were served, then turned to Clarice.

"You're so kind to indulge an old lady's trip down memory lane. Now tell, me how did you become so knowledgeable about the theater? Were you ever on stage yourself?"

"Oh no, nothing beyond my high school drama club," Clarice said. "It was my uncle, actually. Jack Breen. He worked in the theater his whole life. Not a big star—a working professional. He did a little bit of everything and filled in wherever he was needed—chorus, small parts, costumes and makeup—you name it. Mostly Broadway, but he'd go on the road too. Sometimes I'd get to spend school vacations with him if he was in town."

"How delightful!" Caro said, and then talked some more about her favorite shows, skillfully drawing more personal information out of Clarice. I was impressed. Either she had a natural gift, or she'd learned quite a bit about extracting information from that MI6 guy she'd dated. Even Isabelle, normally shy, chimed in with a few stories. If I hadn't been investigating my husband's murder, I'd have been enjoying myself.

Apparently, Clarice was having a really good time too. As coffee was being served, she said as much, adding, "Honestly, this is the first non-work-related gathering I've been to in ages. I'd forgotten how much fun normal conversation can be."

"Well, I imagine in your position you have to spend a lot of time with the financial masters of the universe. That's not nearly as much fun as an afternoon out with the girls," Caro said.

"No, it isn't. What's worse is how nervous the venture capital guys—and they're always guys—get if I don't have a man on the New Leaf payroll with me. Sometimes I have my assistant, Austin, in the room serving coffee just so they'll relax. It's ridiculous," Clarice said.

"Looks like some things never change," Caro said. "I don't know how you sit through all those meetings."

"I'm looking forward to being done with them soon, that's for sure," Clarice said. Then her face lit up. "Listen, I'm having some people over for cocktails on Saturday. All investors and people connected to the business. I know it's short notice, but why don't the three of you come? I'd love it, and it will certainly liven up the crowd. I can show you some of my Uncle Jack's mementos. I inherited the place from him, so I still have a lot of his things."

"We'd love to!" Caro said before I could open my mouth. "What time?"

In for a penny.

"Sounds like fun," I said. "Want to text me the details when you have a minute? I'm going to run to the ladies' room."

Time for part two of the plan—while I was out of earshot, Caro and Isabelle would bring up Danny's death and how great it was to see me out and enjoying myself, yadda yadda. They'd try to shake loose something about Clarice's whereabouts that night. It was a long shot, but it had been a convivial meal, so who knew?

I returned to the table to find that Clarice had treated all of us to lunch. We walked out of the restaurant together. It had started to rain, so Caro and Isabelle decided to hail a cab.

"I'm much too old to start summoning cars with my phone, wherever I've put it," Caro said. "Thanks for lunch, darling, and I'm looking forward to Saturday."

Clarice's car had not yet arrived, so I said I'd wait with her and see if the rain slowed down. If not, I'd hop in a cab too, since we were going in opposite directions. We had a few minutes, so I decided to try one more foray into detection.

"You know, I'm so glad you suggested this, Clarice. I enjoyed lunch, and I'm really looking forward to Saturday night. It's been good for me to get out. I thought seeing people I only knew through Dan would be painful, but instead it's been therapeutic."

"I'm glad too," she said. "We did worry when we invited you to the office. We thought perhaps a restaurant instead, but decided to let you make the decision."

"I was nervous, but it was fine. There was one awkward moment, though. There were a lot of familiar faces, but one guy—mid-twenties, dark curly hair—looked especially so. I felt like I should know him. The name Steve came to mind. Malloy, Murphy? Something like that. I'm sure Dan mentioned the name a few times, but I can't place him. I'm hoping I didn't inadvertently snub someone."

Clarice shook her head. "There was a Steve Malloy with us several years ago, but he's been gone a while. Dan might have known him, but they didn't work together."

"Oh, okay. Maybe the guy I'm thinking of needed to talk to Austin, and I happened to be there. Here's your car. Thanks again! See you this weekend."

I hailed my own cab and went straight home, grateful to be out of the damp and anxious to exchange notes with Isabelle and Caro. We'd prearranged a call for later that day. Right on time, my phone rang.

"So, what do you think?" I said.

"I think that for most of lunch she was telling the truth. Caro thinks she's hiding something about her parents or her childhood—more what she didn't say than what she did."

"Hmm. I got the impression she didn't have a good relationship with her parents, and that's why she spent so much time with her uncle. She's an only child. That dynamic can go either way."

"I agree, but you know when Caro asked her if her parents came to her school plays? She just waved her hand and said they traveled a lot for work. Her uncle came more often. I thought it was sad, but Caro thinks it's something more. 'Wanting for nothing but attention, and desperate for that' is what she said. Clarice reminds her of someone she knew when she started modeling. Same kind of family, and the girl ended up being the type—and I'm quoting here—'for whom too much is never enough.' I know what she means, though it's a lot to infer from one lunch."

"She's channeling Miss Marple, for sure, but I think her instincts are good. I'll do some research on the parents. Any luck with the alibi?"

"Now this is interesting. Caro said how glad she was that you were out seeing old friends again, making it sound like she thought the two of you had been tight before Dan's death, and how it must have been such a shock when you called Clarice with the news that night."

"What did she say?" I asked. I hadn't called—Beau had, and he'd spoken to William Warren. But he'd called early the next morning, and I'd told Caro and Isabelle that before lunch.

"She looked surprised, but just for a minute. Then she said it was actually William who called her. She had a bunch of messages when she left the theater, so she found out quite late. Then I said Frank Benson had told me the next morning. That was true—and he was very upset. His hands were shaking. He apologized for springing it on me at work. He said he would have called me at home, but he just found out himself. Now this is what made me wonder—Clarice said Frank had gotten a call the night before, she thought from the police, and then let everyone know. And then she stopped, and said, 'Or maybe it was William who got the call,' and added that she'd sort of blocked it out because it was so awful."

"That is interesting," I said. "Do you think Frank was telling you the truth when he said he'd just found out that morning?"

"I think he was," Isabelle said. "He was obviously very upset about something."

"I can check with his wife about the call. They were still living together then. Do you or Caro think Clarice was lying?"

"I'm not sure, and neither is Caro. I would say she seemed startled, and then lost in thought. But she could have been scrambling for an answer to a question she hadn't expected. Oh, hang on."

I heard some conversation, and then Isabelle was back. "That's Caro. She's going through her closets, trying to decide what to wear on Saturday." Isabelle lowered her voice. "She wanted me to wear one of her vintage outfits, but thankfully nothing fit."

"Too bad—that could be fun," I said.

"Not my look—I'm sticking with my basic black dress. But I had to promise to let her accessorize me."

"Hard to go wrong with the little black dress," I said. "I'm sure you'll look fabulous."

"Right," said Isabelle, without conviction. "Anyway, Caro thinks we should try to search the place for evidence while we're there. I told her I'd tell you."

"If only we knew what we were looking for," I said. "Tell her I like the idea, but I'm counting on her to provide a distraction if things look dicey."

"I'll let her know," Isabelle said.

We hung up. Caro had a point—this was an opportunity to do some serious snooping. But how? The three of us would be getting personal attention from our hostess—tough to disappear for any length of time, or even to coordinate our efforts once we were there. We needed someone unknown to Clarice, someone who could do a fast, thorough search.

We needed Grim.

I looked out the window. The lights were on in the brownstone. I leaned on the sill and called. When he answered, I said, "I might have a job for you. It's kind of sketchy and not without risk, but at least it's legal. I think."

He laughed. "Sounds like fun. What do you want me to do?"

"Your mission, should you choose to accept it . . ."

Chapter Seventeen

April's cannabis expert was not what I'd expected. But then again, I hadn't been sure what to expect. Willie Nelson braids and a suit? Jeans, a hoodie, and a Grateful Dead T-shirt? An overcompensating, straitlaced Brooks Brothers ensemble? It was none of the above. When I was shown into Noah Leonard's office, I was greeted by a middle-aged, silver-haired gentleman with a broad smile and twinkly blue eyes. He was wearing standard business casual—jeans and a sport coat over a crisp shirt. He was tieless, but a spiffy square of patterned silk peeked out of his jacket pocket. No tie-dye in sight. I confess to being somewhat disappointed, but I was glad I'd stuck with my own basic black business casual.

Once we were seated, Noah said, "So, April tells me you have some questions about the legal cannabis industry. Both your husbands once worked for the same company, and you have some concerns?"

April had told me that Noah was discreet, so we'd decided to share our suspicions in order to get as much relevant info as possible. "He's been around the block a few times," she'd said. "He won't be fazed by a potential murder. He knows what money does to people."

I laid out the basics of the case, handed over one of the filched folders, and said, "I'll be honest—I don't really understand this business. If the New Leaf management is up to something, I'm not sure what or how. I thought initially that it would have to do with the fact that, on the retail side, it's all cash. But they're not to that point yet—no dispensaries. The more I learn, the harder it is to fit the pieces together. I guess what I need is cannabis dispensary 101. I know that's probably a lot to ask."

He grinned. "Not really. I'm teaching a course on cannabis entrepreneurship this summer. I'm working on the outline now. I'll give you an abbreviated version of the first class. You can be my guinea pig. Let me know if I start to lose you."

I pulled out a notebook and pen. "Ready," I said.

Noah was off and running. He started with a definition of terms. "A lot of weed terminology is used interchangeably, but there are key differences," he said, and briefly explained each. "Now, you've heard the term 'green rush.' That's used to describe an expanding global economic opportunity that started at the end of 2012 when the first states legalized cannabis. It covers everything from the product itself to all the ancillary businesses involved in producing that product and getting it to market. You can divide those businesses into two categories—those that touch the plant, and those that don't touch the plant."

He went on, tossing around terms like vertical integration, multistate operators, and social equity. When he rattled off the phrase IRS Code section 280E, I threw up my hands.

"My head is spinning, and this is just the tip of the iceberg, right? I mean, it's fascinating, and I can see the potential for profit and for abuse. But where do I start? I'd love to take your class, but I'm running out of time."

"You're right—there's a lot more involved in this than people think," Noah said. "Let me take a closer look at what you brought."

He picked up a pair of reading glasses from his desk, and once they were perched on his nose, he began flipping through the New Leaf folder. I'd included a copy of the spreadsheet Dan had sent, on the theory that something on it might be meaningful to a person in the industry. He made occasional notes as he read. While he worked, I put down my pen and pad, stretched my fingers, and rolled my shoulders.

"Spending too much time at a desk?" Noah said, looking at me over his glasses. "Grab one of those green bottles off the shelf behind you. Arthritis, tendonitis, general muscle inflammation—it's good for all of that. One of our clients. I take one every night. They're only ten calories," he added, and went back to his reading.

I stood and went to the shelf. There was an assortment of products designed to help with a range of issues—focus, anxiety, insomnia, and pain. I looked them over and took one of the green bottles as instructed. It held flavored CBD gumdrops with some vitamins thrown in. At least they weren't shaped like bears. Alcohol had always been my drug of choice, with caffeine and sugar running a close second, depending on the day. None of those would help with inflammation, so it couldn't hurt to take a closer look at this. I slipped the bottle into my tote bag and sat. Noah finished with the glossy New Leaf folder and picked up the spreadsheet.

"What's this?" he said.

"I'm told it's a list of suppliers, out of date and incomplete," I said. I explained how it had arrived and the various theories around it.

"I recognize some of these names," Noah said. "But not all. It's possible that some are already out of business—you'll want to read about that tax code issue. It's not hard to follow; it has to do with deductible business expenses. It's a problem for a lot of small operators. I'll email you my class syllabus. You'll find some helpful sources."

"Thanks. There's nothing a reference librarian likes more than verifiable sources of information," I said. "It's not like I had plans for the rest of the day anyway."

"Now, back to this." Noah gestured at the folder. "From everything I'm seeing here, right now they're on the side of not touching the plant. New Leaf has expanded into CBD products that you can get pretty much anywhere. It fits in with the natural products history of the company."

"They've got a built-in customer base," I said. "Hemp products were always a significant part of the business."

"That makes sense. So they're currently operating in an area with less regulation, but once they move toward dispensaries, they're touching the plant and that's a whole different ballgame. That's where you get into the banking regulations and the social equity requirements, among other things."

Noah went on to explain that the social equity piece was baked into the legislation and designed to counteract the harm to certain populations and communities caused by the "war on drugs."

"So licensing preference goes to disabled veterans, minorities, women, and people with prior convictions?" I asked, writing as fast as I could. I felt a headache starting at the base of my skull. "That would seem to be hard to get around."

"You would think," Noah said. "But it's happening. You have people providing funding and then insisting on the license holders using certain vendors with whom they have a financial relationship. I've even heard of Russian oligarchs bankrolling all the licensees in an area and effectively cornering the market."

I looked up. "Seriously? Russian oligarchs?" My concern about the mob branching out from olive oil and fine art now seemed positively quaint. I massaged my temples. My headache had taken off with a vengeance.

"So I've heard," Noah said. "But given that your husband sent a list of suppliers, it's more likely that there's money changing hands behind the scenes somewhere."

We talked for a few more minutes. Noah emailed the syllabus to me. I thanked him for his time, and he invited me to get in touch if I had any more questions.

"No one likes to talk about it because the people who cover the industry don't want to see it get a lot of negative press, but there's real fraud going on. I've given you some simplistic examples, but there's a lot of potential for crime. Any company can hire a squeaky-clean compliance officer or someone with a similar title, to make it look like they're on the up and up. Meanwhile, there's something sketchy going on under the radar. That's true in any business. I think legal cannabis has a lot of potential for good, so if I can help take out a bad actor, I will."

With that, he walked me to the elevator and said goodbye. I took something for my headache and headed home, stopping at my neighborhood deli to pick up lunch. I had a few hours before meeting Carl Guenther, so I'd take a look at Noah's syllabus and see if any lightbulbs went off. Headache fading and food in hand, I waded into the required reading for Green Rush Entrepreneurship—An Introduction. Some of it looked pretty dry so I put on some coffee in case I got bored.

I was anything but. There was a lot to cover, but Noah had organized the information well. Some of the government documents were a little dense, but I skimmed them to get the gist. The social equity requirements were detailed. I still thought they'd be tough to get around, but could see how it could be done. The tax code issue was interesting; cannabis producers couldn't deduct typical business expenses when calculating income—only the cost of goods sold. This contributed to a lot of smaller operators not being able to make a go of it. That could be why New Leaf had a continually changing list of vendors—supply chain disruptions. So it was feasible, but worth looking into further. I agreed with Noah's assessment that back channel deals with vendors would be the easiest place for money to be changing hands.

I ran through the rest of the syllabus, reading articles here and there. The ancillary business opportunities were numerous. You didn't need to "touch the plant" to reap the rewards of what was projected to be a multibillion-dollar industry within a few years. I was embarrassed that I hadn't figured a lot of this out—I followed the business news and, in spite of changing careers, still had a talent for marketing. In my defense, I'd been reinventing my life and solving a few murders. But I hadn't taken this seriously enough. I'd been more focused on the mechanics of the murder, not what other crimes might be going on around it. The mechanics were important. As Jennie Webber had told me many times, you couldn't go to court without having them buttoned down. But in this instance, I needed a motive. If I had the why, I was sure I could get to the who.

I shut my laptop. The why was all about money. A great deal of money. New Leaf was profitable already, and if their expansion plans took off, they'd be on the ground floor of a new and lucrative business. That's where the venture capital came in—lots of money thrown at businesses that weren't making any money, and wouldn't for years, but had the potential for a big payout down the road.

I tried to wrap my mind around adult-use lounges adjacent to "wellness spaces." I kept coming up with a mental image of my sister Frances in one of her Lululemon ensembles, finishing up her exercise session and stopping off for a CBD-spiked kale smoothie before heading off to pick up some groceries before the kids got home from school.

I sighed. As crazy as I'd at first thought it, it could work. I could even see myself doing it in the right circumstances. Except for one part.

Nothing would ever induce me to drink a kale smoothie.

Chapter Eighteen

I got to the Hungarian at the appointed time and looked in—no Carl Guenther. I did spot Grim. He was at a table along the wall, facing the entrance, seemingly absorbed in a paper copy of the *Times*. He was wearing his signature black but had traded turtleneck and jeans for a button-down shirt and chinos. There was a sport coat draped over the back of his chair, and dark horn-rimmed, square-framed glasses perched on his nose. He was rocking the geek-chic look, and while I wasn't buying him as your average adjunct professor, no one seemed to be paying any attention to him. As disguises went, it wasn't bad.

Unlike my partner in crime, I was in my usual jeans, sweater, and down vest. I'd brought my gym bag—it had emerged from the alley in better shape than I expected—and loaded it with an old book, a bottle of water, a Chapstick, and some printouts of library materials budget spreadsheets, mixed with cover pages of books I needed to catalog. In other words, nothing important. I didn't think Carl would be showing up with a stack of paper, but if whatever he brought was too much for my inside vest pocket, I wanted a place to stash it where it wouldn't be obvious. He'd acted like a man who thought he was being followed. That might be paranoia, or it might not. Once I had the information in hand, I wanted to get it safely home to study.

I loitered outside, scrolling through my phone and occasionally looking around, like any other person waiting for a friend who was running late. Five minutes passed, then ten. I was getting impatient. If Guenther stood me up, he'd be sorry. I knew where he lived. It hadn't taken long to track down his address and confirm that his girlfriend, Gwen Jeffries, lived with him. Neither had much of a public social media presence, but it was enough for me to find pictures of both and cross-reference a few details.

I was ready to give up the wait and hunt Guenther down, when my phone buzzed. It was a text with a number, but no name: *its carl. someone following hiding in peoples garden please come.*

I hesitated. It was a classic setup—change of location and from the wrong phone. If I saw this on TV, I'd be yelling, "Don't go, you moron!" at the screen. On the other hand, I didn't have a lot of options, and I did have backup. I didn't want to wait.

"Looks like this moron's taking the bait," I said to myself as I sent a message to Grim.

Change of plan. People's Garden. Sketchy but no options. Follow out of sight.

I got back a thumbs-up. I looked in and saw Grim fold his paper and stand up. I responded to Carl Guenther: *Stay hidden. Watch for me.* As Grim came out the door, I started up the street.

The People's Garden was a pocket of greenery on the corner half a block away. It was a community garden, complete with gates, winding walks, and benches. At this time of year, there wouldn't be much blooming, but there were still trees and shrubs to provide cover. Not a bad place to hide—you could enter or exit on either the street or the avenue. I chose a gate on the avenue. It was open and well lit, and there was foot traffic behind me.

I stood at the entrance, getting my bearings and in full view of anyone who might be hiding—and watching—in this part of the park. I didn't hear anything unusual—no voices or sounds of footsteps. The only light came from streetlamps; no telltale gleam from a cell phone in the hand of someone tucked behind a bush. Not yet anyway.

I took a few steps farther in, then sent a text: *I'm here. Where are you?*

I turned in a half circle, alert to any light or sound. Nothing. Then a response.

someone's watching i'm near center

Unlikely, as the center was where the paths converged. Not a lot of cover. But there was a clump of shrubbery not far from it, so maybe. Still, if there were three of us here, the other two were doing a good job of remaining motionless. Or Carl was here alone and paranoid. Either way, leaving wasn't an option.

I tucked my phone away and got a good grip on my bag. I walked toward the middle of the park, stopping every few feet to scan the shadows. I'd reached a circle of dormant plants in the center of the park and was staring into the bushes off to one side when a breeze set all of them into motion. The rustling noise of dry branches filled the park, the wind moaned among the tree-tops, and right behind me a twig snapped.

I took a quick step sideways and turned, swinging my gym bag. I heard a grunt as I connected. The figure behind me staggered and then came at me. I saw nothing but three white circles where the face should be—a ski mask. A gloved hand grabbed for my gym bag and pulled. I hung on tight and lunged forward, reaching for the mask with my other hand. My attacker didn't expect that—the pressure on my bag faltered. He shoved at me with his other hand. I could see a hairy wrist between his dark glove and sleeve. I hung onto my bag and launched myself at him again, desperate to get a look at his face, but he got a grip on my wrist and wouldn't let go. I'd started to kick when I heard a yell and the sound of running feet.

"Hey, lady! You all right? Leave her alone! I called 911!"

I twisted my arm and broke the grip on my wrist. I tried for the mask one more time, but the guy threw all his weight behind a pull at my bag, yanking it free and sending me spinning. I fell face-first on the ground. I rolled sideways in time to see my attacker running for the gate. A slim shadow appeared on the path. Grim, deciding whether to come to my aid or follow.

"I'm fine," I yelled. He took off in pursuit.

"I don't think so, ma'am. You're bleeding," my good Samaritan said. I looked up. A young man with a ponytail was kneeling next to me. An equally young woman with a pixie haircut and a nose ring was peering over his shoulder, holding up her cell phone.

"I didn't actually call 911," she said. "But I will if you're hurt."

"I'm okay," I said, sitting up. I examined my hands and touched my face. He was right, I was bleeding. "I think it's only some scrapes. Got a tissue?"

They did not, but produced some crumpled napkins. I dabbed at the scrapes, which still stung but stopped bleeding. They helped me up and over to a bench, peppering me with questions about whether or not I'd hit my head. We concluded I was not concussed, and they offered to find me a cab or walk me home. I told them I would text a friend to meet me here, and then did so, hoping Grim was having some success. That done, I asked my rescuers if they'd gotten a look at the person who mugged me.

"Definitely a man," said the girl. "But I didn't get a look at his face. I think he had some kind of mask on, don't you think?" She turned to her companion. He agreed and added, "I hope he doesn't go after anyone else."

"Doubt it," I said. "I think the two of you scared him. I appreciate your help. I'm Greer, by the way."

They introduced themselves as Laura and Sebastian. Both were students. "I'm also an influencer," said Laura. "You can follow me on Instagram." She pulled a business card out of her pocket and handed it to me.

"Wow," I said, comparing my twenty-year-old self to her and coming up short.

"Yeah, it's kind of retro, right? Business cards, with everything online. But a lot of people like them."

"Cool," I said, feeling kind of retro myself. A few minutes later, Grim arrived. I raised an eyebrow. He shook his head. No luck.

We thanked the kids again and told them we'd catch a cab. Once in the taxi, Grim gave the address to the driver while I tried calling Carl and then sent a text. No response to either.

Back at my apartment, I washed my scrapes thoroughly and told Grim to open the wine he'd brought to the brunch and have a glass. It was the least I could do. Once I was cleaned up and changed, I poured one for myself and joined him in the living room. He was standing by the window, looking out.

"Anything going on out there?" I asked. "Any guys in ski masks? Shadowy figures prowling around the brownstone? Nervous-looking techies lurking in doorways?"

"None of the above," he said, turning toward me. He winced. "You're going to have a bruise on your cheekbone."

"I know. I can cover it with makeup. It should be better by the dinner party."

He looked skeptical. "If not, you've got a good story. I'm sure some of the other guests will want to compare muggings."

"Yep, and we can see if anyone acts guilty. Though I doubt it."

Grim came and joined me on the sofa. "You think it was one of them? Warren?"

"It was a man, but all I saw was an inch of hairy wrist. No watch, no tattoos, not even a whiff of cologne. Right height for William Warren, but he's pretty average. Could be him, could be hired help. Like Perry."

"What do you think happened to Guenther?" Grim asked. "Have you heard from him?"

"No, other than the texts he—or someone with his phone—sent from the park. No response to the voicemail or the text I sent on the way home. He might have ditched the phone if he was in the park, but I think someone else had it."

"So what do you figure? Are they on to him, or is he in on it?"

"I'm not sure. He seemed genuinely frightened when I saw him. He kept looking around, like he expected someone to be watching him. It could go either way—they coerced him, or he's part of the plan and nervous, or he really is scared and ready to bolt. There's one other possibility. It's a longshot, though."

I told Grim about how envious Carl sounded at the thought that Steve had gotten paid off to get out of town, and how he'd hung onto those files as a "kind of insurance." Grim nodded.

"So you think he was after money, and when you didn't offer him anything, he went looking for another buyer?" he said. "It's possible. Kind of dumb, given everything that's happened, but possible."

"Agreed, but I get the feeling he's only smart about one thing—cybersecurity. A little naive otherwise. And for all I know, he's got a ton of student loans. Here's the thing, though—whoever mugged me didn't get whatever it was Guenther had, or they wouldn't have taken my bag."

"Unless they wanted to take you out entirely and make it look like a mugging gone wrong." Grim said.

True, but unnerving.

"What now?" he asked.

"I'm going to go to his apartment. You know, just to make sure he's okay. And if he is, to make him cough up the information or tell me what he's up to."

"Count me in," said Grim.

"You don't have to. You're already going above and beyond, especially with what we've got planned for Clarice's dinner party."

"I want to. I miss the adrenaline rush of performing. This is the next best thing."

"All right. Tomorrow. I'd rather not wait, but all I've got is an address—nothing else—and I don't want to go in blind. I'll keep trying to reach him tonight, though. He's supposed to be at work tomorrow, so later. I need to get some work done myself. Ava's going to start wondering what's going on."

"Okay, we'll work out the details in the morning. I'll get in early. See you then."

Once I'd triple-locked the door behind Grim, I got myself organized for the next day. While I was putting my wallet back in my tote bag, I found the card Detective Stewart had given me. He'd told me to call if I thought I was being followed again. Well, I had been. He didn't need to know I'd flattened my follower in an alley, but the fact that I was later mugged when meeting someone from New Leaf should get his attention.

I called and left a carefully spun version of events on his voicemail, strongly suggesting he talk to Carl Guenther. Then I had another glass of wine while sitting in front of the television with some ice on my cheek. I tried calling Carl a few more times—no answer. Wineglass empty, I gave up and went to bed. With any luck, I'd see the man himself the next day. I still wasn't sure how I was going to get him to cooperate, but I'd figure something out.

"'*Sufficient unto the day is the evil thereof,*'" I said, and turned out the light.

Had I but known . . .

When I arrived at the brownstone the next morning, Grim opened the door before I had my key in the lock. For some reason, he was wearing both the glasses and sport coat he'd had on the night before.

"Morning!" he said in a cheery voice. "You've got some visitors. Cops," he added in a whisper.

Stewart and Kopp walked into the hall from the dining room. I sneaked a peek at my desk—no lock-picking equipment in sight. I turned my attention back to Detective Stewart.

"Did you get my message?" I asked. "Have you spoken to Carl Guenther?"

"I did get your message," he said. "And based on what you said, I would like to talk to him. Unfortunately, I can't do that. We pulled his body out of the Harlem Meer this morning."

Chapter Nineteen

It took me a few seconds to process, then I asked the first questions that popped into my head.

"How did he die? Someone killed him, right?"

The two men looked at me. Kopp's expression implied that my question was not what he'd expected. He reached for his notebook. Neither answered.

"Well, you wouldn't be here if it was an accident, would you?" I snapped, impatient for some kind of concrete information. Carl Guenther had been my best chance to find out what was going on at New Leaf, and now he was dead. I should have insisted on going with him the other night.

"You're right, Ms. Hogan. Someone killed him. Someone shot him in the head and dumped his body," Stewart said.

"Hmm," I said. That's not what I'd expected. Both Dan and Jackson had gotten blows to the head, an enraged reaction to their unexpected presence. This was different, but I was convinced it was related. The officers exchanged a glance.

"Is there somewhere we can sit and talk?" Stewart asked.

"Oh. Yes, of course," I said.

"Coffee's perking downstairs," Grim said. "I'd just put it on when these gentlemen arrived. Should I keep working on the inventory in the dining room while you talk?"

Where he could more easily hear what was said in the kitchen. Good thinking.

"Yes, that would be fine. Thanks."

I led Stewart and Kopp downstairs. They took the same seats they had the other day. The offer of coffee was once again accepted. I collected my thoughts as I put cream and sugar on the table and poured. Blurting things out in front of law enforcement was a bad habit. It had gotten me in trouble before.

I sat and waited. They weren't here to answer my questions, and at this point I probably knew more about Carl Guenther than they did. I'd see what they asked me. Maybe now that they had another body on their hands, they'd take the connection to Danny more seriously.

"Tell me how you knew Carl Guenther," Stewart said.

"I didn't, really. We met for the first time two nights ago. But I'd seen him before."

I told them about my meeting with Clarice and William at New Leaf, and that Guenther and I had seen each other twice during my visit.

"I thought he recognized me, but I couldn't place him. We'd never met, but he knew who I was. He'd worked there for a few months before Dan was killed. He followed me from the office to the gym that day. My instructor saw him. I've told you about that."

Stewart nodded.

"Yuri, my instructor, saw him loitering near the gym the other night." I then gave them an edited version of what happened, saying I'd confronted Guenther in a public place and he'd said he was following me because he wanted to tell me something about my husband.

"So we went to the coffee shop right down the block. He was nervous—afraid really. He kept looking at the window, and he jumped every time someone came in the door. He told me something had happened at work, a couple of weeks before Dan died, and he was worried."

I told them everything Guenther had told me, winding up with the plan to meet the previous night and the last-minute change in location. Kopp's eyebrows went up.

"It made me a little nervous," I admitted. "But my colleague had agreed to stay nearby, and I didn't feel I had any other options."

"Looks like your colleague wasn't close enough," Stewart said, gesturing toward my bruised face.

"Guenther was paranoid. I didn't want to scare him off. And everything happened very quickly. Mr. Grimaldi was close by when I fell, and when I said I was fine, he tried to find the guy who attacked me."

"And the kids who stopped to help you? Did you get their names?"

"I did, and I can give you contact information for one," I said.

Stewart asked some more questions, double-checking things we'd already covered. Finally, he said, "So all of this over a print-out of a computer file. What was on it, and why the paper?"

"The second part is easy—security. Guenther said these files were only on one computer, or at least not on a shared drive or in the cloud. If you email it or save it to a drive, there's a record. There is if you print it too, but Frank Benson was always print-ing files, and everyone knew it." I threw up my hands. "I'm sure you have someone in the department who can explain it better than I can."

"Then back to the first question—what was in those files?" Stewart said.

"Something worth killing over," I said. "And honestly, I don't think it's so much what's on those printouts, as what it means. That's what we have to figure out."

"Why don't you leave that to us, Ms. Hogan," Stewart said.

Because I'm not convinced you believe me, or that you can figure it out, I thought. I decided it was time for some questions of my own.

"If you're asking me about the paper trail, you didn't find anything like that on his body, right?"

"We did not," Stewart said.

"Which means whoever killed him took it, or he didn't have it on him. What time did he die?" I asked.

"We don't have an exact time yet."

"Did he show up for work? Or did someone kill him right after he met with me? Because I'm starting to feel a little bad that I didn't go with him and make him hand it over right then."

Stewart pursed his lips and looked at me. He nodded and said, "Guenther made it home, and to work the next day. He left at his usual time, and that's the last anyone saw of him."

"So he didn't have it. He told me he hid it in a safe place at home. He wouldn't have taken it to work. He was too paranoid. But whoever killed him couldn't count on that. Have you searched his apartment? Does his girlfriend know?"

"We've just come from there. I'm sure if there's anything to find there, we'll uncover it."

I doubted that. Given the little I knew of Carl Guenther, he would have hidden it well. And Stewart hadn't fully answered my question. I moved on.

"Did you find his phones?" I asked.

"Phones?" Stewart asked. Kopp looked up.

"He had two. His work phone, and he said he didn't want my number on it, so he'd use an old disposable to get in touch with me. But that's not the number that sent the texts. Was it his work phone, or did someone make him send them?"

"We'll look into that. Thank you for that information and for your help. We'll let you know if we find anything related to your husband's death. Mr. Grimaldi is upstairs? We'll talk to him on our way out."

So that was all I was going to get. I picked up coffee cups until they were out of sight, then scooted over to the bottom of the stairs. I heard Grim telling them the same thing I had, then the voices moved down the hall. When I heard the front door close, up I went.

"Whatever Carl Guenther had, it's still in his apartment," I said. "You heard Stewart, right? Nothing on him, and he went to work yesterday but never made it home. He works on the East Side and lives on the West Side. He went through the park to get home, and ended up dead in the Meer. I've got to get into his apartment."

"I agree with your reasoning, but the building is probably crawling with cops," Grim said. "I didn't get the impression Detective Stewart was looking for your help."

"He's not, but they won't be there all day, and I don't think they're going to do a thorough search. If the girlfriend, Gwen, is there, she might let us in."

"Or not. And if not, what are you willing to do?"

"At this point, pretty much anything. I checked the address—okay neighborhood, and it's not a doorman building, so there's not going to be a lot of security."

"Have your lock-picking skills advanced that far?" Grim asked.

"I'm not sure," I said. His were up to it, but I couldn't ask him. I could only hope he'd volunteer. I held his gaze, trying to look innocent. He stared right back, then quirked an eyebrow. He smiled.

"I'll come with you," he said. "And I'll carry the lockpicks—I can say they're for my work, if it comes down to that. But we're going in with a plan. What's the address?"

I gave it to him, along with any other information I'd come up with about the building and the neighborhood.

"Okay, give me a few minutes. Meanwhile," he said, looking me over, "you go home and change. Dark clothes, gloves, and travel light."

I looked down at my Kelly-green scarf. It was nearly St. Patrick's Day. "I can do head-to-toe black. Let me email Ava and tell her something came up and we're both out for the rest of day."

"Good. I'll meet you in your lobby."

I went to my desk and sent the email, all the while running through various scenarios for getting my hands on the evidence. None of them seemed like a sure thing. At this point, being surrounded by adrenaline junkies willing to come to my aid wasn't enough. I needed a flash of insight, dumb luck, or both. I didn't want to rush Grim, but I was getting antsier by the minute. What if the New Leaf crowd got there first?

I was home, changed, and downstairs in a flash. I'd added big sunglasses and stuck a soft knit hat in my pocket. I'd even pulled out my Italian leather gloves, which were so thin and supple they could've been a second skin, in case I did have to employ any lock-picking skills. Grim nodded his approval, and we were on our way. We talked tactics on the subway as we sped uptown.

"You're right about the building. Small enough that there's no doorman, big enough that we can get someone to buzz us in. It's not far from the subway, and there's a diner on the corner. This is what we're going to do."

I was buzzing with excitement when we got to our stop. I put on my hat and sunglasses and strolled down the street while Grim went to the diner. There was one nondescript car double-parked in front of the building. It pulled away as I approached. I circled the block, and by the time I got back to the front, I was sure the police were gone. I saw Grim heading for the door, a plastic bag in hand. He bounded up the steps. I followed more slowly. By the time I got to the door, he was opening it.

"Nice work," I said.

"Someone's always waiting for food. Besides, I told the waitress at the diner we were friends of Carl Guenther and wanted to bring food to Gwen, if she was home. So I've got her favorite sandwich, and according to my new friend, she's there, the cops are gone, and everyone's shocked about what happened."

I was sure it helped that Grim was both handsome and charming, and that when something like this happened, everyone wanted to talk about it, but still. It was impressive work.

"What's the apartment number?" he said, as we got off the elevator on the third floor.

"Three C." It was the door directly across from the fire stairs. I looked around the hall—no cameras, so I took off the hat and sunglasses. The place was older, but clean. We'd decided on the direct approach. Gwen might be a sobbing mess. Or angry or numb. Regardless, I was hoping the food would soften her up. If that didn't work, it was on to plan B. Whatever that was.

Grim knocked. The door was flung open. A red-haired, red-faced woman in her mid-twenties, wearing leggings and a tank top, stood in front of us with her hands on her hips.

"What do you want now? Your sergeant said you were finished. I guess you can come in, but honestly! This is harassment!"

For a split-second I considered it, then reminded myself that impersonating a police officer was a felony, and stuck with the plan.

"We're not with the police. Carl used to work with my late husband. I only wanted to ask you—"

"You work for New Leaf?" She reached for the door, ready to slam it.

"No, I'm trying to avoid them actually. Can we talk inside?" I said.

She pushed her glasses up, looked around the hallway, then gestured us in and closed and locked the door behind us. She marched down the hall to a combo living and dining room, then turned to face us once again.

"What do you want to know?" she said. "I don't have a lot of time."

"Time for a Reuben and fries, extra Russian dressing? We thought maybe you could do with something to eat," Grim said, holding up the bag.

Gwen hesitated, then bit her lip. She nodded, and gestured to the table.

"Okay. We can talk while I eat. Thank you," she said, as she sat and opened the bag. "I haven't eaten since last night. The police woke me up this morning—well, you know." She dipped some fries into the container of Russian dressing, then added, "I eat when I'm nervous."

"So do I," I said. "I'm sorry about Carl. I only met him once, but he seemed like a nice guy. I know my husband liked him."

She looked up, then concentrated on her sandwich. I took the opportunity to look around. The place was a mess. A laundry basket was upended on the couch, its contents spilling onto the floor. Drawers were open and books were stacked on their sides on the floor near empty shelves, mostly sci-fi and thrillers. There was television on a stand, with a bunch of unplugged cords on the shelf beneath it. No computer. I could see into the bedroom, where clothes were strewn from the closet to the unmade bed. There was an open suitcase on the floor, with a few things hanging out of it.

"What was your husband's name?" Gwen asked. She reached for a nearly empty bottle of kombucha, then started to get up.

"I'll get it. Fridge?" Grim said, moving into the kitchen. Gwen nodded.

"Dan Sullivan," I said. "He and Carl worked together for a few months four years ago."

Grim set a bottle down on the table and then wandered over to the window.

"I know. Someone killed him too, right?" Gwen opened the bottle of kombucha and drank, not meeting my eyes.

"Yes. I think it's related to New Leaf, but I can't prove it. Carl told me he had something that might help, but he'd hidden it. He was supposed to meet me last night, but he didn't come. Do you know anything about any of that?"

Gwen shook her head. Tears started to roll down her cheeks. She sniffed, and said, "I don't know about any of it. I know there was something. He's been really jumpy lately. The same thing happened last fall when the other guy died. Frank. But everybody said he had a heart attack, so Carl calmed down. This past week, though . . ." Gwen shook her head and dove back into her fries.

I gave her a minute, but I wanted to keep her talking. Grim was drifting around the apartment, giving it a once-over, occasionally stopping to shift something. He didn't make a sound. Still, Gwen could call time's up at any moment.

I leaned toward her. "What happened this week? Did he say anything about anyone there? Mention any files, or papers from work? Anything?"

"He said something about an insurance policy. Doesn't look like it helped, does it?"

The tears came faster and she started to hiccup. I found a clean napkin and handed it to her. She blew her nose and continued to sob.

"Do you have any tissues?" I asked. "In the bathroom, maybe?"

"Uh-huh," she said.

Grim moved into the bedroom, and returned a minute later, tissue box in hand. He then faded back toward the bedroom. I touched Gwen's hand, and she looked up at me.

"What about yesterday? Last night? Anything unusual?" I asked.

"I wasn't home last night. I do shift work—I'm a nurse," she explained. "I had the night before off. Carl came in late—he said something came up at work. He was a mess. He told me he tripped and fell, hurrying for the bus or something. But he was really amped up. He sat up playing video games for a long time. I went to bed."

That all fit.

Gwen continued: "Yesterday morning he woke me up before he went to work. He said he had to take care of something that night, but if anything strange happened, or if he didn't come home, I should leave right away and not tell anyone where I was going. He told me to use the money he'd hidden in his suitcase, and there was a phone there too and I should use it. I was pretty groggy, and I thought he'd really lost it. He reads a lot of spy novels, and he's weird about security, phones, and computers, because . . ."

She stopped.

"Because he's a hacker, and he's good at it?" I said. "It's okay. He told me. So, he kept a lot of cash, and a pay-as-you-go phone, just in case?"

"Not cash, those generic gift cards." She looked dubious. "There was some money, a hundred dollars or so, but I don't think anyone uses cash much anymore."

Now cash was retro, too. I sighed.

"Did you find the phone too?" I asked. "Anything else there?"

"The phone was there. Nothing else. I told the police to go ahead and look around. Whatever he was hiding, I don't want anything to do with it."

"And they didn't find anything?"

"I don't think so. They took his computer, but he mostly used that for gaming. They asked about phones, flash drives, any kind of paperwork, but I told them there wasn't any. I do everything on my phone, and if I need to print something, I do it at work. I didn't tell them about the phone he left, though. I guess I should use it."

"It can't hurt, Gwen," Grim sat down at the table. "Do you have someplace to go?"

"Yeah. The police asked me the same thing. I told them I was going to go stay with a friend for a while. But I'm never coming back," she said, "I'll have someone pack up. The super can let them in. I'm going to a friend, but out of state."

"Sounds like a good plan. You're a nurse—I'll bet you can work anywhere."

"I can," she said. "Look, I have a plane to catch. I'm sorry I couldn't help more, but I have to leave in an hour."

"I understand." I tore off a piece of the bag and wrote my number on it. "Please call if you think of anything. The sooner this is solved, the safer you'll be."

"Okay," she said. "Thanks for the sandwich. And if you don't mind—maybe you could take the stairs? One of the neighbors might come out. I don't want anyone to know we talked."

"Sure," I said.

Gwen watched us go into the stairwell. Once the door closed behind us, we heard hers shut and the sound of the dead bolt being thrown. We went down a flight and found a small laundry room off the landing—one washer, one dryer, neither running. We stepped in.

"Did you find anything?" I asked.

"No. I couldn't do a thorough search, but it doesn't look like the police did either. I can tell you one thing, though. She's going someplace far from here. She's got shorts, T-shirts, bathing suit—warm weather clothing piled in her suitcase."

"I can't blame her. I'd be going as far as I could, as fast as I could if I were in her shoes. I don't think anything we saw was acting. She's terrified."

"I agree. She's smart to move fast." Grim leaned back against a washer, his hands in his pockets. "What now, Greer?"

"We have to search the place," I said. "I don't see any other option. And we have to do it soon. We're going to have to break in."

I should have felt bad, or at least hesitant. Instead, I was excited. I even planned to try the lock first myself. I'm not sure what had come over me in the last few months, but if I was going over to the dark side, I was going all in.

"That might not be necessary," Grim said. He pulled his hands out of his pockets and dangled a set of keys in front of me. "I found these on a hook in the kitchen. The keys are the same brand as the lock set. I think they're spares."

"That would be great. But what if they're Gwen's? She's got to lock up when she leaves."

"I saw a set of keys with an ID attached to it on the dresser in the bedroom. Pretty sure those are hers with her work badge attached." Grim shrugged. "If not, she'll be in too much of a hurry to look. In her shoes, I'd just leave and call the super to lock up."

"Me too," I said.

"And if they don't work, we'll pick the lock. It's not a tough one. For now—"

"We wait and watch," I said.

Chapter Twenty

We decided to split up, with Grim keeping watch on Gwen's apartment from the stairwell, and me out of sight. He could make himself scarce more quickly and quietly than I could. Gwen would most likely use the elevator, but in case she didn't, I'd wait one floor up, since she'd be heading down the stairs if she came that way.

Grim kept the fire door cracked to keep an eye on things. I went down to the main floor to check the building exits. From the fire stairs there was an exit to the lobby and one to a narrow alley that ran the length of the block. Gwen would have to get her ride to the airport in front. I went back up to see if there was a laundry room on the fourth floor. If not, I'd stay in the stairwell and pretend to be coming or going if someone came in. We lucked out, though; there was another small laundry room on the fourth floor.

Probably every even floor, I thought. I sent Grim a text letting him know where I'd be, and then perched on the dryer, hoping no one planned to spend their Friday afternoon doing wash. I checked the time—based on what she'd said, Gwen should be leaving in about forty minutes. I killed some time checking my email and trying to convince myself that I was not thirsty and did not have to pee. I had come prepared for breaking and entering, not a stakeout.

Minutes ticked by. I hopped off the washer and did some stretching, making sure I was ready for action. I even wiggled my fingers and rotated my wrists, making sure my hands were limber, just in case. There was one bad moment when I heard someone coming down the stairs, but they went by so quickly, they didn't even look in my direction.

Finally, my phone vibrated. Grim.

She's waiting for the elevator.

I went down to the third floor. Grim was still peering through the barely open fire door. He held up a hand. I waited, and a few seconds later heard the elevator ding, then the whoosh of doors opening and closing. Grim opened the door and looked down the hall, then nodded to me and walked over to Gwen and Carl's apartment. By the time I'd eased the fire door closed, he had the apartment unlocked. We slipped in.

"Nice work grabbing those keys," I said. I went to the window, which looked out on the front of the building, standing to one side so I couldn't be seen. Gwen was in the street, stowing her luggage in the back of a Toyota. Either a friend or an Uber. Once she was in and the car had pulled away, I turned and surveyed the living room. Grim was in the kitchen, searching silently and methodically.

"She's gone," I said, keeping my voice low. I hadn't thought she'd come back for anything—she was in too much of a hurry—but I'd wanted to be sure.

Grim came out of the kitchen and grabbed one of the dining room chairs.

"Nothing here. I'll check on top of the cabinets—they don't go all the way to the ceiling."

The apartment was a mess. Where to begin? The clothes from the laundry basket were clearly Gwen's. The remains of her lunch were still on the table. The coffee table held a notepad, with some ripped sheets scattered around it, along with a pile of torn cardboard sleeves, the type that gift cards came in. There was a trashcan next to it with more of the same. I picked up the torn sheets—Gwen had been figuring out her flight options. She hadn't wasted any time. The disarray from one end of the place to the other spoke more of desperation than untidiness.

"I'm sure he would've hidden it in something that only he used," I said.

"Or someplace she couldn't easily reach," Grim said. "Nothing on top of these but dust, though. You want to take the closets? I'll go through the dressers."

I nodded and went to the entrance. There was a coat closet near the door. I went through every coat and pair of boots, saving the more feminine ones for last and giving them a cursory glance. I searched the floor and the top shelf, using my phone flashlight. Nothing but some baseball equipment. I felt inside the glove and searched a canvas bag of balls. Zip. On to the bedroom.

Grim was pulling out drawers, looking under and behind them, as well as going through their contents. The bedroom closet was a decent size, though not a walk-in. Keeping in mind what Gwen had said about finding the money and phone Carl had left in an old suitcase, I started with any luggage, backpack, or carryall I could find. When I came up empty, I repeated my methods from the coat closet. Still nothing. Finished, I headed to the bathroom. Grim was searching under the bed and mattress.

The bathroom was small, but the vanity had a couple of drawers and a cabinet. I made quick work of it. No fake shampoo bottles, nothing in the various boxes and containers of personal items or cleaning supplies, and the dullest medicine cabinet I'd ever seen.

I walked out to the living room, where Grim was surveying the mess.

"We can divvy it—" I began. An angry buzzing filled the room. Someone was ringing from downstairs. I froze. It stopped, and then the noise began again in a series of short bursts. Then silence. I looked at Grim. "We may not have much time," I said. "It could be the police again. Of course, we've got the keys. I'll say she told us to go ahead and look around, and to lock up after."

"Sounds good," he said. "Maybe she'll be in the air before anyone checks. Or maybe it's not the cops. If you take the bookcase, I'll work on the rest."

Finding things tucked in books or hidden among them is a librarian's specialty, although normally those things were lost, not concealed on purpose. There was some sports memorabilia on the top shelf, a couple of awards with Gwen's name on them on another, and Star Wars figures mixed in with both. I ran my hands over the empty shelves, and then I knelt on the floor, where all the books were in tidy piles. It looked like the police had done a basic search, but I doubted they'd gone through every volume.

I started with the larger books and hardcovers, since it would be easier to conceal several sheets of paper in them. When I'd finished fanning the pages, running my hands over the endpapers, and peering between the spine and the text block, I stacked them neatly back on the shelves. I'd started on the paperbacks, which only needed a quick search, when I heard a noise at the front door. I looked over at Grim, who was completely still, listening.

Someone knocked. My heart jumped. Silence. More knocking. Another sound—metal on metal. Jingling. Keys. The turning of the doorknob. Had I locked it behind me? The bottom one I wasn't sure about, but I thought I'd turned the dead bolt out of habit. Grim gestured to the kitchen, pulling me to my feet as he went past. He turned off the light once we were both in and out of sight.

I heard scraping and rattling. It sounded like a key not quite fitting a lock. The knob turned a few more times. Definitely not the police—they'd either have keys, probably Carl's if they were still on him, or they'd be with the super. The door rattled again. There was a bang, like a fist hitting the wood. If whoever had killed Carl had taken any keys off him, they weren't working. I felt like a sitting duck, standing in the dark kitchen. I looked around and grabbed a cast iron skillet off the stove. It was better than nothing.

Someone banged at the door again, and then again. Then I heard a man yelling: "Hey! What are you doing?"

The banging stopped. I heard muffled voices and strained to catch a few phrases.

"—friend of Carl's—forgot something—wrong keys—"

It was a low voice, also a man's I thought, then "suffered a loss, you know? I'll check."

A few seconds later someone pounded on the door.

"Hey! Gwennie! You in there? A friend of Carl's is here. Gwen?"

I heard the second voice again, a murmur of conversation. The first man spoke again.

"Yeah, well, she's not here. Doesn't matter how important it is. Try talking to the super—he's in 1A. First floor in the back. Go on. If I see you up here without him, I'm calling the cops!"

Silence. Grim eased around the corner, went to the door, and listened. I thought I heard the elevator ding. The sound of a door slamming seconds later was clear. Grim came back and said, "We need to finish and get out."

"Right," I said, my nerves still singing.

Grim looked at the frying pan I was still gripping with both hands.

"Right," I said again, setting the pan down. I went back to the bookcase and finished the paperbacks. It had to be here, somewhere. Grim came over.

"Nothing in the furniture."

"Behind the pictures?"

"I've checked all of them but these." He started working on some framed photos of Gwen and Carl. I grabbed an autographed publicity shot of Jacob deGrom in his early long-haired days with the Mets. As I worked to loosen the back, something Carl had said about Dan floated up.

"We talked about sports and stuff." He'd sat there, talking and pleating his menu into a small, thick square of paper.

Dan had kept a Mr. Mets bobblehead and a signed picture of Keith Hernandez on his desk. They'd been in the box Lucy from HR had given me. I'd looked at them the other day. I pulled apart the deGrom picture. Nothing behind the photo but a piece of cardboard. I set it down and scanned the rest of the shelf. Collectibles still in their boxes. The Star Wars action figures I ignored for now. It was the other ones that interested me.

I picked up a Rangers model Zamboni and flipped it over. The box looked untouched, but I pulled it open anyway. Just the Zamboni. I closed it and put it back. Next, a Francisco Lindor bobblehead. This box also looked mint. I opened it too, and sent a silent apology to Carl when I came up empty. There were three bobbleheads left—the current Mets announcers, two of them former players. It was a set. Each in its individual box, but designed to go together, the three of them sitting in the booth, with the team logo on the wall behind them. Gary, Ron, and Keith. Dan, like other hardcore fans, had always referred to them by their first names.

My hands tingled as I flipped the first box. This one wasn't mint—there was a tiny tear in the cardboard, and the bottom bulged. I pulled it open. Wedged between the bottom and the back of the figure were folded sheets of paper.

"Got it!" I said. Grim came over as I opened the sheets. These were the ones I had. I needed the other two. I stuffed them in my pocket and reached for the second box. This one looked untouched, but when I pulled it open a piece of folded paper fell out. This one was from a yellow legal pad. I unfolded it—everything was handwritten, just as Carl had said.

I handed it to Grim. "Get good clear pictures—on your phone, not mine. I'll keep the originals, but I want a record somewhere else."

He nodded and took the page to the coffee table. I opened the third box. One more spreadsheet, one I'd never seen. I handed it to Grim. I was turning back to the bookshelf, when I heard a siren, faint but growing louder.

Neither one of us said anything. Grim kept taking pictures. I closed the boxes and put them where I'd found them. Grim handed me the last two sheets, and I tucked them away.

"Let's go," he said.

I spotted the trash can with Gwen's notes and the empty gift-card sleeves. I swept the remains of her lunch off the table and into the bag, then knotted the top. I didn't want anyone figuring out where she was.

"Just two residents taking out the trash," I said. Grim nodded. He eased open the door and looked down the hall. All was quiet. We slipped out. He was locking the dead bolt when we heard the hum of the elevator. We were across the hall and into the stairwell in a flash. The elevator dinged as he carefully closed the fire door. I was tempted to wait and peek out to see if it was the mystery man coming back to Gwen's apartment, but Grim seemed to read my mind.

"Too risky," he said. "The guy down the hall might have called the police." He handed me the keys. "We'll split up. I'll meet you at the subway station."

Down the stairs and out the back I went. I hung a right and tossed the trash bag into dumpster halfway down the block. I put on my sunglasses, tucked my hair into my hat, and strolled out onto the side street at a reasonable pace.

A police cruiser passed me, lights on, siren moaning, and turned the corner toward the front of the building. I wasn't worried about Grim—he'd be out of sight by now.

I crossed the street and headed for the subway, high on the adrenaline from my first successful break-in and the feel of the evidence in my pocket.

The siren wailed and cut off behind me.

I didn't look back.

Chapter
Twenty-One

When we got back to my apartment, the first thing I did was send pictures of the new information to Isabelle. She said she'd look at it that night and let me know what she came up with. I spread the pilfered papers out on the coffee table, along with the timeline, the card from Danny, various other notes, and a pad and pens.

"Okay," I said to Grim. "I'm going to rule out Frank Benson as anything other than an accomplice to fraud. I might be going out on a limb, but I don't think he's a killer, and I don't think the timing works for Dan's murder. So that leaves us with Clarice Phillips and William Warren, together or separately. And the question we need to answer is, why? What did Dan know?"

Grim was squinting at the handwritten notes. "It would help if Frank's handwriting weren't so cramped. And he used a lot of abbreviations."

"Hang on," I said. I dug around in my work tote and pulled out my fold-up magnifying glass. "Here you go. It has a light too."

"Nancy Drew lives," Grim said.

I sniffed. "It's not for detecting. Well, not only for detecting. It's also handy for old books and very fine print."

"I stand corrected," Grim said with a smile, applying himself once more to the notes.

I went back to the spreadsheets, comparing the new page I'd found with the six pages I'd already had. I didn't find anything in common, with the exception of one line. On the six-pager, there was an entry for "Juno Holdings." It showed a dollar volume in line with the others on that spreadsheet. The single page had Juno in the header, and then about twenty entries beneath it. Some had names, others were abbreviations—letter and number combinations. There were dates next to the first five and dollar amounts next to that. The rest had months, some followed by question marks. The column for dollar amounts was blank.

I opened the calculator app on my phone. The first five entries on the Juno sheet added up to the total on the "Juno Holdings" line. Beyond that, I found nothing in common between the two. Maybe it would all mean something to Isabelle.

"Anything?" I asked Grim.

"I've deciphered a few words. This looks like 'cash' and here there's 'tax reg' and 'legal entity.' Also 'interstate banking' and 'MSO.' Lots of arrows and underlining, a column of numbers, and a bunch of abbreviations. And here in the corner some doodles—a beach scene in a circle, with the word 'magic' written in the sand. There's a British magician's group called the Magic Circle, but somehow I don't think that's what he's referring to. Also a bunch of dollar signs, a smiley face, and McLn720s."

"A smiley face? Seriously? Let me see." I took the sheet and the magnifier.

"It's the 720s that interests me," Grim said, pulling out his phone. "Ha, I knew it. He was looking at a McLaren. It's a sports car, but one that sells for about three hundred thousand. The 720S is entry level, though. The really nice ones go for much, much more."

"Wow. Glad he wasn't overreaching. Still, it looks like he was expecting a big payoff." Big enough to kill for? I was sure the car was the tip of the iceberg, but I still didn't see Frank as a killer. William Warren, that I could see. Clarice? Maybe. She was a dark horse in many ways. Vast sums of money changed people, though. Or so I'd heard, having never experienced it myself. I'd be willing to give it a try, though. That had been part of the appeal when Dan had taken the job. Stock options and a potential IPO could add up to a comfortable retirement fund, not to mention an upgraded lifestyle.

Grim was looking at the Juno spreadsheet. "I think some of these abbreviations are the same," he said, gesturing to the handwritten notes. He pulled the pad over and started a neat list of whatever he could interpret from Frank's notes.

"I think so too. It looks like he was trying to come up with a system. Carl Guenther said he did the same thing with passwords." I took the magnifying glass and scanned the paper. "Some of these other things make sense based on what the expert I spoke to said. 'Cash' and 'Interstate banking' relate to each other. You can't use a credit card to buy cannabis in a state where it's legal, because of federal regulations and rules about interstate commerce. Or something like that. He explained it pretty well, but it's confusing."

"I know. I've been following what's going on here in New York. It's a lot to keep track of, and it's only one state."

"True. I guess this legal entity note has to do with the business structure? Or maybe setting up new vendors. I know the investors like to see growth, but this is an awful lot of new suppliers in a short time."

Grim shook his head. "I'm sorry. I don't know enough about how any of this works. It sounds like a great opportunity, but I don't understand what's behind it. CBD oil all comes from big labs, doesn't it? Would legal weed come from small, local growers?"

"I'm not sure. Maybe to start? Even Ben and Jerry's had to scale up to bigger farms once they increased their distribution. As for the CBD products, someone's got to make it into supplements and edibles and whatever else they're selling."

We tossed around a few more thoughts, more questions than answers. Then Grim had to go. I thanked him again for helping.

"Thank *you* for the exciting afternoon," he said, grinning. "I'm looking forward to our outing on Saturday night."

"Oh, right. But you won't have to break in, or even sneak in."

"No, I'll be masquerading as one of the catering staff. Don't worry—I've got it covered. You'll barely know I'm there. See you."

After I'd locked the door behind Grim, I briefly considered just how flexible my morals had become of late. Not that I was a rules girl to begin with, but lately I'd managed to surround myself with like-minded others. Everyone seemed to be jumping on the bend-the-rules-bandwagon without a second thought. *The ends justify the means,* I told myself. Good enough. I fixed a snack and returned to my evidence.

Grim was right. All of this was hard to follow. It was an incredibly complicated business. How was it that these few sheets of paper, which told only a fraction of the story of a growing company, were worth killing over? It didn't make any sense.

My phone rang. Isabelle. Maybe it made more sense to her.

"This doesn't make sense," she said without preamble right after I said hello.

"I was thinking the same thing right before you called," I said. "What part of it doesn't make sense to you?"

"Well, I've been thinking back to what was going on around the time of Dan's murder. I hadn't been there for that long, but I know the shift from standard natural personal care products to CBD oil, to the plan for cannabis dispensaries was new."

"That's true. Dan had been there a little over a year. A lot of the previous management team left or retired when the company changed direction. Though to be honest, some of that had to do with contracts and the original owners selling."

"Right. So you've got a niche business with a strong regional following, some retail outlets, and a nice online business. You're ramping up for expansion. One area is a wild card because of politics and regulations and whatever. You've got regular suppliers, and you're adding new ones. Why is a list of them so important?"

"I was wondering the same thing. Do the numbers tell you anything?" I asked.

"No, not these. I do remember telling Dan that, based on the history of money in and money out, there were some big jumps. He thought so too, but Frank was in charge of vetting new vendors and the—what do you call it?—due diligence. The relationship between some of the numbers always seemed strange to me."

"Hadn't Dan noticed that?"

"He had, to a point. But he didn't have a lot of time, so he put me onto it. I looked at the history and the projections, but whenever I brought up something, or he did, we were told it was because we were adding new areas to the business. It was a volatile industry because of regulations and the tax code or whatever."

"That doesn't necessarily follow, but I'm not looking at a sales plan. I learned that, due to tax regulations, some producers can't afford to stay in business. So maybe that explains the churn. I'm sure they spelled it out well enough to the investors." I said.

Or did they? How many of them understood the business any better than I did? From what Noah had said, many did; others—not so much. But since no one expected this to make money anytime soon, there was some wiggle room.

"There's only one thing here that stands out," Isabelle continued. "This Juno Holdings. That was something new, and a comparatively big investment for a new supplier, based on history. There could be some reason for that I'm not aware of. As I said, I'm only looking at the relationship between numbers. I don't know what's behind it."

Join the club.

"And this may be nothing, but it looks like 'Juno' is an abbreviation. In a couple of places, there's a period after the last letter. In others there's not."

"Really?" I grabbed my magnifier. She was right. "I see that. But what does it mean?"

"I don't know. Why bother with the period? Usually people run things together in spreadsheets to save space. Could just be Frank. He was always complaining that no one used proper punctuation anymore except for old-school guys like him."

"Well, he has a point. I've gotten sloppier since I've started to text so much. It may not mean anything, but I'm glad you noticed."

"You know, Greer, I'm wondering if we're looking at this all wrong. Maybe this information is important for a different reason. It's not complete, right? I finally came up with Gloria's last name, you know, Clarice's original assistant? I called her. When I was talking to her, I asked her why she left. She wasn't old enough to retire. She said it was the new direction the company was taking, along with the new management. I asked if she didn't approve, and she said she had no issue with the dispensary concept, but she didn't think they—the new team—could pull it off. She said something like 'It's all big talk, but they're just blowing smoke.' And then she laughed."

"Did she say anything else?"

"Only that she thought I was well out of it, and she was sorry to hear about Dan. She said he was one of the good ones."

"He was. That's interesting, but I'm not sure what it means."

"I know. I wish I had more to offer," Isabelle said.

"You've gone above and beyond," I said. "I appreciate your help."

"Thank you, but I want to see them caught, whatever they did. You know, I think Great-Aunt Caro is rubbing off on me— I'm looking forward to the dinner party. I'm even trying to come up with a few ways to get information out of those investors Clarice mentioned."

This was a big deal. Isabelle had confessed when we first met that she felt awkward in almost any social setting. She was brilliant, but as she put it "math camp isn't big on social skill development."

"Caro does have that effect, doesn't she? I'm glad, though. I don't know what we'll get out of it, but it's worth a try."

We talked for a few more minutes about plans for the next evening and what time the two of them would pick me up, and then hung up. I stared at the pile of paper on the coffee table. What now?

"Back to basics, Greer," I said. I moved it all into the alcove, opened up my evidence board, and pulled out everything I had. I decided to start with something I hadn't looked at in a while— the collection of newspaper articles and notes that Millicent Ames had left for me.

Millicent had been in her eighties when she compiled this, and not in the best health, but there had been nothing wrong with her mind. I smiled when I read her admonition on the first page, "Follow the money!" Her comments, both insightful and acerbic, were sprinkled throughout the series of articles she'd left.

"The girl is brilliant, just not in the way those fools thought."

"Real estate is real estate—there is nothing magical about renting an office."

"When did dressing badly and having poor personal hygiene make you a boy genius? Might as well stockpile Monopoly money. Maybe I'm too old . . ."

"People believe what they want to believe."

Someone else had said that, recently I thought. Grim. And April, I thought. About different things, but still.

Millicent had made some good points. She'd covered a wide range of events, from the Panama Papers to Bitcoin mining. It was the last thing she'd written that tied it all together. She'd even underlined it several times:

"Cui bono?"

Cui bono? Who benefits? It always came down to that. In this case, anyone who had a share in New Leaf when it went public, but especially Clarice Phillips and William Warren, who had been there from the beginning. Dan would have, and Frank Benson, and to a lesser extent, the Carl Guenthers of the company.

What could stop that from happening?

Having the investor class figure out that New Leaf was, to quote Gloria, "blowing smoke." About what? The sales potential for a nationwide chain of dispensaries? The time it would take to make it happen? Frank, at least, had expected a big payoff in a short time frame. I didn't think that had happened. He wasn't driving a McLaren when I saw him. He had invested heavily in his fiancée's business and in her enormous engagement ring, but that wasn't in the same league.

I found Frank's notes and my magnifying glass. His doodles weren't much more legible than his handwriting, but he'd crammed in a lot of detail. The beach scene in the circle even had a little conch shell and a seagull. The word 'magic' written in the sand—that had to mean something, though I agreed with Grim that it wasn't about magicians And it seemed like the beach was key. Beach magic circle. Seashell magic circle. Seashore magic circle. There was something about it, that last one, that rang a bell. Millicent had noted something like that—where?

I didn't want to start going through the folder again, so I plugged different word combinations into a search engine, trying to find something that made sense. The closest I could get was 'offshore magic circle.' It referred to a group of law firms that specialized in offshore financial centers. Not everyone hid money in Switzerland. Corporate entities had other options. Frank wasn't that caliber of lawyer, so his interest in this lay elsewhere.

A swooping arrow pointed toward it from the collection of dollar signs above the smiley face. Looks like he was planning a beach house to go with his new car. Deciding I'd gleaned everything I could from it, I put the sheet away, along with the other files. I kept the card Dan had sent to me, though, and propped it up next to my bed. It was the only direct message I had from him.

I made a grilled cheese sandwich and poured some wine and took it to the living room. I flipped through the DVDs, hoping a change of focus would clear my mind. *The Prestige* and *The Illusionist* I set aside—I'd watched them when I first arrived and was trying to get into a conjuring-arts frame of mind. I chose the newer version of *The Thomas Crown Affair*. Both were good, but I had a soft spot for Pierce Brosnan. Besides, I loved the scene at the end when the museum is flooded with men in bowler hats carrying briefcases, all of them ringers for Thomas Crown. Such brilliant misdirection.

I settled in with my dinner and movie, and let my mind drift. In the absence of dessert—how had I let that happen?— I poured a second glass of wine. While I drank, I looked up the portrait of the bowler-hatted man who had appeared in the film. I could never remember the name. I always thought of it as The Company Man, but no. It was *The Son of Man*, by Rene Magritte. The scene I loved was based on *Golconda*, by the same artist, in which identical bowler-hatted men rained down on a suburban neighborhood. Golconda, I read, was the name of a ruined and abandoned city in India, and translated to 'mine of wealth.' Not anymore, apparently.

I went back to *The Son of Man*. Magritte had painted it as a self-portrait, and said of it, "Everything we see hides another thing, we always want to see what is hidden by what we see." I agreed with the first half of that statement, but I wasn't so sure about the second. I thought Grim had nailed it when he told me that magic, conjuring, illusion—whatever you called it—worked because most people see what they want to see. No one truly wanted to see the man behind the curtain. I'd add that most people believed what they wanted to believe. I bookmarked the Magritte page and went back to the movie.

I was feeling more upbeat by the time the credits rolled. A good art heist had that effect on me. Maybe if we couldn't find any hard evidence tomorrow night, Clarice would have some fine art small enough to make off with. At this point, I was sure

Caro and Isabelle would be in, and I suspected Grim had done it before. While I got ready for bed, I entertained myself by making up scenarios in which the four of us smuggled art—or evidence—out of Clarice's apartment.

I got into bed, propped myself up with some pillows, and picked up the card Danny had mailed to me the day he was murdered. I read the message again, then flipped it over and read the fine print on the back. I returned to the picture. What was he trying to tell me? In all the time I'd known him, Dan Sullivan had never been a cryptic message kind of guy.

I put the card back on the nightstand, leaned back, and thought in depth about my husband for the first time in a long time. I still thought of him that way, as my husband, though I tried to remember to add "late" when speaking about him. Would that ever change? Maybe, when this unfinished business was resolved, I could let him go. Meanwhile, who was Dan Sullivan, and what was it about him that had brought about his murder?

Dan had not been someone who saw what he wanted to see, or believed what he wanted to believe. He'd seen what was in front of him and believed what that told him. He wasn't a creative thinker—he was all logic, no leap. He'd used me as a sounding board, to reason through things, but also when he'd felt he was missing something and needed what he'd called a "crazy connection" between facts or situations that didn't add up. He'd indulged my love of mysteries and watched hours' worth of them at my side, but he'd rarely solved them. His talent for puzzles had been word games—no crossword or rebus defeated him.

As for his work, he'd been meticulous to a fault. He'd been honest and presumed the same of others. Though not naive nor excessively trusting, he gave the benefit of the doubt. Once he'd decided someone was on the up and up, his opinion hadn't wavered unless he'd had evidence to the contrary. His faith in his own judgment hadn't factored in that people, and circumstances, change. He had been less cynical and much nicer than I was, and I'd thought that might be what had gotten him killed.

This brought me to an uncomfortable truth: If I were in charge of hiring for a start-up, would I have chosen Dan? I wasn't sure that I would. But then, I wouldn't have hired Frank Benson either. That choice I now understood—Frank was both competent and willing to be bought. Dan was very competent and as honest as the day is long. Perhaps that had been part of his appeal—no one would question the financials because of Dan's squeaky-clean reputation. But he had, at heart, been an accountant, and he'd liked to make sure every little thing added up. Which had become a problem for his employers.

Dan had been hired quickly, when the previous man in the position had retired. Ian Cameron had given him a glowing recommendation because he liked the fact that Dan could be relied upon to build a solid financial foundation under any of Ian's visions. But that wasn't what Clarice and William had asked for. They had wanted someone with a "sterling reputation." Dan had that too, and Ian had said so. Noah Leonard mentioned that companies who wanted to get away with fraud often hired someone with a good reputation, someone on the up-and-up, and put them in charge of compliance or something similar. New Leaf didn't have a compliance officer, but the financial officer could serve the same purpose.

Dan had arrived at New Leaf to find things in reasonable order, but without the kind of detailed history he preferred. It might never have been there, or it could have been gotten rid of. Either way, the fact that a lot of the old guard had left at the same time provided an opportunity for the new management team to rewrite history if it suited their purpose. But Dan was interested in the actual history. There had been some late nights, and eventually he'd been given the okay to hire Isabelle.

Isabelle Peterson, mathematical genius, had done similar work for her brother's company when she'd left her PhD program. On paper, she looked harmless. In reality, she grasped numerical relationships and patterns like no one I'd ever known. She also frankly admitted that she'd never understood the polite lie, the social nonsense that greased the wheels of life. She'd told me that she liked numbers more than people because numbers didn't lie, and people did. If the math didn't work, one of your presumptions was wrong. Her entire tenure at New Leaf, she'd said, had been an exercise in keeping her mouth shut when she saw actions and words that didn't match or didn't make sense.

So Isabelle had reinforced Dan's sense that things weren't adding up, and then he'd found that spreadsheet, and something on it had triggered a realization. "I can't believe I missed it," he'd said in a tone that implied he couldn't believe what he'd found at all. I'd left for work that day, promising to listen to him later. He'd called Ian, who had been tied up in meetings. But sometime before that, he'd gone to Frank, someone he'd thought was either too honest or too dense to be involved. He'd miscalculated.

I took one more look at the card—lighthouse, seashells, sand—and turned out the light. Sleep eluded me. Instead, I spun through everything I'd read and thought, sometimes dozing and sometimes staring into the dark.

"I can't believe I missed it."

I kept coming back to that phrase. Dan had said it, and I'd forgotten until it surfaced while I was at New Leaf. Missed what? The cannabis industry was complex—even with careful study, it wouldn't be that hard to miss some detail. It was new to everyone in the company. Which was odd in and of itself. If they'd hired a specialist, or even employed an outside firm like Noah's, I would have heard. Certainly April would have known and told me. Eventually, they'd have to have some experts. An IPO would bring increased scrutiny, which they didn't want, along with all the money, which they did.

"I can't believe I missed it."

If Dan couldn't believe he'd missed it, maybe it was something more basic. Maybe the new business model was a bright, shiny, lucrative distraction. But from what?

I watched images move through a weird dreamscape, a surreal film unwinding in my mind.

Clarice, winking at me: *"Time for the old razzle-dazzle! Honestly, these men!"* Millicent, in a voiceover, *"The girl is brilliant, just not in the way those fools thought."* William and Frank, cigars in hand, blowing smoke so thick it obscured their faces. Clarice again: *"Have you learned any sleight of hand? I love magic shows."* Grim, in top hat and tails, smiling at me, holding my gaze, and then presenting me with a bouquet of seashells he'd conjured out of thin air as I laughed.

And then, I stood in a room full of men in suits and bowler hats, moving here and there, a constant distraction. The crowd shifted and revealed Frank, in shorts and a Hawaiian shirt and a Panama hat, gathering shells in a bucket. It shifted again and there was Dan. "People believe what they want to believe. I did," he said. Then he morphed into Grim, who tipped his hat to me.

"It's not all smoke and mirrors, but a lot of it is," he said. "There's a sucker born every minute."

That was a line from *Barnum*, the musical we'd done my senior year in high school. I came fully awake. There was something in that scene. Frank—the Panama hat.

The Panama Papers. Shells. *Juno. Looks abbreviated. I found a Junonia.* Legal entities. Offshore law firms.

I sat up.

Shell companies. That was it. Right in front of me. Cannabis dispensaries? Smoke and mirrors. Ugh.

"There's a sucker born every minute, and here I am. Ugh!'"

I smacked my hand against my forehead and got out of bed.

Chapter
Twenty-Two

After my brainstorm, I spent several hours online looking up every name on the Juno/Junonia Holdings list. True to form, Frank had used a naming system for the fake companies. All had some relationship to the beach or to seashells. I had never heard of the murex or wentletrap, and had forgotten Saint James was a type of scallop, but I should have spotted cowrie even if he spelled it wrong. I found addresses for some, rudimentary websites for others, and for a couple I drew a blank. I sat, drumming my fingers and wracking my brain. There was a government site where you could find every business in a given state. They all needed to register somewhere. Department of State? That was it. I got into the business entity database and went back to the top of my list.

Once again I got a variety of results. Within the first half-dozen entries, half listed the New Leaf office address as the principal address. The rest listed locations elsewhere in the state. Two had names I didn't recognize as the chief executive; two listed Frank Benson as registered agent; one listed Shelby Travis, Frank's fiancée; and one listed Steven Malloy. I did a search of the addresses I didn't recognize. One linked to a website for a nursery, now closed, and the next brought up an address, phone number, and picture of a dingy strip mall. The last gave coordinates and a picture of forested land.

I tried the phone number. Out of service. I panned around the picture of the empty land but found nothing that looked like a business or even a building close by. The nursery made a certain amount of sense, but that number, too, was disconnected. What was going on here? I looked at the rest of the list. There was a lot to get through; the process was slow going, and I wasn't even sure what any of this meant. I was a reference librarian, not an attorney.

But April Benson was an attorney, and she worked with this kind of thing all the time. I checked the time—still the middle of the night. I'd email what I'd found to her work address and then text her in the morning. I put together the information, along with my theory and some questions, and hit "Send." Then I crashed.

I was on my second cup of coffee and about to text April when she called me.

"You're onto something," she said without preamble. "I can't believe I didn't think of this."

It was such a close echo of what Dan had said that any uncertainty I felt vanished. This was it.

"We were all distracted by the cannabis angle, but that was all smoke and mirrors," I said. "It's been an old-fashioned con all along. They're paying fake invoices from made-up vendors to redirect money to themselves, right?"

"I think so. There will be a few more entities in between Clarice, William, and whoever else is involved, but the end result is the same. Those suppliers don't exist, and the money is going right into their personal accounts. Somewhere in the islands, I'm guessing."

"But why move toward an IPO? Wouldn't that bring a lot more scrutiny? Unless they never intended to go through with it."

"Could be. A lot of these IPO companies don't make money for a long time. The New Leaf balance sheet is not bad in comparison, even with profits being siphoned off. I think William and Clarice will milk it as long as they can and then take the money and run. They wouldn't be the first," April said. "You've made a good start here, but I'm happy to take over. I've got a paralegal who's always up for some overtime. She should be able to start on this today. I'll let you know what I find, and send any documentation."

"That would be great. You can do this a lot faster than I can." I told her I'd be at Clarice's for a cocktail party that evening and asked her to let me know if she found anything new. "One more question," I added. "On the night Dan died, after you got home from your daughter's play, did anyone from New Leaf call and let Frank know what had happened?"

"No, I'm sure they didn't. He would have said something. In fact, he called me from the office the next morning and said he'd just found out. We may have been fighting, but old habits die hard, and he knew that I knew Dan."

"Thanks," I said, and told her why I'd asked.

"Looks like they haven't got their stories straight. Your friends caught her off guard. I can't wait to hear what else you come up with."

After we hung up, I went to the brownstone to catch up on a few things. Grim stopped in and I brought him up to date. When I was done, he let out a low whistle.

"That's quite a scam. Do you think they're really going to clean out the accounts and leave once they get closer to going public?"

"I don't know. It's possible. Or they may be arrogant enough to keep going. A lot of these start-ups don't make money for years. Who knows how long they could get away with it? Since I don't have a few spare million to invest, I've never paid much attention."

"Same," he said. "Should be interesting to see what we find tonight."

"If anything. Of all of them, Clarice is the cleverest. If she's hiding something, it won't be easy to find."

Grim left about an hour later. I did a few more things, chatted with the crows, and then went home to take a nap and doll up. Caro and Isabelle were right on time. I'd let them know that I'd come up with something, so as the car pulled away from the curb, I started filling them in. I told them what I'd learned and what April—or her paralegal—was working on.

"So it was an old-fashioned con all along?" Caro asked. "They've been skimming off money, and all the talk of cannabis dispensaries was a distraction?"

"Maybe that's what Gloria meant when she said she thought they were 'blowing smoke.' She must have suspected something was up," Isabelle said.

"It looks that way," I said. "It makes me wonder about the man Dan replaced. He left suddenly—he might have smelled a rat. I've still got some questions, though. They've been talking about an IPO for a while. That would bring a lot of attention. How does that fit into the plan?"

"There was a lot of excitement about it when I was there," Isabelle said. "But the timeline kept changing. That was always blamed on what they called the evolving regulatory environment."

"Sounds like they didn't want to give up their cash cow," Caro said.

"Yes, it does. Which begs the question—what's the story now? Tonight's dinner is for investors. Clarice mentioned something about the 'last round of financing.' What's the end game? One last big haul and then they disappear?" I said.

"Excellent question," Caro said. "I guess we'll have to do some subtle digging tonight."

"*Careful* digging," I said. "Don't take any chances. And the question I'm most concerned with is, who killed Dan? And Carl? And maybe Frank?"

"More important, how do we prove it?" Isabelle said.

And there was the problem. "I don't know," I said. "We'll have to keep our eyes open and hope we come across something."

"She really does live in the back of beyond, doesn't she?" Caro said. "What's it called? Marvin Gardens, or something like that?"

"Hudson View Gardens," I said. "It's in Washington Heights. The views of the river should be spectacular. It's the highest elevation in Manhattan."

"Well, I've taken the train through it, but I'm sure I've never stopped," Caro said. "Looks like we're almost there—I can see the bridge."

We were indeed almost there. The Tudor Revival complex was coming up on our left. Our driver navigated through the one-way streets and took us to the door of Clarice's building. Once we were in the elevator, Caro said, "It's not bad, really. I've never been a fan of Tudor anything, but there's lots of green space. Still, wouldn't have thought this was Clarice's cup of tea. She strikes me as more of a steel-and-glass contemporary type."

"She inherited it from the uncle she mentioned," I said. "I think she spent a lot of time here as a kid, so she's attached to it."

"Hmm," said Caro, looking around as the elevator door opened. "I think I'll ask some nosy questions. Wonder what the apartment looks like. Redecorated? Or still full of the late uncle's stuff?"

The answer was neither, or maybe both. The door was opened by one of the catering staff, who took our coats and directed us into a large room to our left. The foyer in which we stood was ten or twelve feet long, with closets and doors opening on either side and at the end. I looked into the den to our right. It held nothing but a love seat and chair facing a large flat-screen television. On the other two walls were marquee-sized, framed theatrical posters. One was for *Phantom of the Opera*, the other *Les Misérables*. The furniture looked new; the posters were old. There was a door halfway down the back wall. It was an odd place for a closet, and I decided to take a closer look later.

I turned back to the foyer and came face-to-face with a large, silver wildcat. It seemed to be looking right at me. As I walked toward the living room, I could see it was a sculpture, nearly four feet long. My best guess was a mountain lion, stretched out on an Art Deco side table, and it looked ready to spring. Beyond that, the foyer was bare.

There was another knock at the door, so I followed Caro and Isabelle into the living room. Clarice was holding court at the far end and gave a little wave when she saw us. The view from the windows was indeed spectacular. The three of us made our way across the room to take a look. Though there was another apartment complex between this one and the river, the placement of the buildings gave Clarice a direct line of site across the Hudson.

"It's wonderful, isn't it?" Our hostess appeared, gesturing to one of the catering staff to bring us some drinks.

"Really lovely," said Caro. "And the place is quite spacious."

"Two units were knocked together decades ago. Honestly, I use about half of it. I've only got the view from the living room and my bedroom. The rest looks onto either the courtyard or the street."

"Still cleaning out and bringing in your own stuff, I see," I said. "That's so hard, isn't it? Especially when you spent a lot of time here as a kid. It must have been so much fun to come stay here with your uncle."

"It really was," Clarice said. "And it is hard to let go of things. I've gotten rid of the old furniture, but I'm still sorting through Uncle Jack's theater memorabilia. I'll keep some, but the rest may go into storage for a while."

"Well, if you can tear yourself away from your guests later, I'd love to see those things. I'm sure your uncle and I must have crossed paths at some point," Caro said.

"I'll make some time," Clarice said. "Once everyone's had a few drinks, I can sneak away for a while. I'll find you later."

"Neatly done," I said to Caro once Clarice was out of earshot. "Now we mingle and see what we can pick up."

I turned and came face-to-face with Grim, who was sporting a beard and a ponytail and holding a tray of champagne glasses. I stopped short and blinked, but managed to keep a straight face.

"Ladies, may I refresh your drinks?" he said. As we traded empty glasses for full ones, he informed us that there were hot hors d'oeuvres in the dining room, and then continued to make the rounds with his tray.

"Nice looking, if you go for the dark and mysterious sort," Caro said. "Good luck, girls. I've spotted my first victim— I'm sure I dated him a few times forty years ago when he was between wives."

Caro sailed off in the direction of a well-preserved gray-haired gentleman. I told Isabelle I was headed to the dining room. I wasn't three feet away before a thirtyish man in geek chic glasses started chatting her up. I got myself a plate full of nibbles and started circulating. I normally hated engaging in polite chitchat with strangers—I found it awkward. This was easy, though. The crowd of investors was heavily male, and each and every one of them the smartest guy in the room. All I had to do was mention that I was a friend of Clarice, confess I was confused by the ins and outs of the cannabis dispensary business, and ask what they thought of New Leaf, and they were off and running.

During nearly an hour of this, I was told repeatedly that the growth potential of the company was enormous; that dispensaries were the newest, shiniest, most profitable opportunities around; and that New Leaf's focus on the wellness community was brilliant. Sometimes this information was imparted with a condescending look and a brief, simplistic summary. Other times it was more detailed and accompanied by an invitation to discuss it further whenever I was free. I went ahead and exchanged contact information with a few people, on the theory that you never knew who might come in handy. I could always block them later if need be.

There was one conversation that interested me more than the others. I was taking a breather and had drifted to the corner of the living room to examine a colorful piece of abstract art. It was familiar, but it took me a moment to come up with the name.

"Mondrian. *The Burglar Who Painted Like Mondrian*," I said. That was why it seemed familiar—I'd looked up the painter after reading the Lawrence Block novel.

"I'm not convinced it's real either."

I turned to find an older couple standing behind me. It was the man who had spoken. The woman sighed and said, "You really shouldn't say things like that." She smiled at me. "We're not experts on Mondrian, after all."

"Neither am I," I said. "I was thinking out loud, trying to remember the artist's name. I've associated it with that novel for years."

"I've read it. I love a good art heist," said the man.

I warmed to him immediately.

"Anyway, when I first saw it years ago I'd have said it was genuine. Now I'm not so sure." His wife sighed again. He continued, "Bert Winzler. This is my wife, Rose. Are you a collector?"

"Greer Hogan," I said, "No. I'm not. I'm an acquaintance of Clarice's. My late husband worked for New Leaf."

"Ah, I see. Investing in the company?" Bert asked.

"I'm a librarian, not a venture capitalist," I said with a smile. "I'm in town cataloging a private collection, so Clarice invited me. I have to confess I don't really understand the business."

Bert snorted. "Join the club. I follow Warren Buffet's advice. I never invest in what I don't understand. None of this adds up for me. I can't imagine it does for any of them," he said, waving his hand at the crowd behind him, "but they like to be first. No sense."

His wife gave him a look and then smiled at me. I had the feeling she was trying to cut off a speech she'd heard before. She said, "So you're a librarian? I've always loved libraries. And you're working on a private collection, you said?"

I gave them the short version of my current situation. They seemed genuinely interested. Rose's next question told me why.

"We have rather a large library," she said. "It could do with a good going over. I'm sure there are things we're not caring for properly, and others that should be donated or recycled. The shelves are overflowing. Is that something you could advise us on? Or perhaps you know someone?"

"It's hard to get rid of books," Bert said, an obstinate set to his jaw.

"It is. But sometimes it's better to weed out the old or damaged so you can take better care of the rest," I said. "I don't think I'm the person you need, but I can ask around, if you'd like."

"That would be lovely. Thank you," Rose said, taking out her phone. Bert didn't look convinced.

"I don't want someone who'll come in and tell us to get rid of things to make the place tidier," he said. "We tried that. I didn't like it."

"You'll be happier with a librarian, then. Someone who values books and understands how to care for them, rather than, say, a professional organizer. Some of them are bibliophiles themselves, but that's not what you're hiring them for," I said.

"Humph. Well, I guess that makes sense," Bert said.

I understood where he was coming from. I had a great appreciation for professional organizers. There were a couple upstate who had saved me days of labor by taking a first pass at collections their downsizing clients wanted to donate. But in my own home? I was not one of those librarians with a ruthlessly alphabetized spice rack. My books were in order, but I tended toward clutter and keeping items with sentimental value. It sounded like Bert was the same.

Once we'd exchanged contact information, the Winzlers said they were going home.

"We only came because we were friendly with Jack Breen, so we've known Clarice since she was a little girl," Rose said. "We wanted to show support."

"And I wanted another look at Jack's collection. Small but very nice—mostly contemporary," Bert said. "Some of it's missing. I'd swear there was a Rauschenberg right here. I hope she didn't sell it without calling me first."

"I'm sure she's packed them away while she redecorates," Rose said. "It looks like she's right in the middle of it."

"She mentioned something like that," I said. "I'll be sure to take a look around at what's left."

Bert looked appeased. We said goodbye and turned in opposite directions. A second later Bert was back at my elbow.

"If you want to see something nice, take a look at the sculpture in the foyer. It's the real thing—very small edition. Tim Cherry. Canadian. He lives out west. That Art Deco table it's on is the real thing too. And don't count yourself out as a collector—remember Dorothy Vogel!" He took one last look at the Mondrian. "Fake!" he said, and turned to follow Rose toward the door. "Give us a call about the library, Greer." He waved and disappeared into the crowd.

I certainly would call. They were not only the nicest people I'd met all evening, but they also had an interesting take on New Leaf. Bert was not a fan. He smelled a rat about something. None of it added up for him. He'd noticed some of Jack Breen's art was missing, and he suspected that one of the items left was a forgery. I eyed the Mondrian and decided to take a look at what was left of Clarice's uncle's collection.

I went back to the dining room. Now that I was paying attention, I could tell that all the walls had been recently painted. The color palette was the omnipresent gray that realtors loved and I loathed, but Clarice had at least chosen a silvery satin shade that brightened rather than dulled. The downside to this was that if paintings had been removed or shifted, it wouldn't be obvious—no telltale spaces or marks.

There were a handful of pieces hanging in the dining room. I recognized a Warhol that was signed "to Jack" and a Cindy Sherman still photo. There was a small Keith Haring original in one corner. The other artists I was less familiar with. I also found a swinging door, neatly concealed in the paneling. It was on the wall nearest to the hall that led to a couple of bedrooms. That might be handy later. I moved into the living room. In addition to the Mondrian, there were a couple of large works, but not names I recognized. That room was all about the view, so bare walls were easily explained.

Back in the foyer, I walked around the sculpture I'd noticed earlier. It was so lifelike I expected to see its tail twitch. The table that held it was gorgeous, and as Bert had said, the real thing. The effect of the two together was stunning. I stood back to admire it. If I ever won the lottery, I'd check with the artist and see if any of that small edition was left. Then I'd hunt for a similar table—I couldn't stick this magnificent beast on top of my battered old bookcase. In spite of what Bert had suggested, I wouldn't be the next Dorothy Vogel, a librarian who, along with her husband, another civil servant, had amassed an enormous and important collection of contemporary art. But perhaps I could aspire to the kind of collection Jack Breen had, small but nice.

I heard footsteps behind me and looked over my shoulder. William Warren. He stopped beside me and studied the sculpture.

"Snake in the grass," he said.

I'd put money on someone having said the same thing about William at some point, but I doubted this was a moment of self-awareness on his part.

"Is that what it's called?" I asked.

He nodded. "I don't remember the artist's name. He waved a hand over it. "Mountain lion. It's an apex predator."

And I'm an alpha bitch. And you're a bottom-feeder, I thought.

"I keep trying to get Clarice to sell it to me, but she won't budge. It's the last piece her uncle bought before he died, so she's attached to it."

His tone implied that such sentiment was a waste of time. I fought the urge to yank his chain and lost.

"Tim Cherry," I said. "The artist," I added when William looked confused. "I was talking to Bert and Rose Winzler earlier. They're quite impressed with this too. Do you know them?"

"We've met. Billionaire philanthropists. He made it all himself. Now he spends his time collecting art and giving away his money."

He sounded incredulous. William Warren had probably never given away so much as a dime unless there was something in it for him. Like an alibi.

"So you're not a collector yourself?" I asked.

William made a face. "No. Neither is Clarice. She inherited all this stuff."

"Well, that could explain it, then," I said.

"Explain what?"

I stepped closer, looked around, then whispered, "Bert Winzler thinks the Mondrian is a fake."

William looked blank, so I gestured toward the living room. "The big, colorful one," I said.

"Oh, that one. Looks like a giant Rubik's Cube if you ask me. Right. I doubt it. She had everything appraised when she settled the estate last year."

"Last year? Plenty of time, then," I said.

"For what?"

"To have a forgery made and sell the original. Is your fundraising going well? Yes? Then maybe she's fed up, selling off Uncle Jack's art collection, and getting ready to skip town. The place is looking pretty stripped down, and she did say she was sick of meetings."

William's face went white, then red. Then it twisted. I thought his head might explode. Interesting. I reached out and touched his arm.

"William! Kidding! Honestly, you should see your face. I read too much crime fiction, I really do. Sorry!"

I gave a little laugh. After a second he joined in.

"You had me going for a second," he said.

"So sorry. Well, I've enjoyed our chat." I really had. "Now, I'm going to find the restroom and some more champagne."

"The bathroom is there. I'll get you a drink," he said.

I made quick use of the facilities. When I came back, Clarice had joined William. He had two glasses of champagne and handed me one. Grim was standing a few feet behind them, holding a tray. He started to shake his head when I glanced over, but a couple walked up to him and blocked my view.

"Are you enjoying yourself?" Clarice asked.

"Yes. It's nice to get out, and it looks like things are going well," I said.

"They are. I think we'll have new funding in place within a week. Now I'm going to send William off to entertain our investors while I spend some time with your friend Caro. Here she comes now."

"Lovely party, Clarice. I've actually bumped into two people I know—can you believe it? Now you must show me your uncle's theater memorabilia. Such an interesting man. Greer, darling, have you seen the Warhol?" Caro asked.

"I passed it earlier, but I'd like to take a closer look."

Clarice and Caro walked toward the den. William turned to talk to someone who had just arrived. This was my opportunity to snoop. Caro had said she'd keep Clarice occupied as long as she could, and create a diversion if necessary. I think she was hoping it would be necessary. I was hoping it wouldn't. Isabelle was going to be my lookout. I nodded as I went toward the dining room, and she detached herself from the man she was talking to and followed. I stood near the Warhol and sipped my champagne.

"How's it going?" I asked.

"Some interesting tidbits, but nothing major," she said. "I did talk to someone with a bad case of apartment envy. He said that Clarice's bedroom and home office are on this side. The area to the right of the foyer is two bedrooms, the den we saw, and a storage room off the den."

"That must be the door I saw in the middle of the wall," I said.

"Probably. It was the kitchen in a smaller apartment that got merged with this one. There are also literally a dozen closets."

"Anyone who's spent time counting closets *does* have serious apartment envy, but it's useful information. Okay, my story will be that I need a quiet place to take an important call. If anyone heads in my direction, call and hang up. I'm going to try this door first. If it's more storage I'll go through the one in the living room."

"I should be able to keep an eye on both doors," Isabelle said.

I was about to slip away when Grim came toward us.

"Sorry about the delay getting your drink, ma'am," he said loudly. As he plucked my half-empty champagne glass from my hand, he muttered, "Humor me," and replaced it with a rocks glass full of something fizzy. "Here you go—club soda and lime. Would you care for another drink, ma'am?" he said, turning to Isabelle.

"Sure," Isabelle said after a brief hesitation. "I'll have a club soda too. Thanks."

"Coming right up," Grim said, taking her glass and moving fast toward the bar in the corner of the dining room.

Isabelle looked at me and lifted an eyebrow. I shrugged and stepped back toward the wall. I stood, drinking my club soda, and watched the crowd. For a moment, everything shifted. The smartly dressed crowd became a group of men in overcoats and bowler hats. Some of them seemed to float, drifting in front of the big windows. "Golconda," I said. I blinked, and the men were gone.

A passing member of the catering staff turned toward me. I raised my drink and smiled. She moved on. When no one was looking, I set my glass down, reached behind me, and pushed at the swinging door I'd spotted earlier. It opened easily. I slid through, grabbing the edge and closing it quietly.

The hall light was off, undoubtedly to discourage guests from wandering in. I flipped on my phone flashlight. There was one closed door behind me, two to my right, and one open in front of me. The one in front was a bathroom—a small, frosted glass window at the far end of it provided enough light to see the fixtures. I'd plan to dive in there if necessary.

I opened the door behind me. It was a shallow linen closet. It held one extra set of sheets and a pile of fluffy towels. The door to my right led to a room illuminated by two windows along the back wall. The light coming in was dim. From what Clarice had said, that must be the courtyard side of the building. Still, it gave me an idea where the furniture was, not that there was much of it. Covering most of the wood floor was a threadbare patterned rug. An old wooden library table pushed against one wall served as a desk. A large monitor and a docking station sat on top, along with an antique wooden document box. No laptop. A modern, ergonomic desk chair was in front of it. Catty-corner to these was a love seat in the same pattern and fabric as the sofa and chair in the den.

"Must have been a package deal," I muttered as I examined the document box. There was no lock, and nothing inside but some pens, pencils, sticky notes, and appointment cards. Those were for painters and floor refinishers, so nothing helpful there. The inside didn't look as deep as I would have expected, so I closed the box and felt around the outside. I was rewarded with the outline of a small drawer. All that time investigating the nooks and crannies of Raven Hill Manor had paid off. I pushed at it in a few different spots. The drawer popped out. It held Clarice's passport, and nothing else.

I flipped through the passport. It was good for another five years. She'd visited the Bahamas recently, and Mexico. Europe over three years before. Nothing untoward there. I put it back and checked the closet. A couple of power strips, a printer, and random office supplies. For someone with an abundance of storage space, Clarice lived a minimalist existence. Other than large, heavy pieces of art with sentimental value, she did not have much in the way of possessions. Not here, anyway.

I peeked out into the hall. Still dark and quiet. I turned the knob on the remaining door. By process of elimination, this had to be Clarice's bedroom. I took a step and lost my balance, but caught myself on the doorframe. I'd been searching for less than five minutes, but my heart was thudding, and I felt hot. Maybe I'd had too much champagne. I really should stick to martinis.

I closed the door behind me and leaned on it. The bedroom was brighter than the other rooms or the hall because of the large window facing the river. It seemed too bright, and the room was full of strange shadows. I squinted and looked away for a moment, then back. There was another, smaller window in the same wall, a few feet away. My eyes finally adjusted to the difference in the light, and I realized it was a door. It had to lead to a fire escape—I hadn't noticed any balconies on the building. I still felt wobbly, so I felt my way along the wall. My hand hit a doorknob.

Another closet. I tried to turn the knob. It moved a fraction of an inch and stopped. I jiggled it. Locked. And me without my burglar tools. I started to giggle and put my hand over my mouth. This was serious. I took a deep breath and moved down the wall, to where I could see another door. This knob turned easily. I held onto the door as I opened it, and flashed my light inside.

Clothes, shoes, handbags on the top shelf. I moved things around and got a whiff of Clarice's perfume. Nothing of interest. I didn't have time to open every handbag, but they all felt empty. I bent to search the back corners of the closet and the floor spun up toward me. The next thing I knew I was on my hands and knees, half in and half out of the closet. I'd dropped my phone. I thought I could see some light, but it was blurry. I felt around and was able to grab it, and then twist around until I was sitting, leaning against the doorjamb. The room continued to spin. So did my thoughts, but I was able to grasp and hold one.

Someone had spiked my drink.

Chapter
Twenty-Three

⁓

I concentrated on my breathing and tried to focus. I knew who I was, where I was, and what I was doing. I also knew I needed to get out of there. I didn't think I'd lose consciousness, but I couldn't be sure. How much of that last glass of champagne had I drunk? Less than half, I thought, maybe only a third? That's right—I'd had a few sips before Grim showed up and took it, and urged me to drink some water. An image of Grim swam up out of my memory. Grim, standing behind Clarice and William, starting to walk toward me. He must have seen something. That was for later, though. Right now I needed to get moving.

I rolled back to my hands and knees and waited for the floor to stop gyrating before I tried to get up. My stomach rolled. The thought of barfing all over Clarice's bedroom floor and then running away set off another fit of giggles. *No noise, Greer,* I thought. I put my hand over my mouth and promptly fell, landing on my side facing the bed. Well, as long as I was down here.

I'd managed to hang on to my phone. I turned it toward the bed so I could take a look underneath. Not even a dust bunny. Wait, there was something. I moved the light around and found a dark bundle with a trailing strap under the far side of the bed. Knapsack? No, more like a carry-on. If I were in better shape I'd investigate. Instead, I'd be happy to be able to stand.

I rolled back to my knees. I was going to need both hands for this, but I also needed to be able to feel my phone vibrate. Putting it in my little swingy crossbody bag wouldn't cut it. I sat back on my heels and tried to think. I looked down, contemplated the neckline of my dress, and tucked my phone in my bra. You could see the outline if you looked, but I was hoping no one would have the chance to look before I retrieved it.

I braced myself on the bed and stood. So far so good. I reached for the bedpost and then took a step. Another wave of nausea hit me. I breathed through my nose until it receded. I made it to the door and looked out. All clear. Once in the hall I evaluated my options. It was a slow process—I felt like my thoughts were swimming through sludge. I decided the swinging door to the dining room was a safer bet for stealthy reentry to the party than was the pocket door to the living room. The only problem was that I'd have to let go of the wall and walk several steps on my own to get to the opposite side of the hall. Worth a try.

I took a step, and then another, one hand on the wall. Almost to the crossing point. I was even with the bathroom when the nausea hit again with a vengeance. I made it to the sink and vomited up champagne, fizzy water, and mini quiche. I felt better immediately, still wobbly but not as dizzy. By the time I'd rinsed my mouth with cold water, reapplied my lipstick, and cleaned up as best I could, my head was clearer. My balance wasn't great and I wasn't thinking fast, but I could hold my train of thought.

Back to the plan. I made it across the hall and was pulling back the swinging door when I felt my phone buzz. No time to check. I looked through the crack in the door and saw the back of one of the catering staff. Male, dark hair, ponytail. Grim. He was positioned between me and the entrance to the living room. I figured I had just enough room to get out. He must have sensed movement behind him as I slithered through the swinging door, because he took a step forward and shifted sideways. I managed to get the door closed and stood, swaying a little, in front of it. No one seemed to have noticed my arrival.

Grim turned, and said "Can I get you something, ma'am?" and then in a lower voice, "Are you okay?"

I nodded. "Drugged. Didn't get too much."

"Thought so."

"Barfed."

"Good."

I heard Caro's voice in the next room. I glanced over and saw Isabelle in the entrance to the dining room. She looked relieved when she saw me; then she turned in the direction of Caro's voice. Clarice came into view a second later. I turned back to Grim.

"Clarice's bedroom. Locked closet, bag under the bed. Nothing else I could find."

"I'll do what I can," he said. In a louder voice he added, "Certainly. I'll be right back with that."

I took a deep breath and exhaled slowly. I still felt lousy—everything was too bright and too loud. This evening had been a fishing expedition, but now that someone had taken the trouble to spike my drink, I wanted something to show for it. I swayed again and decided standing upright unaided was overrated. I stepped back to lean against the wall, but misjudged the distance and hit the paneling with a smack.

"Oof," I said, wincing. I pushed myself upright. Clarice sped across the room.

"Are you all right?" she asked.

"I'm okay. A little dizzy. And the lights . . ." I waved my hands around my face.

"Sounds like a migraine. I used to get those. What you need is some fresh air. Come with me."

Clarice took my arm and guided me through the swinging door.

This is not a good idea, I thought, but part of me was relieved to be in the quiet darkness of the hall. Clarice kept the lights off and walked me down the hall at a sedate pace. I thought she'd head for the office, but she opened the door to her room. Perhaps I'd be invited to lie down? No, Clarice went straight to the door in the corner and opened it. The cool night air rushed in.

"You aren't afraid of heights are you? Good. Follow me. I come out here whenever I need to clear my head," she said.

This is an even worse idea. But the fresh air was making me feel better, and the fire escape was surrounded by brick columns and a low wall. It would still be possible for someone to fall—or be tossed—off it, but not easy. Another benefit to an older, upscale building. As long as I stayed between Clarice and the door, I should be okay. Besides, I had friends not far away. Surely someone had seen us leave the dining room. I walked out onto the black metal platform, glad I wasn't wearing heels. After a few deep breaths the dizziness started to fade.

"Better?" Clarice asked.

"Yes, thank you. Still can't quite keep my thoughts straight, but getting there." I was clearer by the minute, but she didn't need to know that.

We stood quietly. The night was cool, but after feeling so sick and hot, it didn't bother me. Clarice leaned against a pillar, looking out across the river.

"This has been helpful, but I don't want to keep you from your guests," I said a short time later.

"It's all right. I've made the rounds. I'm tired of talking to these people. I'd rather enjoy the view."

"It *is* lovely. And the apartment's great. I've never been in this complex before—it's very nice."

"Do you miss the city, Greer?" Clarice said, turning to face me.

"Sometimes," I said. "I like where I live now, though. I used to think having the city place and the country place sounded like too much work, but now I think it's the best of both worlds. If you can swing it."

"That's the key, isn't it? Money changes everything. I'll always keep this place, but I want a house on an island, somewhere warm, with balmy ocean breezes. What about you?"

"The only island I'm interested in has a cool, misty climate. I'm not a warm-weather girl."

"Ireland?" Clarice asked. "Hmm. It has a favorable corporate tax structure. And you have connections there, don't you? Family? I'm sure something could be worked out."

"What do you mean?"

"I mean you could always go back to sales and marketing. You were good at it—I remember the work you did for your old company. You could get in on the ground floor somewhere, make a bundle. I've got plenty of ideas for my next venture. What do you say?"

"Are you serious?" I asked. She couldn't be. What was she up to?

"Completely. I'm ready to start something new. Of course, it'll take a little while to wrap all this up, but I've already got some irons in the fire. I've always liked you—I could tell you were smart and ambitious. Smarter than the people I'm working with now. Tell me you wouldn't enjoy making asses of the financial masters of the universe in there. We could have fun! Name your price—I'm sure we can come to an agreement."

Clarice had moved closer while she spoke. There was a peculiar glitter in her eye. She *was* serious, at least about some of it. But it also had a ring of "an offer you can't refuse." I decided my best bet was to play along.

"Well, when you put it like that," I said, "I do have rather expensive taste for my current salary. And I have to confess—I miss the pace, the whole game."

"I knew it," Clarice said. "I thought when you came to the office you might be open to something. You've been away long enough, Greer." Clarice laughed. "We'll make a great team. I'd love for you to be my next partner in crime."

That's what I was afraid of, but I smiled and said, "I'm flattered. This is all a surprise to me, though. Let me give it some thought—job title, compensation, location. Then we'll get together, just the two of us, and talk it through."

"As long as it's soon, Greer."

"Of course. Now I'd better get back—Great-Aunt Caro talks a good game, but she's not the night owl she used to be." I reached for the wrought iron door. Clarice didn't try to stop me.

"Oh, but she's delightful! I've had more fun with the three of you this week than I can remember having in years." Clarice locked the door behind us, and we went back to the party. Caro was holding court in the living room, Isabelle at her side. Grim was gathering glasses. The crowd was thinning. I spotted William in a corner, being lectured on something by an older, red-faced man in a suit whose volume suggested he was hard of hearing. He gave Clarice a pointed look.

Caro excused herself from the group she was with. "There you are, Greer darling. I was beginning to worry."

"I got a little overheated, is all. Clarice took me out to the fire escape. Some fresh air helped, but I'm still not feeling my best. Would you mind if we made it an early night?"

"Not at all. I'll call for the car now. Should only be a few minutes. And Clarice, as soon as I've done that, I want your opinion on that show you mentioned."

"I really should go rescue William," Clarice said.

"Leave him," I said. "He's a big boy. Come down with us to wait for the car. Caro wants to chat some more anyway."

"Deal," said Clarice. "You could become a terrible influence on me, Greer," she added in a conspiratorial whisper.

"I would never," I said, and laughed. Clarice joined me. You would think we were lifelong besties. Caro ended her call, and I said, "Clarice is going to walk us down to wait for the car. Let's get our coats."

I glanced over at Grim, who caught my eye and gave a subtle nod. He picked up his full tray of glasses and headed for the kitchen. I wanted to give him as much time as I could, so I moved toward the foyer. The longer we were downstairs, the better.

Fate was on our side. The elevator was slow to arrive, and so was Caro's driver. It was a full twenty minutes before Clarice left us to go back upstairs. As the car pulled into traffic, Isabelle turned to me and asked, "Are you really okay? Someone put something in your drink, didn't they?"

"Yes. Either Clarice or William, probably William," I said. "I'm feeling much better now—I didn't drink that much of it."

I recapped what had happened, and added, "I shouldn't have taken a drink from William, but I didn't think they'd try something like this. Not in public."

"Desperation, or perhaps this William doesn't have much impulse control. You might have said something that set him off."

"I think I did, and I know what it was," I said.

Before I could continue, my phone buzzed, and I realized I'd never removed it from my bra. As I fished it out, Caro said, "Mobile phones. Another reason never to wear flimsy lingerie unless you're sure it's coming off quickly. If that's your operative on the catering staff, tell him to meet us at my place. We can have an official debrief." She rattled off her address.

Grim had sent a text.

*Found something interesting. I'll be
out of here in an hour. Your place?*

I gave him Caro's info and he gave me an ETA, which I shared with the others.

"Good, we have time for something to eat. We'll go to the diner on my block—breakfast all day. And night. You need a little bland protein and starch. Fix you right up," Caro said.

She was right. The meal was exactly what I needed, and by the time I was settled in her apartment, drinking ginger ale, I was almost completely recovered. Grim arrived and accepted a beer. He was still wearing his disguise. I wondered how long it would take him to get rid of the beard and hairpiece.

"All right," I said, "let's see what we've got. Grim, don't keep us in suspense. What did you find that was so interesting?"

"Clarice's passports," he said.

"I already found that—wait—passports, plural? You found another one?"

"I found two, both in the bedroom, both with her picture, neither with her real name. I've got the aliases. Also credit cards in names that matched the passports, as well as one with a company name—Breen Phillips LLC—and a couple wads of cash," Grim said. "She had one set in a carry-on under her bed, and another in a packed suitcase in her closet. Spare phone in both. She's very organized."

"I'll say. So what do you figure—the small bag in case she has to leave fast, and the larger if she has time and wants to look like she's going on vacation?" I said. "That fire escape could come in handy."

"Looks that way," said Grim. "She's got all warm-weather clothes in the suitcase, more of a mix in the carry-on."

"Not surprising. She told me her next home's going to be on an island," I said.

"One without an extradition treaty," added Caro.

"Undoubtedly," I said. "Anything else?" I asked Grim.

"Small gun safe in the closet, and a portable lock box. I didn't have time to get into either."

"I'm surprised she didn't keep the passports and such in that lockbox," Isabelle said. "Although, I guess if I were robbing the place, I'd grab that and the gun safe on the theory that any valuables would be in them."

"I'd do the same," I said.

Caro raised her eyebrows. Grim, who had probably made that judgment call before, grinned.

"I was right about what set William off, though. I was kidding around, and said it looked like Clarice was getting ready to flee the country. I even suggested she was selling off her uncle's art collection and replacing it with forgeries to fund her escape," I said. "He took me seriously until I said I was joking."

"I think he took you seriously, period," Grim said. "I saw William tamper with the drinks. You weren't there, but he was having a spat with Clarice. Not obvious, but low voices and a lot of tension. He waved me over and asked for three glasses of champagne, and set two down on the table with the sculpture. She turned to speak to someone. I saw him slip something into one of the glasses, but then another guest asked me for something and I lost sight of what was going on. I thought he handed the spiked drink to her, but she must have set it down again because the next time I looked her hands were empty. Then she gestured at the sculpture, and she picked up a glass, and William took the other two. That's when you came back and he handed you one."

"I shouldn't have taken it," I said. "Or at least, I shouldn't have drunk any of it."

"How could you have known?" Isabelle said.

"Exactly. It was a risky move on his part, no matter who that drink was intended for. And if he had a drug at the ready, he's done this kind of thing before," Caro said. "In fact, I heard exactly that from someone I knew who was there tonight. He's interested in the business and thinks Clarice is brilliant but doesn't trust William. But what was his endgame? Another body would be a bad idea."

"Information," said Isabelle. "Those drugs all cause loss of inhibition, right? Even more so than alcohol. Both would make you too honest. It's why I don't drink at faculty parties. I'm too honest already," she added.

"So the question is, did he want to know what I might know, or does he really believe Clarice is going to double-cross him?" I asked.

"I like the falling-out-among-thieves theory myself," Caro said. "I don't trust either one of them."

"What happened when Clarice took you out for some fresh air?" Isabelle asked.

I told them about our conversation. Grim gave a low whistle. Caro nodded and muttered, "I knew it." Isabelle frowned and said, "That explains something she said to me."

"Do tell, darling. Did you get a job offer too?" Caro said.

"Sort of. We were only talking for a few minutes. Clarice asked what I'd been doing, and I told her about going back to my PhD program. She was very interested—I was surprised. Then she asked if I'd ever considered applying my math skills to betting markets, using algorithms to capture patterns and create predictions. I told her it had never occurred to me, that it wasn't my field. She said I should consider it, that there are a lot of offshore companies who would pay me a lot if I were good at it. She mentioned Curaçao."

"She did say she had a few irons in the fire," I said. "What else do we have?"

"I found a closet in one of the spare bedrooms with what I think are theatrical supplies. Makeup, hairpieces, that kind of thing. Not brand new, so could be left from the uncle, but not the kind of thing you'd keep if you weren't going to use them. Also a collection of hats and coats, very nondescript," Grim said. "Either Clarice hasn't completely abandoned the theater, or she's got some handy disguises."

"And an excuse for having them," I said.

"That makes sense," Caro said. "If I were planning to flee the country, my first stop would be a good cosmetic surgeon. But Clarice made a comment about how so many actors have had so much Botox and fillers that they can barely move their faces. Said she would never let anyone take a knife or needle to her face. Of course she's still young. That may change."

"Anyone else?" I asked.

"Well, it's nothing concrete," said Isabelle, "but I had the feeling most of the people I spoke to weren't too concerned about the financials. They were enthusiastic about the concept, and could talk about potential, but that's it. Only one seemed to take me seriously when I asked about doing a deep dive into the business. The rest told me it was all too new, or something like that."

"I got the same impression," I said. "None of them expect to see return on investment for years but think that when it comes, it will be big."

Caro agreed. Then she added, "I do have one more tidbit. Clarice gave me a detailed rundown of a play she saw last week— plot, cast, the fact that an understudy went on and fumbled one of his lines. It was the same night that young man was killed. It's possible she saw the play and then went off to commit murder, but depending on the time of death it looks like she has an alibi."

"That leaves William," I said. "But we still don't have anything to tie either one to Jackson's murder or to Dan's."

"You've got enough evidence for some kind of fraud," Caro said. "Once the police start unraveling that, who knows what might come out?"

"True, but I was hoping for a smoking gun, I guess. Though Clarice would be smart enough to get rid of something like that," I said.

"She would. She's very smart and very charismatic. Such a shame that she's probably a psychopath," Caro said.

After that, we wound things up. Grim saw me home and said he'd be at work on Monday, but to call if I needed anything. I went to bed and stared at the ceiling, thinking about Clarice's offer. A life of luxury, world travel, a fast-paced job, and enough money to walk away whenever I wanted. Of course, it would require a certain moral flexibility on my part, but of late I'd been involved in quite a few things that were legally questionable. I hadn't had too many qualms about any of them, and a couple I'd flat out enjoyed. What was the prize, the magic number that would make me throw in my lot with Clarice?

I couldn't count that high. It would be like putting a price on Dan's life, never mind Jackson's and Carl's. Though it might have been William who had done the deed, Clarice had to be involved. Didn't she? I would give a lot to know for sure. I spun through all my options—actions and likely outcomes. I kept coming back to the same thing: Clarice's offer. What kind of deal would make her believe I meant it? What was the amount that would let her buy me off? Was there some combination of things—money, power, prestige—that would buy my silence?

Once, I would never have considered it. Now, I decided it was important to know.

Chapter
Twenty-Four

After another night spent running through my options, I decided going to the police was my next step. Once Detective Stewart heard I'd been drugged, and had witnesses, he invited me down to the station. I was impressed that he was willing to come in on a Sunday morning, and on short notice.

The place smelled like stale coffee and despair. Stewart saw me wrinkling my nose and brought me back to his desk, rather than to an interview room, which probably smelled worse. The office was pretty empty, and the detective was in his version of business casual, so wrinkled that it made Columbo's raincoat look like it had just come back from the cleaners.

"So tell me," he said, as soon as we were seated.

I gave him a factual if carefully edited version of the events that had transpired since our last meeting. I must also confess to a certain amount of spin, mostly relating to how I had gathered some pieces of evidence. My esteemed colleague, Joseph Grimaldi, did not figure in the tale at all. I'd given Caro and Isabelle a heads-up, and we'd gotten our stories straight that morning, right after I'd called Stewart. I showed up at the station with copies of everything, including some things April had emailed me late the previous night. Stewart heard me out, though I got a few raised eyebrows.

"Let me get this straight," he said when I'd finished my story of the cocktail party. "You found all this stuff—passports, credit cards—after someone had spiked your champagne?"

"I found it accidentally while I was looking for the bathroom. Fortunately, I only had a little of the champagne. I started to feel hot and sort of sick, so I got a club soda instead. That didn't help—I thought I might throw up. I kept opening doors, looking for the bathroom. I was disoriented and ended up in a bedroom. It was the strangest feeling—when I wasn't nauseated, I was giddy. It seemed perfectly normal to be there looking at everything. Then I felt really sick and staggered into the hall, found the bathroom, and vomited into the sink. As I said."

"And William Warren is the one who put something in your drink?"

"I think so. He said he'd get me one, and he's the one who handed it to me. Clarice was nearby. She had her own drink and was talking to someone," I said. I repeated the story about how I'd upset him with my comments about Clarice leaving the country. My recital was consistent, but not word for word. This part was easy—I wasn't fudging.

"All right. Now go over this part one more time," he said, holding up copies of what I'd found in Carl Guenther's apartment.

"Once Guenther didn't show up, I went over and over what he'd said to me in the diner. I remembered him mentioning that he liked Dan, that they used to talk about sports. They were both Mets fans. I found those papers tucked into some Mets memorabilia. Dan kept some in his office. A bobblehead.

Collectors say to never open the box, but I thought it looked like it had been opened before, so I took a chance."

True as phrased, and Stewart, having heard it twice, moved on. He asked about the shell companies and said he would contact April. Then he leaned back and sat tapping his pencil against his desk.

"I know you're not going to be happy with this, but there's not enough here to reopen the investigation into your husband's death. You've built a pretty good case for fraud, and I'll hand it over to our people who do that. But murder?"

"What about the things in her apartment? What about Carl Guenther? He was shot."

"A gun safe doesn't mean a gun. It could have been her uncle's. And you said yourself she has a pretty good alibi for the night Guenther was killed."

"But can't you look? Isn't there a way to get a warrant? She's going to leave the country. I'm sure of it. And if she is, William is. He's even shadier. He could have killed Carl or Jackson or Dan!"

"Ms. Hogan, I'm sorry. This is all circumstantial. I believe that you believe it. Hell, I'll even go so far as to say that my gut tells me you've got something here. But the DA will tell me I don't—not for a search warrant, not for anything. Let the fraud team take it. If there's anything there, they'll find it."

"If there's anything there, both of them will be gone by then," I said.

"I'm sorry," he said again. "I promise you, I won't let it drop."

It was what I had expected, but I was still disappointed.

"Sure. Okay, thanks," I said, and stood. Stewart signaled to a uniformed officer at the end of the room to see me out. The detective said goodbye, reminded me to leave it with him and call if anything else happened, and went back to tapping his pencil on his desk. I looked back from the doorway. He was on the phone, spreading out the papers I'd brought.

Fraud. If it could be proven, it would mean a few years in a country club federal prison.

It wasn't enough.

Back in my apartment, I moved on to plan B. I had a short window of opportunity—Caro and Isabelle were going back upstate on Tuesday; Ben and Beau were leaving for their cruise on Thursday; and my parents were back the middle of next week. Grim was a question mark. I wanted to do this while my friends and family were out of reach.

I sent Clarice a text. *Still not feeling great, and I have to deal with some work stuff this week, but your offer intrigued me. Can we get together one night to talk? Friday would be good.*

She responded immediately.

Great! Sooner would be better but I can do Friday. Touch base soon on when and where. You won't regret this!

I hoped not.

I wanted the when and where to be of my choosing, but that could wait. Next I called an old friend of my dad's, a retired cop I'd known since I was a kid doing my homework at the end of the bar. Sure, he was willing to take me to the shooting range. How about that afternoon? The grandkids were coming over for dinner, but he had a few hours. We agreed on a time to meet, and hung up.

I went to the nightstand that Fritz had redesigned and built out. When I pressed and twisted the star-shaped carving on the side near the bed, a section slid out, its movement smooth and silent. Two matching handguns rested in the built-in holsters. One, legal and permitted, I'd bought upstate with Jennie's advice. She'd taught me to shoot with it. The second, its twin, I'd bought with cash when I arrived in the city. I took the legal one and closed the compartment.

I repeated the press and twist on the other side of the nightstand, where I kept documents, extra cash, and my jewelry. I tucked the necessary permits in my pocket. Out of habit, I counted the money and put it back in its envelope. I pulled out my Irish passport. Every time I looked at it, I could hear my grandmother's voice.

"You're eligible for citizenship by descent, Greer, so make use of it. Get the passport and keep your options open."

She'd made my sister do the same, and demanded we send pictures of them when they arrived. A few weeks later, I'd gotten a note from her that included information for a bank account in Ireland in both our names. She'd written, *"Options! One for you, one for your sister."* Kitty Hogan had an interesting definition of keeping your options open, but then she'd had an interesting life. She'd added a PS that began with another set of numbers, then: *"Switzerland. Just you, so don't tell anyone about this account."* I smiled. I'd always been Gran's favorite.

I put the bank account numbers in the passport, put them back, and closed the drawer. I checked the balances regularly. There was always money in them, but never a lot. I touched base with April, who said her paralegal was still hard at work on the information I'd sent. Then I ordered an Uber and headed to the range. I was hoping I'd have better luck hitting something smaller than the side of a barn this time, but unfortunately, my aim was only slightly improved.

"You're taking too long—I think you're holding your breath, trying for the perfect shot. Here, watch my timing. Now try again."

I did as instructed and was more successful. Annie Oakley I was not. I promised to keep practicing, gave an IOU for a beer, and went home. The time at the range had released some tension. I still didn't have a solid plan, but I had the beginnings of one. The end I was up in the air about. Some ideas were improbable, others made me uneasy. Violence wasn't the answer. Not even if the thought of it brought me a feeling of satisfaction that I immediately squashed. I'd have to rely on my wits.

The next morning I updated Grim on my meeting with Stewart. He raised an eyebrow when I told him I was leaving it there for the moment, but he didn't say anything. We went to work on our respective tasks. A few hours passed before I heard from him.

"You've got some decisions to make."

Grim was leaning against the door to the library. I wasn't sure how long he'd been there—I'd been preoccupied. I was cataloging a collection of modern books on card magic, with brutal efficiency. Focusing on getting all the necessary details into the record for each volume kept me from spinning through everything I had found while investigating Dan's murder and trying to find a new angle that would convince the police to reopen the investigation. I'd given everything I had to Stewart, but I was hoping my subconscious would come to the rescue and provide some brilliant insight. So far no luck.

"About what?" I said without looking up. I put the book I'd completed back in its spot on my cart and grabbed the next one.

Grim walked over and sat across from me. He didn't say anything. I sighed and sat back in my chair.

"About what?" I said again. "Because I'm feeling like I'm out of options."

"Not entirely," he said. "You may have exhausted the conventional avenues, but you're not out of the game yet."

"Really? What other avenues do you suggest I pursue?"

"That depends on the decisions you make," he said. He ticked them off on his fingers. "What do you want to do? What are you willing to do? What are you going to do?"

"I want answers. I want justice. But right now, I don't know what I'm going to do."

Grim waited, and when I didn't say anything else, he nodded.

"Okay," he said. "I've got an idea. Let's take a break from this—all of this." He waved his hand around the room. "We'll leave work and hidden secrets and murder alone for a while. I found something I want to show you."

"More magic tricks? New set of lockpicks?"

"Not exactly. Come on. Up to the attic. It'll be fun, I promise," he wheedled.

"Okay, but if I'm climbing all those stairs, it better be good."

"Oh, I think you'll love it."

As we climbed, I asked, "Did you find whatever this is up here?"

"No, I found it in that wardrobe full of hats on the second floor. Some of it was stuffed behind, and the rest was hidden inside a hat on the bottom."

We reached the attic. There was plenty of light from the afternoon sun, but Grim turned the electric lights on anyway. At one end of the room was a small table. It held a polished wooden box and a bulky roll of some sort of fabric. At the other end was a paper outline of a life-size figure pinned to a board. It looked like a shooting range target, but as I went closer, I could see it was a slender outline, a different shape. Instead of the standard bull's-eye in the center, there were X's at regular intervals along the edge of the figure.

"What is it?" I asked, circling the board.

"It's a practice figure for knife throwing," Grim said. "DIY. The figure is paper on cardboard. It folds up. That part was behind the wardrobe. I attached it to some plywood I found up here, and used some two-by-fours to make a stand."

"Looks like it's been used before," I said.

"Some," Grim said. He was over at the table, unwrapping whatever was in the fabric. "Here we go. Throwing knives."

He held up half a dozen blades. As I got closer I could see he had them by the tip, rather than the handle. He presented them to me like a bouquet. I plucked one from the bunch and examined it.

"I expected them to be more ornate, I guess," I said, turning it over. "It's so light."

"Easier to do a lot of throwing with a lighter knife. And these are very well balanced. Want to give it a try?"

"Oh, I don't know. I've got no hand–eye coordination to speak of."

"Nah, you can do it. I'll show you. It's very relaxing. Really. Come on."

Grim walked me a few paces closer to the target. He showed me how to stand, and demonstrated the throwing motion. Then he had me practice without a knife until I had the timing of the release down. Finally he pronounced me ready.

"If you say so," I said.

"Don't worry—I'll take cover. And I've got good reflexes," he said, and handed me a knife.

"Okay." I assumed the stance, held the knife as he'd instructed, and threw. It went into the top corner of the plywood with a thunk. Nowhere near the target, but still—very satisfying.

"I want to try again," I said.

"Thought so," Grim said, and stepped forward with the rest of the knives. He showed me how to hold several at once, "so you can get a rhythm going," and then stood back once again.

I let fly. Throw after throw, most of them hitting the plywood, a few of them near the outline, and one that sailed over the wood and bounced off the eaves. Grim acted as my assistant, retrieving the knives and occasionally correcting my stance or my arm motion.

"Can you actually hit the marks?" I asked. "It seems like you've done this before."

"I can get close, but I've never tried it with a live person, and I never would. Hitting a big target is one thing, missing it with precision is something else entirely."

"How did you learn? This is more circus than magic, isn't it?"

"My mother sent me to Italy as soon as I turned sixteen. My father died when I was young, and I didn't get along with my stepfather," Grim said.

"What did you do then? Run away and join a circus?"

He laughed. "Something like that. My mother's whole family are performers—theater, magic, circus—you name it, I've got a cousin who does it. My mom was a trained opera singer. She was good enough for supporting roles, but not diva material. She didn't mind—she liked to move around. It's a family trait. She met my dad while she was on a tour with an opera company in the US."

"Does she still sing?"

"No, she died when I was in my twenties. Anyway, she retired from performing and gave voice lessons when she had me."

"Oh, I'm sorry." Deciding to change the subject, I asked, "So you learned magic and knife throwing and lockpicking when you were in Italy?"

"I got a head start on the locks. I was always pretty acrobatic, and when I was twelve, my stepfather thought it would be a useful combination."

"Seriously?" I stopped and looked at him. "He had you breaking into things in junior high?"

"Seriously," he said. "I did it to keep my mom safe, though I admit I liked the adrenaline rush. That's one of the reasons she wanted me out of town. Her extended family were eccentric, but none of them were criminals."

"Ah, I see. And your stepfather was abusive? That's awful, for both you and your mom."

"He never hit her, but he was psychologically abusive. Once I understood what was happening, it was hard to stand by. That's another reason she wanted me gone—she was afraid of what I might do. I made her promise to leave once I was out of his reach, but she didn't. She got sick soon after, so she stayed. Cancer. But she died of a broken spirit. The cancer finished the job."

"I'm sorry," I said again. "That's terrible. Is this one of the unbalanced scales you mentioned?"

"It is. And my stepfather is dead, but I had nothing to do with that."

He sounded as though he regretted it, so I didn't pursue it. Instead, I said, "So what's in that wooden box? More knives?"

"How did you guess? Take a look."

We walked back to the table, and Grim turned a tiny key in a tiny lock and lifted the lid of the box. The inside was lined with faded silk. There were knives of various sizes in different sheaths, but not another set like the one I was holding. I set those down and picked through the box.

"Now, this is more what I had in mind," I said, picking up a wicked-looking blade with an embossed silver hilt. I moved on to two shorter knives with scarlet tassels on the end. "And these are nice too, though I think they'd look better in one of those leather gauntlets than this nylon and Velcro thing."

"You've been watching Fritz's collection of assassin movies, haven't you?" Grim said. He took a closer look at the short knives. "Here, I'll take off the tassels, and you can try your luck with these. I've got a pair like this at home, but mine are black."

"Very understated. Very New York. Also in nylon? Or something nicer?"

"Now, now. They're not an accessory, Greer. The nylon and Velcro provide a better fit on your forearm. Here you go. We'll get closer. Now try to hit the figure dead center—the chest or even the throat."

I didn't do much better with the new knife set. Grim took a turn, and then we switched off, using all the knives in turn. My motor memory got better, though my aim did not. The rhythmic workout was relaxing, as Grim had promised. Focusing on one thing, one goal, had freed my mind. I was no longer spinning in circles mentally. I was doing nothing but throwing knives, my brain quiet, my shoulders loose. Moving meditation. I'd even worked up a light sweat in the cool attic.

Grim handed me the original set of knives again and made some small adjustments to my stance. He stood beside me, opposite my throwing arm. I took careful aim, and once again missed.

"Ugh," I said, frustrated.

"You'll hit it when you're ready," Grim said. "Keep going. Don't overthink."

It reminded me of what Yuri had told the class. *"Don't debate in the moment."*

I tried again and again, with the same result: almost, but not quite. *"It's like you're trying to miss."* Jennie Webber's voice this time, at the shooting range near Raven Hill.

Grim gathered the knives. He brought them back and resumed his position beside me. I rolled my shoulders and adjusted my grip. I picked up the first knife, and Grim spoke.

"You've still got decisions to make, Greer."

"What will you do, Greer?" Father Liam had asked. *"What will you do?"*

I threw and missed.

"And what are those again?" I asked.

"What do you want to do? What are you willing to do? What are you going to do?"

Another throw. Another miss.

"I don't know what to do," I said.

Throw. Miss.

"It all stems from that first question, Greer. And then you get to choose."

What was I going to do? I didn't know yet.

Throw. Miss.

What was I willing to do? I didn't want to examine that too closely.

Throw. Miss.

What did I want to do? I took the next knife.

Danny—dead. Jackson—dead. Carl—dead. My life in limbo. Gwen, terrified and running.

What did I want to do?

"I want to kill them," I said.

Throw.

Bull's-eye.

Chapter Twenty-Five

~

After admitting my homicidal desires, my aim improved considerably. I felt lighter, and my mind was clear. We spent another half hour throwing knives and then went back to work, Grim tinkering with Alexei, and me cataloging. Grim took off around five, and I stayed. I moved on to more mundane tasks and let my mind roam. When my stomach started to growl, I tidied up and did my usual walk-around, ending with the dining room.

Grim had remembered to unplug Alexei. I knew he'd had some luck getting the mechanism unjammed but hadn't yet gotten the voice to work. I plugged the fortune teller in and waited. Once the machine was humming and all the lights were on, I pushed the button. Alexei went into action. He raised his hand, swiveled his head, and then spit out a complete fortune card. I took it from the metal slot.

Boldness is the beginning of action, but fortune controls how it ends. ~The Laughing Philosopher

Fortune indeed. I thought good strategy had more to do with how it ended, but I was willing to concede that luck helped.

Either way, it beat a random warning to beware. I unplugged the machine and went home.

* * *

When I heard Grim unlocking the door the next day, I popped up and met him in the hall.

"Meeting in the kitchen. I'll put the coffee on. I've got a plan," I said. "And pastries!" I called over my shoulder.

"I need to get a confession," I said, once Grim sat with his breakfast.

"From?"

"Clarice. She's my best bet—she thinks she's got me on the hook with that job offer. We're already planning to meet."

"She might actually mean that, you know," Grim said. "I think William is becoming too much of a loose cannon. Carl Guenther could have been bought off. Instead, it looks like William shot him. Now they've got a dead employee and the police sniffing around."

"Good point. I can use that," I said. "We still don't know who killed either Jackson or Danny, but whoever it was didn't act alone. She's implicated."

"True. So how are you going to get her to confess? She's a cool one. Easier to rattle William. As you found out at the party."

"Yes. That's what I think too. But I also think that if I can get Clarice to own up to anything, and to point the finger at William in the process, he'll sell her out to save himself once the police start questioning him."

"I think you're right. So how are you going to do this? You know the cops won't help you," Grim said.

"I'm going to record it. That's where I need your help. I don't suppose you've ever bugged anything before, have you?"

"I can't say I have, but I know someone who is very good with all things audio. She started in music and has branched out. Want me to give her a call?"

"In a minute," I said. "There are a couple of things I need to figure out—location and timing. Do you think you could pull some strings at the Hungarian?"

"Sure," he said. "What do you want to do?"

I told him what I had in mind, and he helped me refine my plan. When we had the details worked out, he said, "You know you need backup on this."

"I didn't want to ask," I said. "This could end badly. At the very least, what I'm doing is illegal."

"You may have noticed that kind of thing doesn't bother me."

"I had, actually." I had also noticed it didn't bother me either. I can't say I was shocked or horrified. I'd never been a rules girl. I told myself I wouldn't make a habit of it and would skirt the law only in emergencies. This was an emergency.

"Well, then, you can count me in," Grim said. "One more thing to consider: whether or not Clarice takes the bait, she's going to know the game is up. She'll either leave the country immediately or try to kill you."

"I think murder is more likely," I said. "That's what I'd do."

Grim made his calls. I made a few of my own. The first several were to family and friends, to make sure they wouldn't be in town on Friday. The next was to April. She said she'd be sending me updated files on the shell companies in the next two days. I thanked her and then made my request.

"I need you to do something not very nice," I said. "It involves sending William Warren into a panic. Are you willing?"

"Am I ever. Do tell!" she said.

"He needs to hear that Clarice is leaving town for a long vacation and that you've heard rumors about some accounting irregularities. Maybe you have a client who was interested in investing and now isn't so sure. Something like that. Serious enough that he might consider heading to the airport himself. Friday would be best. Can you do that?"

"Leave it to me," April said with some satisfaction, "I'll have him wetting his pants."

Next I called Detective Stewart, to see if he'd made any progress. The Fraud Department was interested, he said, and would start nosing around. I was to keep that quiet, but he wanted to reassure me that I was being taken seriously. As for Carl Guenther's murder, still no witnesses, and no weapon had been recovered.

The rest of the week I was busy. I spent time every day working on my knife throwing, took another trip out to the firing range; threw myself into my mixed martial arts class with so much enthusiasm that even Yuri was impressed; and worked some late nights at the brownstone, to make up for the time I was spending elsewhere. I'd been neglecting my crow friends, and Charles, Oliver, and Mabel let me know they were displeased, so I had lunch outside every day. I gave them lots of treats and spent time talking to them about my plans. They didn't judge. Crows are like that.

Friday I woke to rain, and a forecast that showed more of the same, along with big temperature swings. Grim was out taking care of some last-minute things for my meeting with Clarice, so

I was alone at work. The only excitement came in the form of a package delivery. It was addressed to me, care of the archives at the brownstone address. I opened it and found a set of small throwing knives with the same kind of nylon and Velcro wrist sheath as the ones Grim had found. These fit better, though. There was a computer-printed gift card enclosed. It read, *"Fortune favors the bold. Good luck."*

Grim must have sent them, and it looked like he and Alexei had the same mindset. Well, my plan was bold, if desperate, and I'd always been lucky. I'd even called Father Liam and asked him to put in a good word, as it looked like the investigation was ramping up. He didn't ask too many questions, but he did remind me that while harming someone in self-defense is forgivable, it is also required to do no more harm than necessary to stop an unjust attack.

"Are you implying that I have a hot Irish temper, Father?" I asked.

"No, I'm stating that you have a cold and calculating temper, and that worries me more," he said. "Now, why don't you come for dinner and the hockey game on Saturday? You can fill me in."

I accepted, was told to behave, and hung up.

I replayed that conversation in my head while I got ready for my confrontation with Clarice. So far, things were going according to plan. Grim let me know everything would be in place at the appointed time. April sent a text saying that she'd talked to William and gotten him so wound up she could hear him hyperventilating over the phone, and ended it with several laugh-until-you-cry emojis.

I really liked April.

Finally, I sent a message to Clarice.

Tied up with a work thing. I think big donors are as difficult as big investors! How about the same time but at the Hungarian. Closer to where I'll be. Thanks.

It took her some time to reply, but then I got an Okay, see you there. I took a deep breath. Almost show time.

I strapped on my new wrist sheaths and inserted the knives. I was doing well in my self-defense class but had never taken on someone who actually meant to kill me. Besides, they made me feel more like a badass than the German steel knitting needle one of my friends swore by. Next I took out both handguns—the shiny new one, legally purchased and permitted, and the older one that had disappeared from official view a few years before. I set them on the bed.

Do no more harm than necessary.

I picked up my new gun, the one I'd taken to the range that afternoon. I could do a lot of harm with one of these. Once I'd admitted that I wanted to, the seething rage I lived with had begun to fade. Or at least I felt I was in control of it. The need to stay alive and to see justice done—those were still strong.

"You've got a cold, calculating temper."

True. And I was okay with that.

I put the new gun back in the hidey-hole in the nightstand. I finished getting ready and then left a voicemail for Detective Stewart.

"I've heard that there are rumors that an investor has discovered some financial irregularities at New Leaf and that William Warren's fingerprints are all over them. Fits a pattern, something he's done before apparently. Anyway, the same source says he's planning on leaving town. Nothing concrete, but you might want to keep an eye on him."

Would he do anything? Hard to say, based on a rumor, but it was worth a try.

After that I sent Grim a text letting him know I was on my way. Then I went out into the rain and hailed a cab.

When Clarice arrived at the coffee shop, I was waiting. With Grim's help I'd managed to get a table in the back, lit by one dim wall sconce. Grim was sitting at the table behind, with his back to me. He was wearing his Clark Kent glasses and professor clothes. Clarice stopped near the doorway after she walked in. I waved. She took a good look around as she came over, but seemed at ease when she sat and ordered a cappuccino. We talked about the weather and how her floor refinishing was going, until the waiter had dropped off her drink.

"Thanks for being flexible about this meeting," I said. "It's been a busy, aggravating week at work."

"All the more reason to make a change," she said.

"My feeling exactly," I replied.

"Excellent. I told you, I have a few irons in the fire. Within a few months, you'll be in a corner office anywhere in the world you fancy. I'll even throw in Austin—he's wildly efficient, and I won't be needing him much longer." She leaned back, smiling like the cat that ate the canary.

"I'm sure he is, and it's very tempting, but—I've been giving it some thought, and a new job isn't quite what I had in mind."

Her eyes narrowed. "What did you have in mind?"

"More of a partnership," I said.

She relaxed. "That's easy enough. We've got a few options to choose from. What kind of business are you interested in?"

"The business I'm already in. Information."

"I'm not sure I follow, Greer. There's money in information, yes, but people have been giving away their data for nothing more valuable than convenience for years. What's your angle?"

"My angle is this: I have information, lots of information, that could put you in jail for fraud and for murder. More than one murder. For enough money, I can make that information disappear."

"Fraud? Murder? Greer, I think your imagination has gotten the better of you. Whatever are you talking about?"

"Junonia Holdings," I said. "The list of shell companies. Frank left notes about it, and he wasn't very clever with his passwords. I've got copies of everything. Carl Guenther didn't know what he was looking at, but I did. So did Steve Malloy. Did you kill him too?"

Clarice laughed. "Steve Malloy took off for Bali. No one's seen him since, but I had nothing to do with that."

That had the ring of truth, though I was still convinced that he'd been bought off. She continued, "I have to confess, you're onto something with Junonia Holdings. That was Frank's attempt to support a lifestyle he couldn't afford. Once it was brought to my attention, we cleaned all that up."

"Sure you did. And while you were at it, you confessed all to your investors? Come on, Clarice."

"All right. We didn't exactly come clean. It wasn't the way I wanted to handle it, but William convinced me otherwise. There's no trace of it now. I'm sure we can make it worth your while. One-time payment—a consulting fee, shall we say?"

"I'd consider it, but there's the matter of Dan's murder. That's something I just can't seem to let go of."

"You can't think I had anything to do with that! I was at the theater, remember?"

"You're using *Phantom of the Opera* as an alibi? Seriously, it's been running for over thirty years. Your uncle was in it for half a decade. I'll bet you know it by heart. Try harder, Clarice."

I could see her wheels turning as she tried to remember if she'd ever told me where she said she'd been that night. She took a different tack. "Greer, I know it's been hard for you. Dan's murder was a terrible thing. It must have been horrifying—walking into your own home, finding him bludgeoned to death and covered with broken glass—I haven't gotten over it myself. But the police caught the man who did it. He's in jail."

Covered in broken glass. There was no way she could have known that. Unless she'd been there. A Waterford vase, an anniversary gift, smashed. By Clarice, who had murdered my husband.

I took a quick breath and tuned back in to what she was saying. I had to step carefully now and stick to the plan.

"I can't imagine what it was like to lose the love of your life, but—"

"No," I said. "Not the love of my life. To be honest, we were going through a rough patch at the time." I leaned toward her. "How do you think I know what show you were supposed to see that night?"

She didn't say anything.

"I was with someone else. Someone you know. Your date to *Phantom.* Ian Cameron."

I watched her face. For a split second I saw rage, then the mask descended again.

"Yes, I know Ian. A mutual friend introduced us. He was supposed to join me, but he called and said he couldn't make it. A meeting ran late. So I went myself," she said.

"So you say, and who am I to try to prove you wrong?" I said. "Besides, I meant what I said about a partnership. I'm not here to put you in jail, Clarice. There's no material advantage in that for me. No, I'm here to make a deal."

"What do you want?"

"Half." Her jaw dropped. "Half of what you've skimmed off the company profits for the past five years. Hear me out," I said, holding up a hand when she started to speak. "In return, I'll give you a scapegoat. William Warren. I've got a witness who can place him at my apartment building right before Dan was murdered, pretending to trip while your guy Perry slips in. And another witness who will swear he wasn't where he said he was."

I had her full attention now. "Go on," she said.

"We both know he's in it up to his neck. He might have been the mastermind behind the whole plan. His shady reputation precedes him. Of course, anyone who knows the two of you won't believe for a minute that he outsmarted you, but maybe coercion? So Frank and William start the scam, and you're in too deep by the time you discover it? It could work, Clarice. Especially since I have another witness who saw him at my parents' house. They had a break-in, and someone died. And William Warren was there, wasn't he? At least, that will be our story, and we can make it stick. Two murders. So what do you say?"

She was tempted. I could see it in her eyes. But as she thought through all of the ramifications, she found the flaws.

"Of course, I've mentioned before, to you and to some other people, that I've grown concerned about William's behavior. But even if any of this little tale you're spinning were true, there's the matter of my liability," she said.

"Tricky, but where there's a will, there's a way. Maybe you could get immunity. You were a naive and trusting young woman with an excellent reputation and great ideas, taken advantage of by a couple of more experienced and less visionary men whose greed got the better of them. You'd get off with a slap on the wrist."

"Unlikely."

"Or how about this? Flee for your life. Leave the country. Make a deal from afar. I'll throw in this: William tried to drug you at the cocktail party. I've got a witness to that too. Maybe it was supposed to be a lethal dose, maybe just enough to get you to sign something to his advantage. Hard to prove either way now, but the fact remains that he tried something."

"What?"

Clarice looked genuinely shocked. Time to run with this.

"You didn't really think I had a migraine, did you? No, my champagne was spiked. The thing is, that glass was meant for you. William handed you a drink, you set it down, then picked up the wrong one. He gave me the other one. Fortunately, I only took a few sips. Another guest saw that I wasn't well and got concerned. He told Isabelle that William had done that kind of thing before."

"He wouldn't dare," Clarice said through clenched teeth.

"Really? He did threaten you, didn't he? It certainly looked that way, according to my witness."

"There was a misunderstanding."

"Hmm. Still, you can't trust him. I'm not convinced you ever have. You're smarter than that. Come on. It's time to throw William Warren under the bus, Clarice. We could make asses of all those people who underestimated us. We could have fun."

I used the same words she had used to try to convince me the other night. Whether it was that or a newfound certainty that she couldn't trust William and was on her own was hard to tell, but I could see the internal debate playing out across her face. I had one last card to play.

"And consider this: once I throw in my lot with you, I'm implicated. I can make this story hang together, mostly with the truth. And who wouldn't believe me? I've got nothing to gain by lying. But I may have to lie, and there are one or two witnesses who might need some coaching. Perjury and witness tampering. So this will be a one-time payment, and then we go our separate ways."

This was a stretch. I wouldn't go for it unless I was desperate. Blackmailers always came back for more. Though to be honest, if someone handed me the wad of cash I'd asked for, I'd be happy to disappear with it and never bother them again. I doubted I'd convince Clarice of that. I wasn't sure I'd convinced her of anything, but I knew I'd sown enough doubt to throw her off balance.

"Well?" I asked.

"Presuming any of this had any basis in reality—and I'll admit that what you've said about William is entirely believable—do you expect me to hand over a suitcase full of cash or something?"

"Tsk, tsk. Cash is so last millennium, Clarice. It's 'or something.' Here. I'm sure you'll know what you're looking at."

I pulled a folded sheet of paper out of my pocket and slid the information for my offshore account across the table. She picked it up and unfolded it. Her eyebrows went up.

"Familiar? It would be convenient if we banked in the same place, wouldn't it?" I said with a smile.

She looked at me, then back down at the paper. Her wheels were turning. She folded the paper.

"When?" she asked.

"Now," I said.

"I can't give you what you're asking tonight. How about a down payment?" She named a figure and told me the balance would follow Monday. My guess was that she figured she'd either kill me or leave the country by then. Probably both.

"Well, I guess that would be all right. Transfer it now."

She took out her phone. I waited.

"I'm having trouble—"

Crockery crashed behind us. Hot coffee hit my hand. Something hit the back of my chair. I turned to see Grim standing, shaking coffee off his arm. A college student with an oversized bag was apologizing. I turned back to Clarice, who was looking toward Grim and the kid with the backpack, frowning. Grim must have noticed because he faced away from us, toward the student. I heard him say, "No worries. I was done anyway." He tossed some bills on the table, tucked his phone into his pocket, and left. Clarice watched him go. She couldn't have recognized him, could she? Time for distraction.

"You were saying?" I said.

She held up her cell. "I can't get a connection. I'll try going outside. Give me a couple of minutes. I'll be right back."

Sure she would.

I smiled and said, "I'll get the check."

She got up and moved quickly toward the door. Once she was out of sight, I plucked the tiny microphone from the light fixture above the table, and signaled to our waiter.

"We're done here. Thanks for your help." I handed him enough cash to cover the check and then some. He looked at the amount and grinned.

"Anytime, hon," he said. "Have a good night."

Chapter
Twenty-Six

I went outside. There was no sign of Clarice. I took a good look around. Perhaps she'd decided not to kill me, and was on her way out of town. I wasn't concerned—we had enough recorded to convince the police. I crossed the street and went toward the Peace Fountain outside the Cathedral of St. John the Divine. Grim and I had agreed to meet behind it. I walked around it and waited. The fog had grown thicker and was drifting in patches all around me. It distorted shapes and sounds, making the street noise into a steady, low rumble and making the fantastic creatures of the fountain look even more uncanny, as car lights created kaleidoscopic reflections in the mist.

I took another turn around the fountain. Had Grim decided to follow Clarice? I checked my phone. No message. I'd give him a few more minutes and then text him.

I stood in the swirling fog. There was a break in the traffic. It created one of those odd pockets of silence you sometimes get in the city. In that brief interval I heard it—the metal clang of a gate closing. I turned. Behind me was the iron fence that surrounded Pulpit Green, another part of the Cathedral grounds. In the center was a gate.

"Grim?" I said.

No answer. The traffic started again. I walked to the gate. I thought they were locked at night, but this one was open. Forgotten about, or had Grim picked it? Why? Had Clarice spotted him?

I looked around—pointless in the fog. I went through the gate, picking my way carefully around dormant plants. In the center of the green was the pulpit it was named for. By day, it reminded me of the delicate spire of a church, its center arches open on four sides, the stepped stone base raising it above the low wrought iron fence around it. Now, in the fitful moonlight, the arches looked like a scream. Beneath it, in front of the fence, lay a pale shape.

Grim.

I moved as quickly as I could across the dark green, scanning the area as the patches of fog crawled around me. I saw no one nearby, and dropped to my knees next to Grim's still form.

"Grim!" I said, feeling for a pulse. There was blood on the side of his head, matting his hair.

His eyes opened. "Playing dead," he whispered, his lips barely moving. "Keep talking."

"Grim—wake up!" I spoke loudly, my tone panicked, then leaned forward, as though checking his breathing.

"Clarice. Alone. Took my phone—figured out recording. Missed the device. She's still here somewhere."

"You're bleeding so much! Stay with me!"

"Head for the street. She'll follow you, and I'll follow her." He was sounding groggy, and blinking. I felt his hand and face—like ice.

"I've got a better plan," I whispered. I got my feet under me and crouched. "I'm calling an ambulance. I'll get help," I said loudly.

I was reaching for my phone when Grim said, "Behind you!"

I turned my head to see Clarice, her arm raised and something dark in her hand. I pushed up and back, hitting her in the gut with my shoulders. I heard the sound of a grunt and of something hitting the ground as I staggered backward and landed on my butt. I rolled to all fours and got up, trying to spot her. Grim was still on the ground. I had to draw her away and attract some attention.

I saw Clarice not too far away, on her feet but looking down, searching the ground for something. Probably whatever blunt instrument she'd tried to use on me. I saw Grim roll to his feet, stagger a little, and then disappear behind a tree. He'd left his jacket on the ground, the light-colored lining visible. With any luck Clarice would think he was still there.

I crouched down again, feeling around for anything I could use to distract her. I found some small rocks and threw them to her right, away from the pulpit. They didn't make much noise, but it got her attention. I edged closer to the gate, but she saw the movement and turned. There was still fog drifting between us. I froze, hoping she couldn't actually see me in the dark.

Wrong.

She'd found what she was looking for on the ground. She raised her arm and pointed a gun at me.

Well, hell. In spite of the gun safe in her closet, I'd been hoping firearms were William's MO and that Clarice would stick to bashing people over the head. If she was within arm's reach, I knew I could take her, and I wanted the satisfaction of hurting her with my bare hands. Now, I needed to distract her long enough to bolt. I remembered the signs of rage I'd seen around

Dan's body, and Jackson's. That's when she got sloppy. I reached for the knife at my wrist. Time to make her mad.

"Did William let you borrow his gun?" I taunted. "He doesn't think much of women, does he? He told me you'd have failed with New Leaf without him and Frank."

"William is a greedy fool! No self-control. And Frank was an idiot!"

Clarice's face twisted. She looked like one of the Cathedral gargoyles. She'd lose control soon.

"And Pete Perry? He couldn't pull off a simple robbery. So hard to get good help these days, isn't it?"

"I had to finish that one myself. But you know that, don't you? I could see it in your face."

"Yes, I know you killed Dan."

"He didn't have to die, you know. If we could have made whatever evidence he had disappear, it would have been his word against ours. There wasn't much, at that point. And he shouldn't have been there. But he just wouldn't let anything go."

"And Jackson, the homeless man on my parents' porch?"

"I couldn't send William. Too sloppy. Someone saw him when he was looking the place over. And he never mentioned that vagrant who sleeps there. Not that he matters."

Oh, but he does, I thought.

"Well, William doesn't think too much of you either. But he's the one who shot Carl Guenther, isn't he? Didn't he think you could handle it?"

"Oh, I can handle it, all right," she said.

Not really, I thought. Her stance was off, and she was holding the gun in one hand. I was balanced and ready.

I pulled my arm back and threw the knife, in one easy motion, as I'd been taught. I aimed for her chest, but she ducked when she saw my arm move. The knife glanced off her forehead and dropped to the ground, but it hit hard enough to draw blood. I could see it, and the horror on her face when she realized what had happened.

It was the most satisfying moment of my life.

"You bitch!" she screamed. She raised the gun, but the shot was wild. No matter what you see on TV, it's difficult to hit someone at a distance with a handgun. Lucky for me. Time to get out of Dodge. I bolted for the gate, weaving to avoid the trees and shrubs that dotted the green.

Another shot rang out as I pulled the gate open. I heard a thud in the tree behind me. I shoved the gate shut behind me and headed for the fountain. A few pedestrians had heard the shot and stopped.

"She's got a gun! Run! Call the police!" I yelled. Clarice fired again. The small crowd scrambled. I went for the nearest cover—the fountain. Where you would normally find water, the Peace Fountain had plants, but the structure was still solid stone and bronze. I jumped over the edge, then flattened myself and crawled through the shrubbery toward the front. I was pulling myself up, using the dangling, severed head of the vanquished Satan, when I heard stumbling footsteps.

Clarice, with blood streaming into her eyes from the cut on her forehead. The gun was in her hand, but down by her side, out of sight. She brushed her opposite arm across her face, trying to clear her vision. She stopped right in front of me, her back to the fountain, and I saw my chance. I eased up and forward.

"Clarice," I whispered.

She started to turn, raising the gun, her arm right in front of me. I grabbed it and twisted, and she spun. Now I had the gun pointing upward and her back to me. I slid my other arm around her neck and pulled her back, my position in the fountain giving me leverage. I had her off balance, her face not far from my own.

"I'm going to enjoy watching you go to prison," I said.

"I'll never go to prison. I'd rather die," she said, renewing her struggle.

"And I'd rather die than let you get away," I said.

"You will," she said. She flung her arm back, and I nearly lost my grip on her.

"You'll have that scar for life you know," I said.

That did it.

"I'll kill you!" she screamed. She squeezed the trigger. Really, she gave me no choice. I pulled her back against the ornamental brass rim of the fountain, then yanked and twisted her arm. I heard the satisfying crunch of bones beneath her piercing scream, and the gun dropped.

I was saved from doing her further damage by the arrival of New York's finest. They pulled us apart, but enough bystanders were telling them about Clarice threatening to kill me that I got more gentle handling than I expected. I spotted Grim, calmly giving his version of events to a uniformed officer on the other side of the fountain. When the ambulances arrived, Clarice tried to take off, and all attention turned to her again. Good. Here was my chance.

The EMTs wanted to examine me, but I said I had to check on my friend, so they gave me a blanket and waded into the fray around Clarice, who was fighting like a rabid animal. I zipped over to Grim, currently being evaluated for concussion.

"Thank God! I thought you were dead!" I said, hurling myself into his arms and covering both of us with the blanket.

"Could we have a minute?" Grim asked. The paramedic sighed and stepped away.

"Are you all right?" he said, pulling me close. His face next to mine, he whispered, "Not that this isn't delightful, but what are you doing?"

"Knife sheath. Right wrist. I need it gone before I talk to the cops."

"I thought you'd know better than to bring a knife to a gun fight," he said, as he slid his hand down my arm.

"I do. I brought two knives. And a gun. Waistband, five o'clock. And you'll need to find the other knife. Near the pulpit. I'd like the knives, but lose the gun."

"And take the cannoli?" he asked. I felt the gun slide away. He shifted our awkward embrace, and I pulled at the Velcro on my left wrist. The nylon sheath loosened. Before I knew it, both had disappeared into Grim's jacket. I presumed the gun had as well, but you couldn't tell looking at him. He really was good at the sleight of hand.

Grim stepped back and pulled the blanket tight around me. He leaned forward, gave me a kiss on the forehead, and said, "I'll find the other knife. They won't be looking back there on the green." Then he said more loudly, "Let the ambulance crew look you over, honey, please?"

I nodded and turned to the paramedic, who started asking me questions. Grim melted into the darkness. I heard another siren and looked toward the road. Stewart was getting out of a car, Kopp right behind him.

This should be fun. I stuck close to the paramedic, who led me to the ambulance. I was sure I had nothing more than bumps and bruises, but I really was cold and had started to shake. The paramedic, who looked like J. Lo and was both efficient and reassuring, gave me another blanket and asked me questions. By the time Stewart and Kopp arrived, she was almost done.

"Ms. Hogan. How are you?" Stewart said. We both looked at the paramedic.

"Shock, bump on the head, should have those ribs X-rayed," she replied.

Stewart began to speak but was interrupted by another shriek of rage from Clarice and a metallic clang from the other ambulance.

"I'll talk to you at the hospital," he said, and he and Kopp went to help their brethren.

My new friend J. Lo sighed again. I had a feeling she did a lot of that in this job.

"Drugs," she said, shaking her head.

"Actually, no. Crazy. Psychopathic, probably. And would rather be dead than caught."

"Great. Just great. I'll let everyone know." Another sigh. She looked around. "Where's your friend? He might be concussed."

Far from here, disposing of evidence, I hoped.

"He didn't want to be taken to the hospital. No health insurance," I said.

She shrugged and bundled me into the ambulance.

Chapter Twenty-Seven

I walked among the tombstones on a bright March day, the kind of day, as Dickens would say, when it was summer in the light and winter in the shade. It was late in the afternoon, and the light was starting to fade, but it was pleasant, nonetheless. I'd stopped on my way in and watched a wedding party on the steps, smiling and laughing and posing for pictures. I'd done the same thing in the same place, what seemed a lifetime ago. It's good luck to see a bride, or so I'd been told, so I lingered until the happy couple and their attendants had piled into limos and left to dance the night away.

When they'd gone I went to the cemetery, taking a round-about way to my destination. I stopped and greeted old friends, now gone, wishing them well, wherever they were, my heart lighter than on my last visit. When I reached Dan's grave, I was glad to see dappled sunlight as the breeze moved in the trees. The daffodils my mother had planted for me in the fall were sending up green shoots. They'd bloom soon, certainly by Easter. I knelt and cleaned away some windblown leaves, then took my usual seat on the bench.

"It's done," I said. "Though you were almost too clever by half with that greeting card. I finally got the message, but it took a while. Longer than it should have."

It had been a week since my confrontation with Clarice. I'd spent the night in the emergency room, being attended to between patients in far worse shape than I was. No concussion; my ribs were bruised, but not broken; and the gash in my arm from one of the bronze creatures around the fountain required a tetanus shot, just in case.

"Ms. Phillips has a cut too," Stewart said during his visit with me before I was released. "Hers is on her forehead. Much cleaner, almost like a knife."

I shrugged. "Must have happened when she was chasing me. Or in the fountain. Maybe you should let someone at the Cathedral know," I said.

He gave me a long look. I looked back. "Right," he said when I didn't blink. He ran me through the whole story again and then told me he'd have more questions. I was invited to the police station on Monday. "We've got several people who heard her threaten to kill you, and we've got Mr. Grimaldi's statement, though we'll need to talk to him again. There are still a few things I'm not quite clear on, though."

"I'm happy to help the police with their inquiries," I said. "And I'm sure Mr. Grimaldi will be too."

Mr. Grimaldi was unexpectedly out of town. I wasn't sure why, but I knew he wasn't avoiding the police. He'd called to check on me while I was in the ER, dozing while my doctor attended to a gunshot wound.

"I took care of that errand. Check the fridge in the office tomorrow. I left the other stuff in the box on your desk. Nice quality on those."

"Thanks, and thanks for the gift. I'm sorry I forgot to mention it earlier. It's great that they're the same kind we've been using upstairs."

There was a brief silence. "When did they arrive?" he said.

"Yesterday. Just in time."

Another pause.

"That's great. Listen, there's something I have to take care of. You may not see me for a few days. Call if you need me, though, anytime."

I was puzzled, but a nurse arrived with my tetanus shot, and I didn't give it any more thought. Grim was mysterious—it was part of his charm. So was his sense of humor. After I was released from the hospital, I went home and slept and then went to the brownstone. When I checked the fridge, I found a bakery box. Taped to the top was a note that said, *"From my favorite bakery, over by the river. Enjoy!"* Inside were a couple of cannoli. The shells were getting soft, but they were still delicious. The knives were in the box with the lockpicks, and Grim had added one of our official index cards on the top. *"Misc. Magical supplies. Inventoried."* Nice touch in case the cops dropped by.

Stewart had said I didn't need a lawyer, but I brought one with me anyway. I'd dated David while he was in law school and I was in grad school. We'd had a good time and parted as friends. His father was a partner in one of the biggest criminal defense firms on the East Coast, and David had joined the family business. We all had a pleasant if somewhat lengthy chat. Grim and I had our stories straight, and witnesses corroborated them, so Stewart said it was unlikely I'd be needed again.

"Her lawyers are looking for a deal, and so are Warren's. He can't talk fast enough. Thanks for the tip on that—we'd been keeping an eye on him, and we picked him up at the airport. The new finance guy they hired is in on it too. Your friend April

Benson has been a big help. She's provided a nice paper trail. Sounds like she's put half her staff at our disposal on this."

It was only one paralegal, but April was working on it too. "They'll never be able to prove anything about Frank's death," she told me. "I'm sure that was Clarice, but she won't talk. Her lawyers are asking for a psychiatric evaluation—can you believe it? That will never fly. Well, as long as she's locked up. As long as all of them are."

Other than Frank, the only loose end was Steve Malloy. If he'd gotten paid off and left the country, it would be a long hunt. I suspected that was the case—Clarice's comment about Bali had the ring of truth about it.

It had been a busy, exhausting week.

Father Liam had given me a raincheck on dinner the previous Saturday, with the expectation that he'd get the full story this weekend. I was expected at the rectory shortly, but he wandered down and joined me on the bench.

"Giving your man all the details, are you?" he said.

"Something like that," I said. "I'll fill you in over dinner. Pizza and beer, right? Then we can watch some hockey."

"Ah, better than that. We had a wedding today, and the bride's mother sent over a feast as a thank-you. Lasagna, meatballs, and a couple of bottles of red. You're in for a treat. You haven't lived until you've had Mrs. Tripoli's meatballs."

"That sounds great," I said.

"So how are you doing, Greer?"

"I'm okay. Tired. Still kind of achy."

He tapped the bandage on my forearm, visible at the edge of my sleeve. "Things got physical, I see."

"They did," I said. "And I might have done more harm than was strictly necessary."

"To the woman that killed Dan?"

I nodded. "She'll be scarred for life, and she hates that. I'm enjoying it."

"Ah, I see."

"I wanted to kill her."

"But you didn't."

I shook my head. "No. I might have been able to, but I didn't."

"Why not?"

"'*The mills of the gods grind slowly, but they grind exceedingly fine,*'" I said. "I wanted to watch it play out. I wanted to watch her suffer. It's better than killing her, I think."

"The lesser of two evils, Greer. I don't blame you. I hope the need to see her suffer fades, for your sake, but I understand. So—supper? I'll go start the oven."

"I'll come in a few minutes," I said.

Liam walked up the path.

I stood and looked down at my husband's grave. I felt sorrow, and an emptiness, not from the absence of Dan—I'd grown used to that—but from the absence of the rage that had driven me for so long.

Now what?

Finish the cataloging project. Help Grim solve his mystery, and perhaps lay his own ghosts to rest. Go back to Raven Hill and help put the library and new archives together.

Target practice with Jennie, just in case.

The last light faded. I stood for a few more minutes in the deepening shadows.

"Bye, Danny," I said, and blew a kiss. I looked up at the archangel Gabriel.

"'The mills of the gods grind slowly, but they grind exceedingly fine,'" I repeated. I'd leave it all to them. Tonight, I'd drink wine and eat Mrs. Tripoli's meatballs, and if the Rangers beat the Devils, all would be right with my world.

For now.

Acknowledgments

A book may be written by one person, but it takes a dedicated and generous group of people to help bring characters to life and to produce the finished product. Many thanks to Jennie Clarke of Rubric Legal LLC, whose decades of experience in corporate law and finance and new and emerging business provided the basis for New Leaf and for April Benson. David Feldman, Esq., of Feldman Legal Advisors, lent his considerable expertise in the legal cannabis and psychedelics industries to the character Noah Leonard and to New Leaf's ambitious expansion plans. These areas of business law are both complex and fascinating, and any mistakes in how they are portrayed are solely the fault of the author.

Jill Sakowitz, lifelong New Yorker and Upper West Side resident, provided invaluable aid by scouting locations and verifying details, from correct cross streets and place names to locks and lighting. She did it all, and I am profoundly grateful. Any errors are mine and not hers.

Greer's temporary employer, the Archive of Illusionists and Conjurers, was inspired by a job listing I saw many years ago from the Conjuring Arts Research Center in Manhattan. While the former is wholly fictional, the latter exists and is near the top of my list of libraries I'd like to visit. I'd also like to thank the staff and volunteers of this and other small and private libraries who devote themselves to preserving knowledge that might otherwise be lost. Our world is richer because of their efforts.

My heartfelt thanks to my agent, Julie Gwinn, for her encouragement and moral support during the unexpected twists and turns of the past year.

Much appreciation is due to my editor, Faith Black Ross, and the team at Crooked Lane Books—especially Madeline Rathle, Rebecca Nelson, Dulce Botello, and Thaisheemarie Fantauzzi Perez. Thanks for taking a chance on Greer Hogan and giving her the opportunity to solve not only her husband's murder but also several others along the way.

Last but not least, many thanks to my husband, Mark, for keeping our household humming along while I was locked away in my office, and to my family for their unflagging support.